SIXTY DAYS FOR LOVE

LIZA MALLOY

DEDICATION

This book would not be possible without the love and support of my amazing husband, parents, and children. This one is for you guys!

1

———

I n retrospect, falling behind the wheel of the car and starting the ignition was not my most brilliant move to date, given the number of Long Island Iced Teas I'd consumed. In my defense, I had no intention of leaving the parking lot. Without the alcohol coursing through my system, though, I probably would have devised a better plan for ditching the loser I'd danced with over the past hour.

As it were, the loser climbed into his shiny green pickup truck and sped off, but not until he saw the police cruiser pull up beside me, lights flashing.

"Crap," I muttered, flailing my head forward dramatically, accidentally tapping the horn with my forehead. I turned to see a uniformed officer approaching and I panicked, yanking the keys out of the ignition, hoping maybe the officer hadn't noticed the car running.

The cop tapped on my window, motioning for me to roll it down. I pushed the window button, but nothing happened. I fumbled with the stupid lever for another minute, cursing the crappy car for failing me, and then finally gave up, swinging the door open.

"Ugh," the cop grunted as I nailed him in the thigh with the door.

"Sorry," I said meekly, realizing I was now certainly going to be arrested. "My window must be broken. It wouldn't roll down."

He rubbed his leg and glanced up at me. "You turned your engine off. Power windows won't work without the key in the ignition."

As he spoke, my key chain rolled off my lap and onto the ground. I inched the door open further to retrieve the keys just as the cop went for them too. This time, I slammed his other leg with the door. He grunted again and handed me my keys, a decisive look of irritation on his face.

"Oh fuck. I'm so sorry," I began, turning away to grimace since I'd just cursed at a cop. "You probably think I've been drinking and I swear I wasn't going to drive anywhere. I just, well, my friend was going to drive me home but then we met these two guys and she just left with one and I was supposed to go home with the other but he was a total loser and I just don't see how sleeping with him would get me over my stupid husband and I couldn't bring myself to go with him." I paused to catch my breath.

"I told him I had to get something from my car and I was just going to pretend like I was driving away in hopes that he'd leave. Then I was going to go back inside until I sobered up." I glanced up at the cop, half expecting to see him pulling out his handcuffs, ready to read me my rights. "I would never drive drunk."

The officer glanced around the parking lot, then gestured towards the spot where the loser had been parked. "Was that the guy, in the green F150?"

I nodded solemnly.

"Well, he left without you. Hope you got his number."

I snorted. As if I'd ever call that guy. I can't believe I even spoke to him. He'd spent the better part of an hour regaling me with tales of his glory days in a garage band.

"Is this your friend's vehicle ma'am?"

"No, it's mine."

"You said your friend was going to drive you home. So why is your car even here?"

"Her car is a piece of crap. She's saving for an Audi. She was going to drive my car."

He sighed. I knew I should stop talking, but babbling was more my style, and I struggled to control my natural instincts when I was drunk.

"I assure you I never go out drinking like this. Well, I mean, obviously I did tonight but that was Jen's idea and it was only because my husband moved out today and my house is all empty and quiet and..."

Before I could figure out where I was going with that sentence, I was sobbing. Long, hard, heaving sobs. I leaned forward again to shield my eyes and instead bumped my head into the horn, honking it again.

Another sigh from the officer. "Can I see your license ma'am?" He crouched down to eye level.

I reached for my purse just as I remembered I hadn't brought it. Another one of Jen's dumb ideas, to leave my wallet at home so I would have to flirt shamelessly and get guys to buy my drinks for me. I winced.

"I don't have it," I said. His eyebrows scrunched together.

"I mean, I have a license. A good one. No tickets or anything. It's just at home now." I raised my hand to my chest, as though reciting the Pledge of Allegiance.

I stared out at him, trying to gauge whether there was even the slightest hint of sympathy in his face. He still wasn't smiling by any means, but his eyes, well, his eyes were like pools of melted chocolate. "You're cute. I should've tried flirting with you," I said, startled to hear the words out loud instead of just in my head, where they belonged.

"Please step out of the vehicle ma'am." He stood up and surveyed the parking lot again.

I cringed. "I wish you'd stop calling me ma'am. It's making me feel old." I glanced down at my legs, gauging whether they'd even support me if I tried to stand now. Sober, I hadn't been the most coordinated in the stupid four-inch high heels Jen had convinced me to wear. Now, I'd definitely have better balance barefoot. I bent to take the shoes off.

"What are you doing?" Now the officer sounded more confused than annoyed. "Leave your shoes on. I just asked you to get out of the car."

I stopped fiddling with my shoes and gazed up at him. "I can't walk in these shoes. If you're going to make me balance on some line or something, I need to do it barefoot."

He laughed. "It's freezing out here and there's broken glass on the pavement. You're not doing anything barefoot."

"Well that's just discrimination. If I were a guy in tennis shoes right now, I'd stand a much better chance at that walking test." I frowned. "Hey, what if I say the ABCs backwards instead?"

Now he seemed truly amused. Maybe it was a good thing I'd called him cute.

"Ma'am, er, Miss, why would I want you to recite the alphabet?"

"To see if I'm drunk." Obviously. What, did he think I'd never seen a cop show on TV?

"Is that why you think I'm here?"

"Isn't it?" Then I froze, horrified. He'd seen me stumble out of the bar in my trampy high heels, obscenely short skirt and borderline indecent top, headed towards the vehicle of a man I clearly didn't know. "Oh God, you think I'm a prostitute!"

This time, when I flung my head forward, I didn't even care that it smashed into the horn. How could I possibly explain this to David...gee honey, sorry to bug you in the middle of the night on the day you moved out, but I sort of need your legal services to get these solicitation charges cleared? Yikes!

When I finally lifted my head, the officer was gone. I heard a click and realized he had walked around the car and opened the passenger door. He opened the glove compartment.

"Hey, what are you doing? You're not allowed to search there without a warrant or probable cause. What are you looking for?"

He held up a small envelope and closed the door. "Your vehicle registration," he said calmly. "Are you a lawyer?"

I snorted again. You'd have thought my outfit would have disproven that theory. "No, but my husband is."

"The one who moved out today?" The officer clearly didn't seem concerned, but I was near positive he couldn't just snatch things from my car without a warrant. Maybe I could use that to weasel out of the prostitution charges without even calling David.

But before I could come up with a decent argument, he spoke again. "David Craig. Is that your husband?"

I nodded.

"This car is registered to him. You said it was yours." He handed the registration to me.

"It's not like I stole it. I'm sure we'll switch the title over in the divorce." I grimaced at the word "divorce." "Oh God, I'm too young for a divorce!"

"What is your name?"

"Chelsea."

"Chelsea Craig?"

I shrugged. "I guess so." I hadn't even begun to think about whether I'd change my name after the divorce. Did I even have a choice? Wouldn't I have to give up his name once we were officially caput? Not that I'd loved his last name or anything. It was just such a hassle to change in the first place and the thought of having to go through all that work over again...

I braced myself on the car door and slowly stood, narrowly avoiding conking my head on the door frame. I wobbled a little, but didn't fall. And then, with the last scrap of dignity I had, I walked to the back door of the police cruiser and tugged on the handle. It didn't budge, so I yanked harder, nearly tumbling backwards. Officer Brown Eyes caught me with a steady hand.

"Now what are you doing?" he asked.

"Turning myself in," I said, although that should've been obvious. "I'm too tired to protest. Just take me in, book me for being a hooker or whatever."

I turned as I heard him chuckling.

"I don't think you're a prostitute," he said.

"Oh." I considered my options. "Wait, do you think I look too old to be a prostitute?"

Now he laughed louder. Are cops even allowed to laugh at you? First an illegal search of my vehicle, now outright mockery. This was beginning to border on police brutality.

"You don't look old at all. How old are you?"

"Twenty-eight."

"That's not old at all. Hell, a lot of prostitutes are well into their forties."

I ignored that unsettling remark, noticing that it wasn't

just his eyes that oozed sex. His voice was pretty hot, too, all deep and mysterious sounding. I turned, finding myself face to face with him. He was taller than me, even with my heels on, and had a slender build that I suspected was solid muscle.

"So are you arresting me or not?"

He smiled, a warm but bemused smile. "I haven't decided that yet. How were you planning on getting home if your friend left and you weren't going to drive?"

I shrugged. "I'll sober up eventually."

He frowned. "You can't just hang out in this parking lot all night. It isn't safe for a young woman."

I smiled. He called me young. I opened my mouth to say I'd just take a cab, but then I remembered I didn't have any money for a cab. Stupid Jen and her stupid idea not to bring a purse. I tried to think of another explanation, someone to call for a ride or anything, but I drew a blank and, instead, started crying again.

"You can't arrest me. Who would bail me out? The only lawyers I know are David's friends. And I can't exactly call him and ask for a ride. He's probably already in bed with Traci." I shuddered at the name.

"Who's Traci?"

"His paralegal," I snorted. "Yup, there you have it. My husband left me for his twenty-three-year-old paralegal. The year David and I got married, she still had to sneak into R rated movies." I stepped around him and collapsed back onto the front seat of my car. I was too drunk to stand in these damn heels while he tried to make up his mind about arresting me.

The officer frowned.

"Hey, what's your name?"

"Officer Gyllenhaal."

I gazed up at him, squinting to read his nametag. His first name was Nicolas. "Any relation to Jake?"

He shook his head, a thin smile crossing his lips. "The address on the vehicle registration, is that your current address?"

I nodded responsibly, then watched as he stared indecisively at his watch. Finally, he spoke. "Scoot over."

"Why? Are you commandeering my car now? Because I promise it's not stolen. It's not even one of those messy divorce situations. David knows I have it and he doesn't care."

He laughed, then leaned into the patrol car, emerging as the flashing lights stopped. "I'm parking it up by the door where it won't get towed if you leave it here overnight. And then I'll drive you home. I'm off duty in ten minutes anyway."

I smiled at this development and attempted to climb over the gear shift and cup holders to get into the passenger seat, determined to ignore the fact that Officer Nicolas could likely see all the way up my trampy skirt as I did so. I fastened my belt and handed him the keys.

After he parked my car, he walked around and opened the passenger door to help me out. It felt a little like we were on a date, except that he was guiding me towards his police cruiser and not a fancy restaurant. Well, a girl could dream. He unlocked the cruiser and I yanked on the back door, this time successfully opening it.

"Get in the front," Officer Nicolas said, making no attempt to hide his eye-rolling as he opened the front door.

I shrugged and hopped in. Never having been in a police car before, I felt like a kid in a candy shop. Or, rather, an arcade. There were flashing lights and cool gadgets everywhere. I reached out to press on a large black knob when I felt his hand on mine.

"Don't. Touch. Anything," he said, those sexy brown eyes piercing into me.

I sighed and leaned back, thinking that if I could've hooked up with a guy like Officer Nicolas, instead of the green-truck-loser, maybe Jen would've been right and I would've felt better about David. In fact, I was sure of it.

We made small talk during the drive to my house, but I was a little too tipsy to recall the details. I kept thinking, boy won't David get a laugh out of this story tonight. He seemed to find the stories about my day dull, and he always had these exciting and funny anecdotes about his day. I never felt like I was pulling my own weight when we snuggled in bed at night, just before falling asleep, and swapped stories, but this one would surely entertain him.

Then I remembered David wouldn't be there tonight, that I was going to a completely empty, quiet house, where I would stay alone, forever. And suddenly, I had no interest in going home.

"I'm starving," I said. "Can we stop somewhere really quick?"

"What?"

"We don't have to go in or anything. I'm fine with a drive-through." Truth be told, I would've preferred a sit-down diner, but even I was sober enough to see that Officer Nicolas might have some issues with escorting a drunken divorcée to an all-night restaurant in his uniform.

"Tacos?" he asked a moment later, as we approached the intersection.

"Um, I'd prefer burgers," I said. "Unless you really want Mexican," I added.

He pulled into the drive-through I requested and turned

to me. I ordered a cheeseburger kids' meal and he ordered a giant burger and fries. He drove to the next window and reached for his wallet.

"I'll treat," I quickly offered. It was the least I could do since he was giving me a ride, well, and not arresting me.

"You have no money," he said dryly, paying the man at the window and driving off.

I thanked him, but waited until we reached my house to eat, not wanting to risk squirting ketchup all over his cruiser. When he pulled into my driveway, I hesitated, half expecting him to help me out and walk me to the door. But he didn't move.

"So you can get a ride tomorrow to pick up your car?"

I nodded. Jen owed me, big time. I fumbled with my belt, struggling to not drop my meal on the fancy laptop propped on the dashboard in front of me. He reached to assist, and our hands touched. I smiled. "I really appreciate you driving me home. And thanks for not arresting me. You won't get in trouble, will you?"

He shook his head slowly. "You don't strike me as a hardened criminal. I'm pretty sure you've learned your lesson and will stay out of trouble from now on."

I nodded solemnly and climbed out of the car. I steadied myself on the hood before setting off down my front path, trying my hardest not to stumble on the way to the door.

"Chelsea!"

I turned at the sound of my name. Officer Nicolas was right behind me, dangling my keys at eye level.

"You dropped these," he said.

"Oh, right. Thanks." I took the keys. "Hey, um, if you hang on a second, I can get some money to pay you back for the food. Or you can come in."

"Don't worry about it," he said.

"I'd bake you some cookies as a thank you, but it's pretty late."

"What kind of cookies?"

"I make amazing cranberry and white chocolate chip cookies," I told him. "Or if you're more of a chocolate guy, I do a mean double chocolate chunk."

His lips curled into a sly grin as he reached into his pocket. "I like cookies," he said, handing me his business card. I read it quickly.

"Well, thanks again, Officer Gyllenhaal. No more drinking from here on out," I said.

He laughed. "Call me Nick," he said, and he climbed back into his car.

2

———

I awoke late the next morning, my head pounding, my back aching, and my left hand completely numb. I sat up slowly, squeezed my fingers together until the feeling returned to my hand, and did a couple slow neck rolls. No wonder David hated this couch. It had to be the least comfortable couch ever constructed. It was too short for me to fully stretch out on and the leather was cold and slippery. But as far as couches go, it definitely looked great. Clearly, I'd based my purchasing decision on that factor alone and hadn't bothered to nap on it before buying.

I wondered how drunk I must have been last night to not have noticed how crappy the couch was before passing out on it. Course, it wasn't like I had tons of options. David had taken the guest bed and I was not about to sleep in our old bed alone.

I shuffled into the kitchen to make myself some coffee. I scooped out a heap of coffee into a filter and then paused, confused. Why wasn't the coffee pot in its normal spot? I considered the possibilities briefly before cursing out loud. "Who takes the fucking coffee maker?"

I shrieked for a solid minute. As long as I was going to be living alone, I might as well start talking to myself, I figured.

Opting to be pragmatic, I opened the refrigerator and retrieved a diet soda. Not my first choice morning beverage, but at least it was caffeinated. I heard my cell phone ring and dashed into the great room to find it. The ringing seemed to be coming from my skirt, a garment which, in the light of day, appeared much shorter than I'd remembered it being the night before.

"Hey," Jen's smooth voice greeted me. "Am I interrupting anything?" She seemed to be whispering.

"Only my self-pity and pounding headache."

"Are you at home?"

"Yep."

"Oh great. Can you come get me?"

"No," I said, before fully realizing why. "My car is at the bar."

"Well my car is at your place," she said.

"Your car is also nearly out of gas."

"You know I love you Chels."

I sighed. "So you want me to get gas in your car and come pick you up at some guy's house?"

"That would be great," she said. "It's an apartment though." She gave me the address and I trudged upstairs, soda in hand. I took a quick shower, barely staving off nausea as I dried my hair, then slipped into jeans and a sweater. I dabbed some concealer under my eyes and rubbed a thin layer of foundation over my face. I returned downstairs and quickly debated whether breakfast would make the nausea better before finally just grabbing a few leftover French fries still in the box from my late-night meal.

I pumped a full tank of gas into Jen's beater, despite the high probability that she'd never pay me back, and picked her up about an hour after she'd initially called. She was still in her clothes from the night before, her hair looking like she'd been electrocuted and her makeup washed clear off.

"Oh, shut up," she mumbled, nudging me out of the driver's seat.

"How was he?" I asked, gesturing to the shirtless man watching us drive off from Apartment E.

"Eh," she said nonchalantly. "How was your night?"

I told her about my night, impressed that I was able to recall as much as I did.

"So was he hot?"

"Who?"

"The cop."

"Actually, yes," I said.

She grinned briefly before turning to me. "I thought the guy I left with was hot last night, too. Today, not so much."

"How do you do this all the time?"

"I don't do this all the time. I was just trying to cheer you up."

"By having a one night stand?"

"No, Chelsea, by encouraging you to have a one night stand. You need to learn to have sex for fun again."

"I had fun sex before," I insisted.

Jen laughed. "No you didn't. The first few years, you had sex that David thought was fun, and the last year, since you started this whole baby-making mission, you had sex that neither of you thought was fun."

I scowled, but she was sort of right. I didn't dislike sex, but it had always fallen into the general category of items on my mental to-do list.

"Maybe we should start slower with the plan to cheer

you up," she suggested. "What if we sign you up for online dating today?"

I shook my head. "Today, I'm buying a coffee maker and new bedding so I can sleep in my own freaking bed without thinking about him."

Jen sighed as she pulled next to my car. "A new man in your bed will distract you a lot more than a new comforter."

I ignored her and climbed out of the car.

She rolled down her window. "You're making him cookies, right?"

"What?"

"You said you promised to make him cookies."

"Oh, yeah. Well, he knows I was kidding."

"But he gave you his card."

"So?"

"So bake the damn cookies and take them to him at work."

"I can't face him sober. I was a mess last night. I rambled on about not being a prostitute and I'm pretty sure I mooned him at one point."

She grimaced.

"Accidentally," I clarified.

"Just take him the cookies. Baking will calm you down and you probably won't actually see him anyway, just leave them at the station for him. Oh, and thanks for the gas. I'll pay you back next time."

I shook my head again as she zoomed off.

Two hours later, I was home from Bed, Bath & Beyond, a new comforter, sheet set, and coffee maker filling my trunk. I knew there must be other things I'd have to replace, but these were the most urgent essentials. Still a little queasy, I fixed myself a small, healthy lunch. Okay, maybe I downed half a box of Toasted Cinnamon Puffs Cereal, but whatever. It was loaded with nutrients. It said so on the box.

I contemplated taking a nap in my newly-decked out bed, but opted instead to try Jen's advice. Sure, she'd been way wrong on the hook-up last night, but baking cookies seemed like a harmless enough plan.

I mixed the dough for oatmeal peanut butter cookies, cranberry white chocolate chip cookies, and double chocolate chunk cookies, the three best in my arsenal. I froze most of the dough, baking about a dozen of each recipe and then selecting the ten best of each varietal to arrange on a sturdy paper plate after they cooled. I'd save the others for a little snack later. I grabbed a ten dollar bill from my purse and tucked it into an envelope with Officer Nick Gyllenhaal neatly printed on the outside. Then, I jotted a brief thank you and wedged it in the envelope before licking it shut.

I covered the plate with that plastic wrap that's supposed to cling to anything but is notorious for only sticking to itself or anything else you don't want it on, ultimately unwrapping about half the box before getting enough stuck on straight to cover the cookies. Then I went upstairs to do a quick self-assessment.

I knew Jen was right, that the chances of him actually being there were slim to none, but I also didn't want to risk him seeing me looking like a mess again. Even if he wasn't actually cute without my drunk goggles, I couldn't live with myself if I didn't somehow improve the impression I'd made the night before. I switched bras, slipped into a slightly more fitted v-neck sweater, and reapplied makeup. I combed my hair, added some jewelry, and gave myself one last glance in the mirror.

I still looked tired, but the makeup helped a lot. My eyes were fiercely green today, in contrast with their paler green hue when I was less hopped-up on caffeine, and my shoulder length brown hair looked smooth and classy. It probably didn't hurt that I hadn't been styling it for months since David and I stopped going to movies and parties. I'd read somewhere that a break from your beauty routine could take years off your apparent age, but I had never before considered that a plus side of a ruined marriage.

The station listed on Nick's card wasn't the closest to my house, but it wasn't far either. I wondered if he lived nearby and then I wondered if he lived alone. Had I even checked for a wedding ring? Futilely, I racked my brain. Anyway, it didn't matter if he was single or not. I wasn't courting him, just bringing him a thank you treat.

The parking lot at the station was pretty empty, which didn't surprise me since it was a Sunday afternoon. There was a row of police cars, all identical to the one I'd ridden in, and a few marked SUVs. And then there was a handful of other regular cars. I parked by those and started up to the main entrance. When I walked in, I saw a small waiting room and a woman sitting behind a desk, a large plexiglass screen separating her from the waiting room like at a doctor's office.

I approached the window and waited for her to acknowledge me. "Hi. I wanted to drop something off for Officer Gyllenhaal."

"What's your name?"

My eyes widened. Why was that relevant? "Oh, it's on the card here. I can just leave it for him with you if it's okay. It's just a little thank you present. He helped me with some car problems." I held up the cookies.

She stood. "I think he's here somewhere. Let me find him."

"Oh, no, that's okay..." I began, but she was already gone.

Still clutching my cookies nervously, I turned and paced around the waiting room. There were some awards and photos hanging along the back wall, but nothing too interesting.

"Can I help you?"

I recognized the deep voice before I spun around to face him. I looked up, glancing straight into those luscious brown eyes I remembered so vividly from my drunken stupor, and promptly forgot how to speak. After a moment, he smiled. He had a prominent dimple on one cheek and the trace of one on the other, covered by a light layer of dark stubble which I hadn't noticed the night before. He was definitely still cute today.

"Are those for me?"

I initially thought he was staring at my breasts, but quickly realized he meant the cookies. Too bad. I nodded like an idiot.

"You didn't really have to bring me cookies, Chelsea."

My heart thudded. He remembered my name. "I just wanted to thank you, and apologize. I'm not normally, well, you know." Actually, I hoped he knew what I meant, because I honestly didn't. Although I'm not always drunk, I had been drinking more than usual lately. And as for the rambling, well, I did normally do that.

He smiled warmly and took the cookies.

I placed the envelope on top. "I wanted to repay you for the food too."

"That's really not necessary. The cookies are plenty."

I glanced down at his hand, confirming the absence of a wedding ring, before gazing back up. He was staring right at me. I knew I had to say something. "No, really, I insist."

He turned around, set the cookies on the counter by the large plastic window, and pulled another card out of his pocket. He jotted something down on it and handed it to me along with my envelope. "If you really want to repay me, you can treat me to a kids' meal sometime. I can't just take your money."

He retrieved the cookies and punched in a code on the door in the corner of the room. "I'm off tomorrow and Thursday," he said, as the door buzzed and he slipped out of the room.

I glanced down at the card, uncertain of what had just transpired or why he had given me his business card again, until I turned it over, finding his cell phone number scrawled in blue ink. I bit my lip and scurried out of the station before I managed to humiliate myself.

BACK AT MY HOUSE, I spent the rest of the afternoon cleaning and pacing. Cleaning was something I always did on Sunday afternoons, ensuring I'd have no excuses to procrastinate on work when the week began. If my house was a mess during the week, or if there was any task I could think of that needed accomplishing, I'd tackle that instead of working. And as a freelancer, paid only for finished work products and not time spent working, I'd quickly go broke if I gave in to every distraction. The big exception to that rule was my office. Technically, it was the third bedroom, but I used it as an office. Aside from a weekly vacuuming, no cleaning occurred in the office. I liked the way the light bounced off the dusty bookshelves and the fact that loose papers coated every surface in the room. It was one of my many quirks.

Today, I was drinking while cleaning, which probably contributed to the pacing. I had my first glass of wine—a cheap, excessively sweet Riesling which David would've likened to curdled apple juice—while dusting the furniture and wiping the windows. A second glass motivated me to clean the bathrooms and kitchen, and a third and final glass had me belting out Bruno Mars tunes while mopping and running the vacuum. By the time I finished, I was facedown, sobbing into my newly cleaned carpet.

Probably it was the combination of bad wine and sappy music, but I couldn't ignore the distinct possibility that I'd reached the beginning of the end. My life as I knew it was headed down the drain, and I was powerless to stop it. The love of my life was gone and without him, I couldn't afford the house. In fact, without him, I might even need a steady job with a fixed income, something I was pretty sure I wasn't cut out for.

So basically, I was going to be homeless, unemployed, single, and broke.

My writing wasn't entirely unprofitable, with my freelancing bringing in between two and four hundred a week, and each book I penned for another author in their name netting me about ten thousand. For a few years, I'd done two books a year that way, but lately, since David's work was lucrative enough to support us both, I'd dropped down to one every fifteen months or so, using my newfound free time to work on my own novel.

The stuff I wrote for other people wasn't fiction. Usually, my agent would fix me up with someone who had a great idea for a nonfiction book and who was qualified and prepared to do all the research. They'd turn all the materials over to me and I'd do the writing. When it was done, their name would go on the cover, with my paycheck and an occasional mention on the Acknowledgments page the only signs of my involvement.

Magazines were usually more interested in my humor articles. I wrote on a variety of easy-to-research topics, like new diet trends or fashion, in a funny, relatable way. I was never a serious journalist and had no desire to ever report actual news. Honestly, I was happiest writing fiction; specifically, sappy romances.

I'd actually finished one novel about a year before. I hadn't told David I was writing it, knowing he'd think it was a silly waste of my time. But when I'd finished, I'd printed out a copy of the first draft and presented it to him with a bow on top. He'd been confused, at first, and then, just when I expected him to sweep me up in a congratulatory hug, he'd lit into me about how much ink I'd wasted from our printer and didn't I know how expensive ink was. He apologized later and promised to read it, but I'm not sure he ever did.

A few weeks after that, I'd mentioned that I was going to polish the manuscript and prepare a synopsis to send to my agent in hopes of finding a publisher. David made it clear that, in his professional opinion, I would jeopardize my reputation with the agent if I followed through with my plan.

In retrospect, he was probably right. It was my first novel, and the manuscript was a little amateurish. I shelved it—literally hiding the completed project on a shelf in my office—and secretly began penning my next novel. That one was still in progress, but I could already tell it was better than the first.

I shoved the mop back into the closet and reached for the bottle of wine only to find it was empty.

Crap.

It was hard to ruminate about the shoddy state of my life when I was out of cheap wine. How did I let my wine supply deplete? And actually, how did I let my entire life sink to this low?

My mind briefly scanned over the last fifteen years. I'd definitely been on track in high school, with good grades, a coveted position on the dance squad, and a cute boyfriend who played varsity basketball. I'd always planned on attending NYU to study creative writing, but said boyfriend was going to a local college. In the end, I joined him at the local college. It didn't have a particularly stellar writing program, but it wasn't like I was *only* there for him. I still got a degree, and my parents saved money on tuition. Of course, the boyfriend dumped me for my freshman roommate, but that was ancient history.

After graduation, with no clear career options, I'd begun law school. That was where I'd met David. He was the most handsome 1L—that's what they called the first year students—with curly blond hair and a hypnotic smile. He was a charmer, too. We started dating before I'd even learned how to brief a case, and by final exams, we were in love. He convinced me I wasn't cut out for law school and I dropped out after the first year. I got a job writing for the local newspaper, and David proposed. We were married a year later, and David persuaded me to quit my job when he graduated.

As romantic as the suggestion had seemed at the time, I went crazy staying at home by myself while he worked upwards of seventy hours a week. To fill my days until he came home, filled with exuberant stories of office politics, crazed opposing counsel, and clients from hell, I started baking. Once I got a little too good at that, as evidenced by the weight gain afflicting both David and I, I started writing again, this time on a freelance basis. It felt great to contribute, however meagerly, to our family finances, and I enjoyed having something to do all day aside from puttering around the empty house.

Where did I go wrong? When had I turned into a pathetic mess that David—or anyone else, for that matter—didn't want to be married to?

Shaking my head, I washed my wine glass, ate a family-sized bag of pretzels, and went to bed. It wasn't until the middle of the night when I saw everything clearly—the link that tied together all of my past mishaps. I sat abruptly, my pillow flying off the side of the bed.

"I didn't fight," I said out loud, startled as my voice shattered the silence of the pitch black bedroom.

But that was it. The moment my life began spiraling downhill was the moment I stopped fighting for what I wanted.

I wanted to go to NYU, but I hadn't fought for it. I hadn't even bothered to try to convince Connor that we could have a long-distance relationship or even to let myself acknowledge the possibility that my education might be more important than a youthful romance.

Later that year, I wanted to steal back my boyfriend from slutty Hannah Hoffman, but I hadn't even tried. I even agreed to photograph them before the spring formal!

After college, I wanted to try my hand at writing, but I didn't fight my parents when they suggested law school. When law school got hard and David mentioned it might not be my thing, I quit without a fight. And even though I actually enjoyed my low-paying job at the paper, I don't even recall telling David that when he asked me to resign.

I wondered what would have happened then, if I'd fought to keep that job. Probably I would've been a more interesting person for him to come home to. Instead of just listening to David, I'd have had my own stories to share over dinner. And I wouldn't have eaten all those cookies. And maybe, with the job to distract me, I wouldn't have gotten so obsessed with our difficulties conceiving a baby. Maybe, just maybe, if I had insisted on keeping that job, David wouldn't be sleeping in Traci's bed right now.

I knew it was too late to go back in time and change my old mistakes, but it wasn't too late to fight for David. I could still save my marriage. I was going to fix myself up, to change myself into a woman who deserved to be with David, and I would steal him back from Traci. My life would not get away from me without a fight. Exhausted and relieved by my revelation, I fell back into a peaceful slumber.

3

The next morning, I awoke feeling calm. I hadn't slept well, but at least I had a plan. Well, maybe not so much a plan as a general idea. I needed to hammer out the details. I rigged up my new coffee pot and brewed a fresh pot of hazelnut roast, then pulled out a crisp sheet of paper and a newly sharpened pencil. I poured myself a mug of coffee, dumped in enough skim milk to turn the coffee pale beige, hearing David's voice in my head mocking "would you like some coffee with your cream?"

I divided the paper into two columns. On the left side, I made a list of everything David didn't like about me—either things he'd outright said he didn't like, such as my inability to cook non-dessert foods, my unwillingness to bleach my light brown hair, my compulsive nail-biting, or my willful obliviousness to current events. I also included traits I suspected he disliked, such as the five pounds I'd added to my otherwise slender build since our wedding or my tendency to ramble. I quickly filled an entire page with my shortcomings and had to start on a new sheet of paper.

Geesh. No wonder David left. I was a disaster!

In the right column, I started brainstorming ways to fix the problems identified on the left. Some of the goals were simple: join a gym, get highlights, stop biting nails, take cooking classes, read the newspaper daily, and so forth. Others were trickier. How could I learn to feign interest when he talked about a case at work? Was it even possible for a non-barrister to be interested in whatever it is that lawyers do? I certainly couldn't compete with paralegal Traci if I refused to even attempt to understand his work. Maybe I'd start by watching *Law and Order* and go from there.

My phone rang and I realized I'd already wasted the first two hours of a perfectly good work day. I set the list aside and went on with my day.

THAT NIGHT, I met Jen for dinner. She was already at the pizzeria when I arrived, which was a first.

"You're late!" she said with an excited grin. I figured she was banking on this one instance excusing her next dozen or so late arrivals.

"Yeah, sorry, I got a little distracted this morning with a list I was making and the day just got away from me."

Jen raised a confused eyebrow but didn't press the topic. "How are you today?" Her tone reminded me of the way a psychiatrist might address a schizophrenic.

"I'm fine, Jen. You don't have to look at me like you're afraid I'm going to have a violent outburst or start crying. I've got a plan now, and I'm going to win David back."

"Win him back?"

I nodded calmly and summarized my chart to her. She cringed as I spoke, her eyes growing wider by the moment.

"Can I talk now?" she asked when I finally finished outlining my plan.

"Sure, but you won't change my mind."

"Fine. I'm not even sure I want to change your mind because you seem to feel better now that you have a plan and I'm certain that sooner or later you will realize your plan is ridiculous."

"Ridiculous?"

She shrugged. "Insane. Wacky. Futile. Whatever. My point is, you weren't that happy with David anyway, and then *he* cheated on *you*. If anyone needs to try to win anyone back, it's David. He is a pandering scumbag and you deserve better, but obviously you aren't ready to accept that fact yet, so let's discuss something else."

I inhaled sharply and tried to ignore Jen's harsh comments. She had always been overly opinionated and incapable of conceding to reason, so there was no point in arguing with her.

"Fine." I finally said. "How was work today?"

"Eh," she shrugged. "That's a boring topic. I have a date tomorrow, though!"

I leaned back as the waitress positioned our large pepperoni, black olive, and mushroom pizza on the center of the table.

"With whom?" I asked, plopping a steaming slice onto my plate.

"Ryan," Jen replied with a mischievous grin.

"The one night stand from the bar?"

She nodded.

I laughed, not in the slightest surprised by this. Although she hadn't given him the best review the morning after their hook up, Jen was a very forgiving person. The fact that he called her the next day earned him big points in her book.

"I thought you said he wasn't that cute in the morning," I reminded her.

She shrugged. "Yeah, but neither was I. I mean, if we're going to start judging men on the day after, I'll be single forever."

I smiled supportively, but in my head, I was remembering how Officer Nick had looked pretty fine the day after my initial encounter with him.

"Have you called him yet?" she asked, reading my mind.

I shook my head. "No, I'm not going to. I'm going to get back together with David."

She rolled her eyes dramatically. "I didn't say you had to sleep with him, although I still think that would be a good idea, but you have nothing to lose by at least going out with him. You said you wanted to make yourself more interesting to David, to get some new hobbies, so this could be one of them."

"You think my new hobby should be dating another man?"

"It wouldn't even have to be a date. And you don't have a choice anyway. You owe him for the burgers."

I smiled, but we both knew I wouldn't call him.

"Do you still have his card?"

I nodded. I pulled it from my purse and handed it to her. "See, he just wrote his cell phone number. It's not like he asked me out," I began, but then I realized she had snagged my phone when I was distracted by the last remaining breadstick. "Don't you dare," I said, just as she tapped something on the phone and slid it across the table to me.

"It's ringing," she said. "And don't even think about hanging up. He's a cop and he'll just trace the call."

I barely had time to glare at her, let alone to panic, before he answered. I cleared my throat awkwardly. "Um, hi, is this Nick?"

"Yes," his voice sounded deeper than I remembered. "Who's this?"

I took a deep breath. "Chelsea Craig, the uh, cookie lady."

He laughed. "Those were really good cookies."

"Thanks."

"I was starting to think you weren't going to call."

I tried to think of a witty response, but drew a blank.

"Thursday is my only other night off this week, so I guess you'll have to take me out then."

"Right, sure," I said. "Do you really want fast food?" He had said I owed him a kids' meal, after all.

"I'm more of a Mexican-food guy, actually." There was a pause, and then he named a restaurant about ten minutes from my house and offered to pick me up.

"I can meet you there," I quickly said.

He chuckled again, but agreed, and we hung up. I glared at Jen.

She smiled proudly.

THURSDAY ARRIVED without me deciding what to wear that night. Truth be told, I'd been so busy thinking about David and my grand scheme to win him back that I hadn't thought about my non-date with Nick at all. Still, I owed the man a dinner, and I might as well look good.

I settled on a denim skirt that fell just above my knee, paired with a long-sleeved fitted blouse, partially unbuttoned to reveal the pale pink camisole beneath. It was pretty, accented both my butt and boobs without looking trampy, and it was casual. I straightened my hair and swiped on an extra coat of mascara before throwing a long, multi-strand necklace over my head and taking off to meet Nick.

I scanned the parking lot for police cruisers when I arrived but didn't spot any. He probably drove a different car off duty anyway, but I didn't know for sure. I didn't see Nick in the restaurant either, so I waited in the front. At five after seven, he brushed in the door. He wore dark jeans that immediately drew my eyes to his hips and a long-sleeved olive sweater that clung to his biceps. I licked my lips hungrily.

Nick's eyes lit up when he saw me. I stood, and we approached the hostess together. As the hostess seated us in a quiet corner booth, it occurred to me that she must think this was a date. Nick ordered a Corona, but I stuck with iced tea. It didn't seem smart to get sloshed in front of a cop again.

"Not a beer gal?"

I shook my head. "I'm really not a huge drinker," I lied.

"Not even the occasional margarita?"

"Well, yeah, but…"

"She'll have a margarita," he said to the waitress.

"Frozen," I added, knowing at least that would slow me down. I could slurp down one of those 24 ounce on-the-rocks margaritas in an instant.

"Give us a couple of minutes," Nick said to the waitress when she returned with our drinks and a basket of chips. When she left, he turned to me. "You're quieter tonight."

"Um, yes. I'm a little embarrassed about how I acted the other night." I said, omitting that I actually didn't remember everything from that night.

"You're an entertaining drunk, all right."

"I'm sorry about all the stuff I told you. I know you probably don't need all those personal details when you try to arrest someone."

He nodded. "You mean the stuff about your divorce? Was that all true?"

I frowned. "I don't remember what exactly I told you, but yes, my husband did move in with his paralegal last Friday."

"Ouch." He sipped his beer. "Were you separated?"

I snorted. "I didn't even know we were having problems, aside from the normal marriage stuff. I was definitely unaware that he was sleeping with someone else or that he had been seeing someone else long enough to actually move in with her."

"Wow. So it was completely out of the blue."

I nodded, and before I had to explain any further, the waitress returned and we ordered.

"What do you do when you're not selling your body for sex outside the bars?" he asked.

"I'm a writer," I said, blushing. "Freelance magazine articles, mostly. I work from home. What about you? What do you do when you're not rescuing drunk ladies?"

He smiled. It was one of those perfect smiles—completely symmetrical, full, and innocent, revealing straight, white teeth beneath. "I'm on the vice squad. We deal primarily with drugs, prostitution, and gambling."

My eyes widened when he mentioned prostitution.

He laughed. "I never thought you were a prostitute."

"What made you decide to be a cop?" I asked, relaxing as the margarita hit my blood stream.

"I did a stint in the Army and studied criminal justice in school."

"Do you like it?"

"Most days. It's a thankless job, though. The pay isn't

great and the people you arrest are never exactly appreciative of your efforts."

"But the people you help appreciate it," I said.

He nodded. "Yeah, but we don't hear from them a lot.
Most people don't bring cookies to the station." Nick leaned
forward and brushed a piece of tortilla chip off the side of
my lip. The intimacy of the gesture flustered me, and he
clearly noticed.

"How'd you get into freelancing?"

I shrugged. "Law school didn't really pan out."

"You went to law school?"

"Just a year. It wasn't for me."

"You don't seem the law student type. You're too
interesting."

I beamed at the unexpected compliment.

"What do you write?" Nick asked me, just as our food
arrived. Before I answered, he turned to the waitress and
asked for another round of drinks. Then he focused his full
attention back on me.

I offered him the brief, generic description of my actual
work, and then mentioned what I'd like to be writing. He
seemed fascinated by my book ideas, and before I knew it,
we'd finished our food. The check arrived and he slipped a
credit card to the waitress before I could stop him.

"Hey, I was going to pay. I owe you." I said.

Nick shrugged.

"That was the whole point of this meal, so I could repay
you."

"I decided the cookies were worth more than your kids'
meal," he said. "This was just for fun."

"Well, thanks."

I was unsure of what else to say as we walked out
together. I started towards my car slowly, and he followed.

Now was the awkward part, where we apparently decided if it was a date or not.

Nick stopped next to my car and smiled. "I'm glad you called. You're a little quieter when you're sober, but still intriguing."

"I'm trying to cut back on the babbling." I said, feeling myself blush. "Well, thanks again for the other day, and for dinner."

Suddenly, he crouched down next to my car. I followed his glance to my back tire, which didn't look quite right.

"You've got a flat. Do you have a spare?" he asked, running his fingers along the tire.

"A spare tire?" And then I remembered. I did have a spare tire, but it was in my garage, at home. I'd taken it out before a shopping spree with Jen a few months ago, after a dispute with David about his frequent business trips. I needed the extra trunk space then, and clearly, I'd forgotten to put it back in.

"I think I do. But it's, um, at home."

This seemed to perplex him, but he didn't say so. "Hang on."

I watched him walk to a silver Chevy Camaro and return a moment later with a large spray bottle.

"Fix a Flat," he explained. "This will hold it so you can drive home."

I watched with fascination as he attached the bottle to my tire and slowly reinflated the black rubber. Once it seemed full, he ran his fingers along the ridges. "I don't see a nail and they might be able to patch it if you bring it in. It's a pretty old tire though. Your tread is worn way down. I'd just switch it out for the spare if I were you."

I nodded. "Right. Definitely. I'll do that first thing in the morning."

A bemused grin crossed his face. "You know how to change a tire?"

"I know how to take it someplace and pay them to change it for me," I said. Of course, I was bluffing. I'd never done that either. Auto maintenance, much like lawn mowing and home repairs, was always in David's purview. Although, I was fairly certain he couldn't have changed a tire himself either.

Nick shook his head. "You don't need to pay someone. I'll do it."

I was going to protest, but he'd already started to his car.

"It should drive fine now. I'll follow you home."

I drove ten miles under the speed limit the whole way home, acutely aware that I'd consumed two margaritas and was now driving home with a police officer on my tail. At one point, he flashed his brights at me and I nearly pulled over to the side of the road.

Nick pulled in my driveway after me. "You're a cautious driver," he teased, following me into the garage.

"You made me nervous. And why did you keep flashing your lights?"

"I was trying to get you to speed up. That drive was like being in a parade."

"I didn't want you to ticket me."

Nick laughed. "If I was going to ticket you, I probably would've done that on Saturday." He spotted the tire and got to work.

We continued the comfortable banter while he changed the tire, and I found I was disappointed that the task didn't take him longer.

"I guess I owe you more cookies now," I said as he wiped his hands on a rag.

He nodded. "Yeah, but since I ended up paying for

dinner, another meal might be more appropriate. Maybe Tuesday night?"

I raised an eyebrow. Was he asking me out?

"You pick the place this time. And I'm picking you up. You're out of spare tires anyway."

"Okay, but you have to let me pay. I don't want to be forever indebted to you."

He waved and drove off.

I watched until his car was out of sight, then shut and locked the door behind me. I rummaged through the freezer until I found a roll of double chocolate cookie dough, sliced off an oversized chunk, and wedged the remainder back into the freezer. Retreating to my bedroom upstairs, I changed into comfy pajama pants and a tank top while the dough defrosted, then snuggled under the covers to watch *Law and Order* reruns while eating the uncooked treat.

THE NEXT DAY WAS FRIDAY, and Jen insisted on dragging me out to dinner with her and a couple other friends. I loved Jen, but she was starting to smother me. Since David moved out, she'd been calling daily and confirming that I had plans for at least two weeknights and all weekend long. It's not that I didn't like going out with friends, but it wasn't the same.

After spending the better part of the day dreading the outing, I decided to call Jen and cancel. "I appreciate the invitation, but I just want a night like I used to have with David," I explained.

"Chels, David told you he was working late almost every Friday night."

"He was, and then he came home and we cuddled on the couch and watched a movie."

"Chelsea," Jen's voice had that obvious tone to it, but thankfully, she didn't say what she was thinking.

"Okay, fine. I get it, Jen. He was working it with Traci Friday nights. But I still miss the cuddling. And the movies." Looking back, it did sound lame, but I had nothing but good memories of relaxing with David and watching funny shows. Really, that was perhaps the best part of marriage, always having an excuse to just snuggle at home. It wasn't like dating, where I'd have to try to impress someone. I could literally just sit on the couch and be myself with David. Those were the days.

"Well, let's go to a movie with the girls after dinner then. I don't know about cuddling, but I'll hold your hand," she offered. She hung up before I could protest.

I sighed with exasperation, but started to change into nicer clothes regardless.

On the plus side, I reasoned, I could use my plans with Jen to avoid going to my parents' house for dinner. I mean, I loved my parents. I just wasn't eager to tell them that the husband they so adored dumped me for his paralegal.

Thankfully, my mother had recently begun texting, so I simply typed a quick message to her informing her that Jen had a dating crisis that she needed to discuss over dinner tonight, not bothering to clarify that the romance in crisis was my own, and that I didn't want to ditch David both nights of the weekend for dinner.

My mom replied almost instantaneously, which she never did, suggesting that I bring David to their house Saturday. Yikes.

"Can we just reschedule?" I replied.

"Tues lunch?"

I gritted my teeth, but agreed. Lunch with my mother would give me a chance to tell her alone, which seemed easier than confessing my marital woes to both of my parents together, even though my dad was probably more likely to take my side in the situation, whereas my mother would surely blame me. And it would keep my mind off my dinner that night with Nick.

4

———

I awoke Tuesday morning acutely aware of my lunch plans with my mother. However, I hadn't anticipated her arriving at ten-thirty for said lunch.

"You're wearing that?" she said in lieu of a more traditional greeting as I opened the door.

I glanced down, certain my pajama pants and tank top weren't the worst thing I could wear to a lunch buffet. Honestly, I was probably overdressed for some of the dumps she frequented with my grandma.

"Hello, Mom," I said, leaning forward and kissing her on the cheek. "I wasn't expecting you this early. I'll go get dressed."

She sighed, as though she'd arrived at a perfectly reasonable meal time, then made her way into the kitchen. I raced up the stairs, nearly tripping towards the top, and yanked on the first outfit I grabbed. The longer my mother was loose in my house, the better her chances of figuring out David had left before I had a chance to tell her myself.

I debated skipping the makeup step, but decided that would raise suspicion in my mom anyway. So, I swiped on a quick coat of mascara and some tinted lip gloss before returning to survey the mischief she'd caused.

"Ready to go," I announced, louder than necessary.

My mother gazed up from the stack of mail she was rifling through. My mail. "You know there are bills in here," she said.

I snatched the stack of mail away from her. "I'll pay them later," I assured her. In all honesty, I'd been avoiding the mail, and especially the bills. Most of our utilities were in David's name, the savings and checking accounts were all in both of our names, and the credit cards were probably a mix of the two. How was I supposed to even handle that? Should I go on paying them from joint accounts and if so, for how long? I contemplated setting up my own savings and checking account, but the majority of the income came from David, and as long as he was still using shared credit cards, I didn't feel compelled to cover all the bills from my own puny income. And what if I did pay the bills and started seeing charges for fancy restaurants David was taking Traci to or slutty lingerie he bought her?

I glanced up and realized my mother was glaring at me.

"Are you even listening?" she asked. "I said men prefer you to stay on top of these things. Don't let David see this pile of mail on your counter."

I rolled my eyes. I'd suggested we set up online bill-pay countless times over the years, but David was the one who insisted on having a paper record. "What sounds good for lunch?"

She shrugged. "What sounds good to you, sweetie?"

I quickly tried to think of a crowded place where she couldn't yell without attracting attention. "Olive Garden?" I suggested.

She smiled and offered to drive. I took the opportunity to butter her up.

"Your hair looks nice, Mom."

"Thank you. I had it styled on Thursday."

"I'm thinking about trying highlights and a layered cut," I said.

She glanced sideways at me. "That's a great idea. You never do anything different with your hair. It couldn't hurt," she added, without clarifying what exactly couldn't be hurt by a new hairdo.

The small talk continued over the next few minutes, and I successfully offered up truthful, albeit vague, answers to her questions about David and his work. Thankfully, the restaurant was close, so the drive was short.

We were the first customers, having arrived at precisely 11:01, so the waitress greeted us and took our order quickly. Now was my chance to tell her, before I lost my nerve.

I swallowed audibly, then began. "I'm glad you invited me to lunch today. There's something I wanted to tell you."

A wide grin broke out on her face. "I knew it!" she squealed, jumping out of her seat to hug me. "You were practically showing in those pajamas of yours, and Italian food is exactly what I craved when I was pregnant with you!"

Her excitement confused me so much that I nearly missed her implication. "I'm not pregnant," I said, quietly.

"What?"

"I'm not pregnant," I repeated louder, just as the waitress deposited our drinks at the table.

The waitress blushed and nearly spilled my strawberry lemonade on the breadsticks. My mother's face fell.

"But you said..."

"I said I had something to tell you." I inhaled slowly.

"David moved out for a little while. We decided we needed some space."

"What? You're married. You don't get space. And even if you did, your house is plenty big. Perfect for lots of children, if you ask me. Have I told you what your father and I slept in the first ten years of our marriage? A full bed. Practically a twin, I tell you."

I nodded, slowly, slurping my drink and wishing I could get sucked into the straw and disappear. "Right, well, actually I didn't have a lot of say in the matter, but he decided he needed to move out for a while."

She frowned. "What did you do?"

"When he left? Well, I went out with Jen."

She shook her head. "No, what did you do to make him leave?"

"It wasn't my fault!"

She reached across the table for my hand. I resisted the urge to yank it away. "Of course not, sweetie. That came out wrong. What I meant was, what happened before he left? Did you have a disagreement or something?"

"He had sex with his paralegal," I said, dryly. Of course, just then the poor waitress had returned with the salad, which she practically threw onto the table in an attempt to get far away from us quickly.

"Oh." My mother calmly helped herself to some salad, tossed the onions into a napkin which she folded on the edge of the table, then served me a heaping portion, too. "Well, that is unfortunate."

"Yep."

"Men can be very challenging sometimes," she said.

"Yep."

She chewed her salad thoughtfully.

"Can we talk about something else?" I asked.

She nodded, and we did, until she drove me back home. And then, of course, she couldn't resist leaving me with her ultimate wisdom as she deposited me in my driveway.

"I know this is entirely his fault, Chelsea. What David did is wrong, and he certainly needs to apologize. But men make mistakes. We're all human. As his wife, your job is to forgive him."

"I'm not sure he wants to be forgiven."

My mother hugged me without unbuckling her belt. "You can do anything you put your mind to, Chelsea. Let me know if you need anything."

I rolled my eyes as I exited the car. Hopefully my second restaurant meal of the day would be more successful.

NICK WAS right on time that evening. I had selected a little Indian restaurant for us to dine at, figuring the spicy food would discourage him from making any moves. That way, I could get through the dinner with him without ever resolving the whole date or nondate issue. After the lunch with my mom, I couldn't handle any more awkward conversations.

He started up to the door, but I let myself out before he reached the front step. He paused and smiled. "You look beautiful," he said.

And that unleashed it.

"Is this a date?" I asked. "Because it feels a little like a date, with you picking me up, complimenting me, and I don't even know why I wore this dress...it's cute, but it screams date, doesn't it? I just, well, I told you my husband just moved out. I'm still technically married, though. I can't be going on dates. My mother would kill me." I stopped talking and realized I was gasping for air.

"Are you done?" he asked calmly.

I nodded.

"It's good to see the rambling Chelsea is back," he said, opening the passenger side door. "Let me lay down my cards here and see if we can't get this straightened out. I gave you my number last weekend because I find you attractive but I wasn't sure if you were mentally stable. You called, which surprised me, and despite the whole tire incident, you didn't raise any red flags as far as your mental status. So yeah, I was thinking this was a date."

I wasn't sure how to react to that so I smiled. Hey, he called me attractive. And beautiful. If it were a date, he'd be doing really well.

"Can I ask you a question?"

I nodded.

"If you don't want to date, why did you agree to go out with me tonight?"

Good question. I couldn't very well admit that he had the nicest butt I've ever seen. "You're pretty persuasive," I said.

"Well, seeing as how we're both all dressed up and en route to a restaurant, why don't we go ahead and eat together. I'm pretty sure the only difference between a friendly dinner and a date is the sex afterwards."

"I would not have sex with you on a second date."

He eyed me mischievously. "I'm pretty persuasive."

THE RESTAURANT WAS CROWDED for a Tuesday night, so we had to wait at the bar for a table. By the time we were seated, the glass of wine I'd sipped at the bar was already in full effect.

"I'm sorry I'm such a nutcase," I said. "I thought I had everything figured out until David left, and since then, I don't know what I'm doing. My friend Jen thinks I need to move on and she swears the best thing to help me forget about David is meaningless sex. My mom, who I had lunch with today, thinks I should be trying to win David back." I paused. "Of course, I didn't tell her he moved in with his girlfriend, just that he cheated."

"Your friend Jen sounds very wise," he said with a grin.

I swatted his hand playfully. "The problem is, I'm not sure I want to get over him. Right now, I think maybe I need to fight to save my marriage."

"You think you could forgive him for sleeping with someone else?"

I gazed down at my half-eaten salad. "No. Right now I can't fathom ever forgiving him. But if I'm being honest, I don't think he's entirely to blame for our current situation."

Nick reached across the table and placed his hand over mine. I looked up and our eyes met. "Chelsea, it is not your fault he left. I don't know all the details, but I know you didn't make him cheat. Any guy that would cheat on you is obviously a moron."

"Thanks," I mumbled. "It's a good thing this isn't a date, because I'd be losing some serious points with this discussion topic."

He shrugged. "It all hinges on the sex later. We'll see how that goes, then decide."

I pierced several lettuce leaves with my fork instead of answering, determined to believe he was joking.

"You know, if you are planning on getting back with him,

it might actually help if you've been with someone else, too, level the playing field and whatnot."

"I'll let you know if I decide to go that route," I said.

He smiled and didn't take his eyes off me as the waiter approached with our food.

I grinned appreciatively at the waiter for the distraction and seized the opportunity to change the subject. "So, tell me something interesting about yourself."

"What do you want to know?"

I shrugged. "Something not everyone knows. Tell me your dreams, your fears."

Nick chewed thoughtfully. "Clowns and detective."

"You'd like to be a clown someday and you're terrified of detectives," I summarily teased.

"Exactly."

"I could've guessed that. Everyone is afraid of clowns. Tell me something unique you're afraid of."

"I'm a cop. I'm not supposed to be afraid of much. Every day, there is the possibility I'll get shot at work. I'm okay with that."

"Yeah, yeah, I get it Mister Tough-Guy. You're really not afraid of anything else?"

We each finished off a few bites while he contemplated this challenge.

"Worms," he finally said.

"Like parasites?"

"Earthworms. It really freaks me out how you can cut one in half and instead of dying, it just becomes two worms. They're like some mutant monster, just waiting to take over Earth."

I considered this. "Yeah, now that you mention it, worms are creepy in that respect. Not as bad as clowns, though."

Nick laughed, drawing my eyes back to his perfectly

straight white teeth. "Mental note not to take you to the circus."

"Any siblings?"

"In the circus? No. But I do have two younger sisters. You?"

"Only child. I suspect that's why I became a writer, so I could invent dialogue and characters to make up for the lack of real interaction in my house," I mused. "I mean, I didn't have a bad childhood or anything. My parents were pretty great and no major complaints, just no one to play with."

He nodded. "My sisters tried to dress me up like a prince whenever they wanted to have princess weddings. I used to envy the only children I knew."

"I bet you were a good big brother, and very protective of your sisters."

Nick swigged his beer. "Not protective enough."

"What do you mean?"

"When I was a senior in high school, my sister Valerie had this boyfriend who used to knock her around. Nothing too serious, but it really messed with her head long after he finally dumped her."

"I'm sorry. That's awful."

"She was only a sophomore, and the boyfriend was a junior. I knew the guy. I knew he was a jerk, a total meathead. But I didn't know the rest until later. And then I got suspended for kicking his ass, but of course it was too late at that point." He took another long sip. "That's actually why I wanted to go into law enforcement."

I nodded appreciatively. "And why detective?"

"It's the next logical step in my career. And I think it will be more satisfying. As an officer, I've got more vague responsibilities. Basically I'm supposed to maintain the order within my jurisdiction. But my specific tasks can change daily and I'm not able to see any one investigation through till the end. A detective has fewer cases and gets to delve deeper into each one." Nick grinned again. "And it pays better."

The rest of the meal was uneventful. We ate, we laughed, and then he drove me home. When he pulled into my driveway, he turned off the ignition, but made no effort to get out of the car. I suspected he was waiting for an invitation.

As much as I'd love a quick fling with someone as hot as Nick, I just wasn't a casual sex kind of girl. I was the type to panic about it and overthink the whole scenario, so I wasn't able to enjoy it at all until at least three months into the relationship. And if I were going to have meaningless sex, I'd probably have to be way drunker.

"Thanks again for dinner," I said finally. "You really didn't have to pay, though."

He shrugged. "It feels weird to let a lady buy me dinner."

"Even if it's not a date?"

"Even if it's not a date."

I sighed. "I'm sorry I'm such a mess. I really enjoy hanging out with you. And if I weren't such a wreck now, I would love to go out with you."

Nick grinned. "I don't really hang out with women, at least not as friends. But you're very entertaining, Chelsea. I suppose I can make an exception, but only since I know you'll change your mind sooner or later."

"Thanks." I climbed out of the car.

"Hey, if you're not busy Friday night, you should come hang out at this club, Dusk. I can get you in free. Bring your friend, the crazy one who ditched you at the bar. She'll love it."

I nodded and waved.

5

On Friday, Jen dropped by a little before eight with sandwiches. She was wearing a skirt and ridiculously high heels. I shook my head before she had a chance to even urge me to change into the same. "No way. I told him I don't dress like a slut."

"I'll ignore the implications about my outfit there," she said with a laugh, setting the sandwiches on the table. "Anyway, I was going to say you looked hot."

I eyed her warily. I had ended up in stretchy black pants that hung low on my hips and a flowy low-cut tee shirt. I had on heels, but they were only an inch and a half high so I could still walk normally.

"Are those pants new? I don't remember seeing them."

I tried to think up a lie but was too hungry to be creative. "No. I just haven't worn them since college." Apparently, the divorcée diet was working for me. Without anyone to share real meals with, most of my dinners since David's departure consisted of Fruit Loops with a side of wine.

Jen shrugged and we ate the sandwiches, reapplied makeup, and took off.

"So why are we going to this club if you're not going to sleep with Nick?" Jen asked as she parked the car. "His mere presence will keep you from hitting on other guys."

"I'm not going to sleep with anyone, so it's a moot point. And we're here because we want to have fun and you're trying to keep my mind off David."

"But why this club?"

"Nick said he'd get us in free."

"Oh, right."

There were only about five or six people in line in front of us, but we had our IDs ready as we reached the bouncer. He didn't even glance at the IDs, merely announcing the cover charge instead.

"Actually, we're here to see Nick Gyllenhaal," I said meekly, unsure of how this whole freebie thing worked.

The guy nodded. "I think he's in the back somewhere."

Jen and I walked on through and then stopped near the bar. "Which one is he?" she asked.

"I don't see him."

"Should we look more?"

I considered this. "Na, it's not like we're supposed to meet him here. He just mentioned it. Let's get a drink."

We hovered near the bar until two seats opened up and Jen swooped in. "Cosmo or appletini?" she asked.

"Appletini," I said, turning to scope out the club again. Right as our drinks arrived, I spotted Nick. He was wearing jeans and a black shirt with a fitted black leather jacket over it. He was standing in the corner, alone, his eyes perusing the room with a peculiar seriousness.

"Hey, there he is," I said, nudging Jen and nodding in his direction.

She sipped her drink. "Not bad," she agreed. "Not bad at all." She turned back to me. "Damn, Chelsea. I'm jealous now. I go home with Mr. Receding Hairline and you end up with that hunk?"

I giggled. "You did not just call him a hunk."

She swatted my arm, nearly causing my drink to spill. "Why are you sitting here with me? Get your ass over there and talk to him. Quick, while he's still alone!"

"I can't just ditch you," I said. "What are you going to do?"

She rolled her eyes. "Don't worry about me. I'll flirt with the bartender."

I smiled, knowing full well the bartender was not her type. I took another big sip of my drink and started to stand when another girl approached him. She leaned in and said something, and then they both laughed. And then he took her by the elbow and they walked towards the back of the club.

Jen's eyes met mine. "I'm sure they're just going to a table in the back room."

She turned to the bartender. "Hey, what's in the back there? Is there another dance floor or more tables?"

He gazed where she was looking and shook his head. "Bathrooms," he said.

Jen and I shared a grimace.

"I'm sure he's not hooking up with a girl in the bathroom," I said.

"Definitely not," she agreed, clearly not believing her words. She ordered us each a cosmopolitan. We finished off the appletinis in silence. I had just started on my cosmopolitan when I felt a tickle on the back of my neck.

"Hey sexy," a voice whispered.

I turned abruptly, and there was Nick, grinning.

"You came," he said.

I nodded, flushed. Jen stuck out her hand. "I'm Jen."

"Nick. Pleased to meet you."

"Do you want a drink?" I asked.

Nick shook his head, a bemused grin on his face. I turned and saw the bartender chuckling, too. I didn't get why that was so funny, or why he was approaching me right after apparently stalking off to the bathrooms with another girl. Although, come to think of it, they weren't gone that long.

Jen cleared her throat and glared at me.

"Thanks for suggesting we come," I said. "Good drinks."

He smiled. "You ladies have a designated driver this time?"

Jen raised her hand. "Me. I'm done after this one, Officer, I swear."

He nodded. Damn he was cute. He looked a little mysterious and super tough in his current outfit, but other than that, he was just as I remembered him.

"You ladies should dance," he suggested. "I'll catch up with you later." He winked and headed over to talk with the bouncer.

"What was that, Chelsea?" Jen screeched.

"What?"

"Have you totally forgotten how to flirt?"

I grimaced. "Maybe."

Jen rolled her eyes, disgusted. "You need more to drink." She ordered two kamikaze shots.

"You told Nick you weren't drinking anymore," I reminded her.

"They're both for you," she said. "And then we're dancing. And then the second that liquor hits your brain, you're dancing with him because he is hot."

I chugged the drinks and followed her to the dance floor. One of Jen's best qualities is her ability to have fun no matter what. Even though the dance floor wasn't that crowded, she immediately started getting down like she was alone at home. Her enthusiasm was contagious, and within a moment, I was dancing, too. Every few minutes, I'd glance over to see if Nick was watching, but for the most part, he was just standing at the front talking with the bouncer. But then the next time I turned, he was staring at us.

The look on his face reminded me of the way a dog looks at a hamburger left on a table just slightly out of its reach. I may not have tons of dating experience, but he was definitely interested. We made eye contact briefly, and he smiled. I turned back to Jen and kept dancing. Even though I wasn't looking for a date, the attention was flattering and I immediately craved more.

"Is he still watching?" I asked a minute later.

"Yup." She sighed wistfully. "Seriously, Chels. If you don't have sex with him, I will. Even if I have to force him."

I turned again, but he was gone. I swiveled back around to Jen, and there he was, right in front of me.

"Not a big dancer?" I asked, relieved that I was apparently now tipsy enough to flirt.

He grinned and pulled me close, his hands on my hips. He swayed back and forth with me for a minute and then leaned forward and whispered. "Better not dance too much," and then he sauntered off.

"What just happened?" I asked Jen.

She shrugged.

We kept dancing, and he returned to a spot near the bar, alternating between hungrily gawking in our direction and scanning the room, a bored look in his eyes. At one point he left with two other guys, an annoyed expression on his face, and he came back alone a minute later.

"I'm going to the bathroom," I said to Jen. She acknowledged my statement, but kept dancing. There was a guy moving in on her now anyway.

I ducked into the bathroom, lingering in front of the mirror after washing my hands. I dabbed a little more lip gloss on and smoothed my hands across my hair. I did a little twirl to check out my butt in the mirror. It was looking surprisingly good, I decided. Maybe even better than in college when these pants last saw the world outside my closet. And the push-up bra combined with the low-cut top was definitely not the problem.

So why was Nick blowing me off? That whole stare from afar thing was sexy at first, but now it was just bordering on creepy.

I started out of the bathroom and someone grabbed my hand. I jumped and turned just as Nick pushed me against the wall.

"Are you trying to drive me crazy?" he asked, his voice low.

"What do you mean? You wouldn't even dance with me."

He leaned in and kissed me before I could protest. Since he had me pinned against the wall, there was nothing to do but kiss him back. His lips were soft and warm and he tasted like peppermint. My hands, with a mind of their own, were on his hips and inching around to his back. I stopped when I felt something cold and hard tucked into his waistband. I pulled back suddenly.

"What is that?"

He reached behind his back and pulled out a gun. I jumped, nearly screaming, and he quickly put it back where it came from. "Calm down. I'm working."

"You're what?"

He lifted up the leg of his jeans, revealing a second gun at his ankle.

"Who are you?"

He laughed. "I told you, I'm working."

"Like an investigation or something?"

"No, private security. For the club."

"I thought you were a cop."

"I am. I moonlight here every other weekend or so. It pays well, and they need actual cops since we're licensed to carry concealed in a bar."

I considered this. "So you couldn't drink because you're working?"

He nodded.

"And you couldn't dance with me because you're working?"

Another nod.

"But you can still hook up with that other girl when you're working?"

He looked confused.

"Or did you just kiss her outside the bathroom, too?"

"Babe, these are the only lips I've kissed tonight," he replied, raising an eyebrow seductively and dragging his finger across my mouth.

"Then why did you suggest I come here?"

"I thought you and your friend would have fun. And I wanted someplace where I could keep an eye on you." He glanced out to the dance floor. "Looks like your friend is hitting it off with someone. You might need a ride home."

"You just kissed me. I'm not riding home with you!"

He laughed. "You're stubborn, you know that?"

I frowned and was about to protest, but he kissed me again and then disappeared down the hall, leaving me bewildered, dizzy, and alarmingly aroused.

I caught my bearings and then returned to the bar, not eager to interrupt Jen's fun on the dance floor just yet.

"Another appletini please," I said to the bartender as I plopped down. He slid another napkin in front of me.

"You better slow down. If you're too drunk to drive home, I can't take you till two A.M. when I'm off," Nick said, startling me as he came up behind me.

I glanced at my watch. It was after midnight already, not that it mattered. Jen was taking me home. The bartender set my martini in front of me. I could tell he heard Nick's comment.

"Thanks," I said to the bartender. "Can I ask you something?"

He glanced sideways down the bar, which wasn't too busy at the moment, and nodded.

"How often does Nick drive home a girl who's had too much to drink?"

He laughed at my question. "I don't know. He doesn't work that often."

I pouted. "Come on, you could at least guess."

He shook his head. "He might shoot me if I ruin his chances with you."

"No, see, that's just it. He has no chance with me. I'm married. Please?"

The bartender glanced around. "It's happened once or twice that I've noticed." He paused. "And usually, the girls he takes home come back another night."

I nodded my silent appreciation just as Jen returned. "What do you think about Bobby?" she asked.

"Is he the redhead or the balding guy?"

She frowned. "The balding guy. Geez, you're no fun at all. We can't all land Channing Tatum look-alikes. Don't be so judgy."

"Sorry. I had a little chat with Nick though."

That admission captured her attention. She stole a sip of my drink as I spoke.

"Yeah, he accosted me outside the bathroom. Apparently, he's working tonight. Not as a cop, but as a security guy for the club."

Jen nodded. "So he wasn't blowing you off on the dance floor after all?"

"Nope." I paused. "And he kissed me. Twice."

She squealed like a preschooler. "I knew it. Promise me you'll have sex with him."

"What? No!"

Jen grinned mischievously and returned to the dance floor.

I finished my drink and followed reluctantly. Forty-five minutes later, Jen unapologetically left the club with balding guy, leaving me stranded. On the plus side, she did return with the jacket I'd left in the car, but a jacket wasn't really going to help me without a ride home.

I caught Nick's eye as she left, and he grinned unabashedly. I popped up from my barstool and walked right over to him. "You can take me home but I'm not having sex with you," I said.

The bouncer standing beside him laughed.

Nick simply grinned. "I can handle that," he said. "But when you change your mind, you're going to regret having been so stubborn all night."

His comment irritated me to the point that I sauntered immediately to the dance floor and shimmied up next to the first guy I saw, who happened to be the redhead who was making the moves on Jen earlier. At this hour, the people remaining at the club who weren't already attached to another patron were starting to get desperate, so he went with it.

Five songs later, I noticed Nick sitting at the bar, watching me. I realized it must be close to two, and not wanting to get stuck with Redhead as my ride home, I excused myself and went over to Nick.

"I thought you couldn't drink," I said.

"I'm off duty now," he said. He finished his drink and did one of those mysterious guy handshakes with the bartender. We walked in silence to his car. He opened the door for me and I stumbled in.

"How much did you drink?" he asked.

"Not enough to sleep with you," I answered.

He chuckled, but started the car.

"You know, your little friend the bartender told me you've tried this trick before."

"Bastard," Nick mumbled. A slight grin escaped his lips. "He said you told him you were married."

"I am."

"You're separated. And if you ask me, the best thing to help you get over your husband would be sex."

"With you?"

"Well, I am the only guy in the vicinity."

"So that's all you've got, an offer of meaningless sex?"

"Yup. I'm not really a relationship guy, but I've been told I'm good in bed. Really good in bed. Like, forget about your loser husband good."

"You're a pompous jerk," I said.

"Fine, suit yourself."

Neither of us spoke for a minute.

"You kissed me back," he finally said.

"What?"

"In the hall. I wouldn't be so persistent, except you kissed me back."

I sighed. "Look, it's nothing personal. If I were going to

have meaningless sex, I would do it with you, okay? But I'm not trying to get over my husband. I've given up so much in life without even a fight, and this time, I'm not taking it lying down. I'm going to get him back." I paused, feeling vindicated. "In fact, he's coming over tomorrow, at three o'clock. And I'm going to show him exactly what he's missing."

Nick didn't answer, so I shut up until we reached my driveway. I assumed this would be the last I heard from him, that I'd finally made my point, but then he unbuckled his belt, leaned over, and kissed me again.

This kiss was just as mesmerizing as the last, and I quickly caught myself kissing him back. I tried to muster the willpower to stop, but I couldn't. I blamed it on the alcohol. And on his perfect, soft lips and moist tongue that knew exactly when and how far to dart into my mouth. And perhaps on those wandering hands that slid through my hair and up against the back of my head in a way that sent shivers down my spine. His hands started to migrate down my arms, and a warm tingling spread throughout my body. I tried to focus on David, tried to remember a time when his kiss felt like this, but I drew a blank.

Nick ended the kiss without warning, leaving me discombobulated and desperate for more. I opened my mouth to speak, but no words came out.

He grinned proudly. "You need help in?"

"No. Thank you for the ride." I stumbled out of the car, fanning myself despite the freezing weather.

6

I allowed myself to sleep in the next morning. When I awoke, I smeared a tea tree pore-clearing mask over my face and arranged teeth whitening strips into my mouth. I plopped down on the floor with the best of intentions to do sit-ups while my beauty tools worked their magic, but I did a bit more daydreaming and staring at the ceiling than crunching. Making a mental note to join a gym with a trainer to motivate me, I rinsed off my teeth and face.

My next stop was the nail salon a few blocks away. I sprung for the acrylic tips since my own nails were too short and uneven to salvage. Sure, maybe buying fake nails wasn't exactly the same as ceasing to bite my own, but it was a step in the right direction. Besides, I couldn't exactly chew on my nails when they were safely hidden under layers of acrylic and glue. I briefly considered swinging by my hairdresser to see if she could squeeze me in for a coloring, but I decided against it. I figured she was busy anyway, and honestly, I wasn't quite ready to go platinum blonde, no matter how much David wanted it.

On the drive home, I stopped to buy a special baking

sheet designed for mini quiches. I also bought some frozen mini quiches. I couldn't learn how to bake them overnight, so I figured the next best thing was to buy some, toss the packaging, and pretend they were homemade.

Once home, I showered and slipped into my Spanx and a pair of jeans that had been too tight for years, but now seemed to fit. Choosing a top was harder. I wanted to make an impression on David, but I didn't want him to know how hard I was trying to impress him. I ended up selecting a clingy long-sleeved tee shirt. It appeared casual and comfortable, but accentuated the new bra nicely.

I moved the quiche into the special pan just as there was a knock at the door. I shoved the pan into the oven, checked my reflection in the mirror and hurried to the door.

"Hey you," I said with a smile. "You didn't have to knock."

David shrugged and brushed past me without a second glance. "I didn't want to walk in on you changing or anything," he grumbled.

I forced a laugh, which came out sounding louder and more unnatural than I'd planned. "You've seen it all before," I reminded him. "Oh, my quiches!" I scurried into the kitchen and pulled the perfectly rounded tarts out of the oven.

"You made those for me?" he asked incredulously.

I shook my head. "Well, I mean, I made them, obviously, but not exactly for you. You can have one, of course. I was really just practicing. I'm starting a cooking class soon and wanted to try my hand at this new recipe first." I held one out near his face, intending for him to open his mouth so I could feed him.

David grimaced and backed away. "I already ate lunch."

I tried to mask my disappointment as I plopped the

quiche back onto the tray. I rapped my nails onto the counter, desperate to draw his attention to my nicely manicured hands.

He sighed. "Could you stop that? It's annoying."

My hand stilled.

"I think I have more stuff in the basement," he mumbled. "Is my extra suitcase still down there?"

"I haven't touched a thing," I replied as he tromped down the stairs.

Once he was out of sight, I sighed, dejected. I tossed two quiches into my mouth and texted Jen a quick recap of my failed attempts. Clearly, winning back David was going to be harder than I thought.

I was just about to check on David's progress when there was a light rap at the door. I glimpsed downstairs, but as far as I could tell, David was still sifting through boxes. I peeked out the side window, expecting to see a salesperson. Instead, I saw a Camaro parked in front of the house. I opened the door, and there stood Nick.

He was wearing his standard issue police cargo pants, but a plain navy blue shirt on top. His badge was tucked into his belt. He wore sunglasses, sexy narrow ones that looked nothing like the kind I thought cops were supposed to wear, and was holding my jacket.

He flashed a mischievous grin. "Aren't you going to invite me in?"

"David's here."

He walked past me into the entryway. "I figured as much. There's a car in your driveway." He glanced around, then hearing a noise near the basement, stepped a few paces closer. "I was in the neighborhood and just thought I'd drop by," he said, in a much louder voice.

I raised an eyebrow, not sure what he was up to.

He shrugged in response, then leaned in. "If you want him to want you, you gotta make him jealous."

"I don't think," I started to say, but then David emerged from the basement, eying Nick warily.

Nick immediately held out his hand and flashed a wide smile. "Nick Gyllenhaal," he said. "Sorry to interrupt. Chels here didn't tell me she was having company."

"David Craig," David said, now eying me suspiciously. "Are you a police officer?" His gaze fell to Nick's utility belt, where a holstered gun was off to the side.

"Yeah. Not just some wacko," Nick laughed.

"Can we help you out with something?" David asked.

Nick shook his head. "Oh, nope, I was just dropping off Chelsea's coat." He turned to me. "You left it in my car last night." And then he proceeded to slowly skim his eyes down my body, making zero attempts at subtlety.

I felt a surge of heat rush to my face, but when I snuck a glimpse of David, I saw that his jaw was clenched, his teeth grinding. So, I went with it, smiling appreciatively at Nick. He held the coat out towards me and I took it, our hands lingering.

David finally cleared his throat.

I turned to him nonchalantly. "You can go finish up in the basement. I'll come see if you need any more bags or anything in a bit."

"Nice to meet you," Nick called as David hesitantly retreated back down the stairs.

"I better hit the road, Cupcake. Gimme a call later," Nick said to me, louder than necessary.

I walked him to the door.

"You look hot. Good choice with the shirt."

"Thanks," I said. "Cupcake?"

He grinned. "I like cupcakes. Especially the frosting. I like to lick it off, real slowly."

I swallowed hard. There was no way David was still within earshot, so this flirting wasn't for his benefit. And then, as if he enjoyed my confusion, Nick smacked me on the butt before sauntering off to his car.

I watched him, breathless, as he drove away. A moment later, David stomped up the stairs.

"I can't believe you're screwing a cop," he scowled.

"He just gave me a ride home yesterday. I'm not sleeping with him," I said.

I went to the laundry room to start a load of sheets and towels, smiling widely. When I'd gotten home last night, I'd been too tired—and too distracted by that damn kiss—to put much thought into how I was going to make David want me back. Thanks to Nick's little visit, though, I was right on track.

David left shortly after that, and the remainder of my day was uneventful. I finished the laundry and cleaned the rest of the house, just like I did every Sunday. Then I ate a hodgepodge dinner of leftover items in the fridge and went to bed early, exhausted from the night before.

I couldn't have been asleep for long when I awoke to a loud clatter in the kitchen. My heart was racing as I opened my eyes. I sat up quickly and held my breath, straining to listen for other suspicious noises, but heard only silence. I glanced at the clock. It was precisely midnight. I told myself it was a safe neighborhood, that there were rarely burglaries. I'd probably just left a stack of dishes in the sink that somehow toppled over.

But still, I stood, knowing I couldn't just ignore the remote possibility that I was not alone in the house. I grabbed my cell phone and clicked onto the phone keypad, determined to be prepared if I needed to call 911. I crept to the bedroom door, inhaled deeply, and slowly poked my head into the hall.

A large dark figure loomed at the top of the stairs. My instincts told me to immediately shut and lock the bedroom door and dial 911 while scooting some large piece of furniture up against the door. But for some reason, my body didn't comply with my instincts.

Instead, I chucked my cell phone at the intruder, screamed loudly, and held my ground, unable to will my feet to move.

"Ow, fuck Chelsea. What the hell?" the figure said, stepping closer.

"David? Is that you?"

"Of course it's me. Who else has a key to the goddamned house?"

I exhaled dramatically and sunk to the floor, my shaky knees no longer supporting my weight. "I thought you were an intruder."

"You're an idiot," he scowled. He walked past me and turned on the bedroom light. "So you're alone?"

I quickly checked that I hadn't peed my pants during my moment of terror and then rose back onto my feet. "Yes, I'm alone. Who else would be here?"

He snorted. "I don't know. You seemed pretty chummy with Officer What's-his-name." He pushed past me, his arm knocking me to the side.

"I told you I'm not sleeping with him. I'm not even dating him. Not that it's any of your business." I refrained from saying that if Nick had been there, he likely would have shot David as an intruder. I leaned closer, smelling booze. "Are you drunk?"

He shooed me away. "No, I'm not drunk. God, Chelsea, you really are pathetic."

"Why are you here?"

"I thought maybe I left something behind," he said, tromping down the stairs.

"It's the middle of the night. If you thought you'd left something, you could have called or come by tomorrow."

He peeked into the garage and then shut the door behind him. "I bought the damn house. I'll come by when I want." He paused, gave me a quick once over followed by a disgusted grimace, then made his way to the foyer. "And you better not be bringing sleazy men back to my house."

"You moved out," I said, my voice wavering despite my best efforts not to cry.

"Whatever." He let himself out the front door. I watched as he drove off, presumably heading back to Traci's.

I turned the deadbolt on the door and then made my rounds throughout the first floor, locking the garage and sliding door too. We didn't have a chain on any of the doors, so David could come in whenever with his key. I returned to my room, collecting my cell phone from the hall, and locked the bedroom door. Still, I knew I wouldn't be able to fall asleep anytime soon.

I glanced at the clock again, noting that less than fifteen minutes had passed since the initial disturbance. I remembered Nick telling me he worked until midnight. Not knowing what else to do, I called.

"Hello there, sexy lady. Reconsidering my proposition?" he asked.

I hadn't been expecting *that* warm of a greeting, and it took me a moment to recover and muster a reply. "No, I was just, well, are you busy now?"

"No. Is something wrong?"

"I'm just a little shaken up. I was asleep and then I heard this loud noise and I thought there was a burglar."

"Are you alright? Where are you?" His voice suddenly sounded very official.

"No, I'm fine now. It turned out it was David. He's gone now."

"Wait, your ex broke into the house while you were sleeping? What did he want?"

"I don't know. I think he was drunk. He just looked around and yelled at me and he left."

"I'll be over in ten minutes."

I disconnected, immediately relieved. I stumbled to the bathroom, quickly swishing around some mouthwash, applying makeup and deodorant, and running a brush through my hair so I didn't look like I'd just awakened. I don't think I looked that bad to start with, or at least not bad enough to merit the grimace I got from David, but a little effort never hurt. I considered getting dressed, but instead just swapped out my flannel pajama pants for a pair of jeans and pulled a blue wrap over the tank top I sleep in.

I reached the foot of the stairs right as I heard a knock on the door. I opened it immediately and Nick came in, wearing faded jeans and a dark long-sleeved shirt, looking sexy as usual.

"I thought you just got off work?"

"I changed at the station. Did you call this in to dispatch, or just me?"

"Just you."

"Which door did he come in?" he asked, swiveling the doorknob and eying it closely.

"Oh, I don't know."

He frowned. "Well, how did he get in?"

"He still has keys."

"You didn't change the locks?"

I shook my head, feeling like an idiot. It had never occurred to me to change the locks. I was still expecting David to move back in. Changing the locks seemed like an unnecessary obstacle to that ultimate goal. Besides, I wasn't even sure that was allowed. "It's still technically his house, too, until the divorce is finalized."

"Did he touch you?"

I hesitated, then shook my head. The shove probably wasn't intentional.

"Did he take anything?"

"I don't think so."

Nick sighed. "You should change the locks, Chelsea. It doesn't sound like he did anything illegal, but if he came in once in the middle of the night, there's nothing stopping him from doing it again as long as his key works."

I nodded.

"What did he want?"

I shrugged, leading him in to the great room. We sat side by side on the leather sofa. "He said he forgot something, but it seemed more like he thought I was cheating on him. I think he was looking for you."

"He moved out, Chelsea. Even if you'd had someone here, you wouldn't be cheating."

"He seemed different. He was angry and mean and I think he meant to scare me." I felt tears begin to swell in my eyes.

Nick rubbed his forehead. "This is my fault. I shouldn't have dropped by earlier. I just figured it would cheer you up to see him jealous. You know, give him a dose of his own medicine."

"No, I'm glad you came by. I liked seeing you and I loved

the pissed off look on his face when you left." I giggled. "He actually accused me of sleeping with you."

He reached forward and tucked a wisp of my hair behind my ear, his hand lingering on the side of my neck. "I don't know why you want him back," he said.

"He didn't used to be a jerk. He used to make me feel like a princess. He's just different now," I explained, noticing that Nick's face was so close to mine that I could feel his breath on my nose. "You think I'm pathetic, too, don't you?" I asked, recalling the look of disgust on David's face when he'd said it earlier.

He shook his head. "There's a lot of words I'd use to describe you, Chelsea, but that isn't one."

We were quiet for a minute, me getting lost for the billionth time in his endless brown eyes while he stared at God-knows-what. "I doubt you can get a locksmith here before morning," he finally said.

I nodded, knowing I'd never fall back asleep tonight anyway.

"I could stay," he offered. "Just in case he comes back."

I broke his stare, turning down to our laps. "I can't ask you to do that."

"You didn't ask me."

"I won't sleep with you," I reminded him.

"That's okay," he replied. "Although, you're going to change your mind eventually, and when you do, you're going to kick yourself for having wasted all these valuable moments."

"My couch is really uncomfortable."

He laughed.

"Do you want anything to drink?"

"You have any beer?"

I stood to check the fridge, delighted to find that David

hadn't taken all the beer. I would've expected him to grab that when he stole my coffee maker. I handed Nick a beer and opened a cheap Riesling for myself, filling the wine glass to the rim.

"Are you hungry?"

He shrugged. "I ate earlier."

I interpreted that as a hesitant yes, so I opened the freezer and grabbed a roll of cookie dough I'd prepared the previous weekend. I defrosted it in the microwave while the oven preheated, then sliced it onto the cookie sheet and set the timer for ten minutes. By the time the cookies were ready, we both needed a drink refill.

I scooped the warm cookies onto a single plate, the chocolate melting into the spatula as I mangled the form. "You're supposed to let them cool on the sheet first if you want them to look pretty, but they taste better warm."

Nick peered over my shoulder. "They tasted pretty good the other day. In fact, you're a pretty popular lady at the precinct now."

I smiled, glad that someone appreciated my baking. I nudged the last cookie onto the plate, my finger now coated in chocolate goo. Nick grabbed my hand, spun me around till I was facing him, then sucked the chocolate off my finger, lingering much longer than necessary.

I felt a rush of blood to my groin, nearly melting to the ground when I glanced up and saw him staring right back at me as his tongue darted around my fingertip.

He released my finger and grinned. "I see what you mean. They are better warm."

I exhaled evenly, then carried the cookies and my wine back to the couch. He followed, beer in hand. "If I made cookies this good, I'd eat them all the time. I'd look like a blimp."

"David always told me not to eat so many. I'd probably lose twenty pounds if I gave up the cookies," I joked.

He frowned. "You're perfect just like this."

We finished the cookies and I stifled my fourth or fifth yawn. It was nearly two A.M.

"You're tired," he observed.

"You really don't have to stay. Seriously, this couch sucks."

He considered this for a moment, then shook his head. "I should at least have a look around the rest of the house before you go to bed, make sure there's nothing suspicious."

I followed him up the stairs.

He stuck his head into the guest room and office before stepping into my room. "How come your room is so much cleaner than the office?"

"I don't spend much time in here." Ever. At all. At least since it became "my room" instead of "our room."

I turned and realized he was lifting his shirt over his head. "What are you doing?"

"I'm not sleeping in my clothes," he said, reaching around his back, retrieving a gun from the waistband of his jeans, and placing it on top of my dresser.

My eyes widened. "You had a gun this whole time?"

He shrugged. "I always carry. And besides, I wasn't sure what I'd find when I got here. This began as an official visit, remember?"

He was now unbuckling his pants, a pretty clear signal that the official part of the visit had drawn to a close. He tossed me the pajama pants I'd draped over the chair by the dresser. "I assume these are yours."

I took them and hesitantly went into the bathroom to change. When I emerged, Nick was in my bed, under the covers. His jeans and shirt were folded neatly beside his gun.

"You're in my bed," I said.

"You don't have a bed in your guest room and you said your couch sucks."

"I can't sleep with you," I reminded him, actually meaning that I was too concerned I might try to have sex with him if I slept beside him.

"Well, too bad. I'm exhausted," he said, rolling over so he faced the windows.

I took this as a sign that he meant for me to join him, platonically. I crawled into my bed beside him, awkwardly perched on my back.

After a minute, he spoke. "You might as well get comfortable. I'm not going to try anything."

I breathed a laugh, but flipped onto my side and eventually fell asleep.

WHEN I AWOKE, I was eerily relaxed. I'd somehow slept till nine and, even more surprisingly, I knew from the arm draped across my side that David had slept in, too, and he never slept in. He was always up by six, even on weekends, and by the time I woke up, he would've snuck out to buy me gourmet coffee and donuts and sometimes even a bouquet of flowers. More recently though, he was always in a crappy mood when he woke up early and seemed to prefer stomping around the house aimlessly until I woke over arranging any sort of romantic surprises.

The body behind me shifted and I realized it wasn't David.

It was Nick.

I was in bed with Nick.

It was Nick's arm wrapped around me, and Nick's hand resting on my breast. I couldn't tell if he was awake or not, but his groin pressed against my back with a firmness that I'd rarely felt from David. Nick's finger raked across my nipple and a tingle shot throughout my body. I must have tensed up noticeably, because he laughed.

"Your hand is on my breast," I said.

"Oh yeah? Well, your ass is on my lap."

My eyes widened in alarm. I tried to inch forward but he squeezed me tighter.

"I wasn't complaining," he said, his breath feeling hotter and damper against the back of my neck until I realized he was kissing me. I shivered again, despite a rush of heat over-taking my body.

"Nick," I said, rolling towards him, but before I could speak, his mouth was covering mine, his warm tongue tickling my lips before pressing into my own tongue. I groaned involuntarily and he propelled himself on top of me. The weight of his perfect body pressed into me with a calming effect, and I realized how much I'd missed feeling a man's body against my own.

I knew I was kissing him back, and I was powerless to stop. I couldn't remember the last time a kiss felt so good or the last time I wanted another person so much. I realized that at that moment, I would've agreed to anything Nick said, and done anything he wanted, if only he'd promise to keep kissing me. I heard myself groan again and then he stopped.

For a moment, I thought maybe I was hallucinating, seeing him climb out of bed and step back into his jeans. But when he tucked his gun back into the back, I realized he was serious.

"Where are you going?" I whined.

He turned to me, grinned, and pulled his shirt back over his head. "I work at noon, and I need to hit the gym before that."

"So you're leaving?" My voice came out sounding a lot more desperate than I'd intended. But seriously, what was he trying to do to me?

He laughed mischievously. "If I stay now, we both know what's going to happen. And I'd hate to put you in the position of doing something you're not comfortable with." He leaned forward and kissed me. I was tempted to rope my legs around him and pull him towards me, but the fact that he had a gun strapped to his hips discouraged me.

"I'm off at eight. If you're free, we should go out for a drink."

I nodded dizzily.

"And call a locksmith."

And then, he left.

I squished my goose-down pillow over my face and screamed with frustration the moment I heard the door click shut behind him and then spent the next hour fantasizing about what might have happened if Nick hadn't left when he did.

7

Once I finally dragged myself out of bed, I called Jen. She fulfilled her friend duty by commiserating about what a jerk David was for a good ten minutes before politely reminding me that she had a real job and was actually working that day. So, I took the hint and hung up without mentioning my mostly-innocent sleepover.

A quick check of my calendar informed me that today was the start of my diet. I groaned, but decided I couldn't postpone it again or I'd never get started. I searched for a calorie tracking app, then poured myself a bowl of cereal. I glanced at the label, shocked that my breakfast was only 120 calories. Who knew Sugar Puffs cereal was so diet-friendly? I started to log my meal while mentally patting myself on the back and then realized to be truly accurate, I needed to measure out the correct portion.

Well, you'd think one cupful and one bowlful would be pretty similar, right? No, siree. Apparently my bowl was three one-cup servings. I grimaced, and entered two servings into my diet app. Obviously I'd burned the caloric equivalent of at least one serving just by doing all this measuring and walking back and forth. By the time I measured out my milk for the cereal and my coffee creamer, I realized that my normal two minute breakfast had now taken nearly a half hour to prepare.

"Clearly people who diet have no other obligations on their time," I commented aloud. Of course, then I realized I had nothing particularly pressing to do, so I quickly added a few tasks to my to-do list for the day so as not to feel unimportant. Finally, I made my way to my office.

I had devised an excellent solution to my fear of paying the bills, or more specifically, my fear of inadvertently funding some aspect of my spouse's affair: automatic bill pay. I'd used it for some of our utilities in the past, but David had never wanted to relinquish control of the credit cards enough to rely on an automatic service for those. But now, the alternative was too frightening. I set it up with each account so that the full balance would be withdrawn from our joint checking account the day before the due date. I'd still receive my statements by email, but I could simply delete them without much temptation to pour over David's every expense.

I was still too distracted by Nick's recent departure from my bed to concentrate on my freelance work, and I was still too angry at David to polish the autobiography I'd been working on for an Olympic marathoner, so I instead dug around on the shelf for my own manuscript.

It was dusty and the ink on the cover had started to fade. The corners of the pages were bent and a small coffee-colored ring made me wonder when I'd ever been so callous as to use my only piece of truly original fiction as a drink coaster. I scooted the rubber band off the stack of papers, grabbed a red pen, and started to read.

The book was more entertaining than I remembered. It was a straightforward plot about a woman who, thanks to her parents' messy divorce when she was young, vowed never to marry. The woman moved to the country with a bunch of dogs and started her own knitting business, thinking she'd never run into men out in the middle of nowhere, but then of course she fell for the town veterinarian, a handsome widower whose wife died during childbirth. It was predictable, sure, but the characters were lovable, the writing flowed easily, and the sex scenes were just risqué enough.

Without meaning to, I read the entire book. I'd come across many typos and other parts which surely needed editing, but my red pen had gone unused. I'd simply been too wrapped up in the story to focus on the revision process. I glanced at the clock and realized it was already two o'clock. My initial reaction was panic—how could I have wasted so much time reading a book I'd written? But then I decided it was a good sign. If my book entertained me that much, maybe other people would like it, too. And maybe, if other people liked it, David would appreciate my talent even if he didn't personally love the genre I chose to write.

I hopped into the shower and got dressed for the day, determined to hit up the library in search of a book about the fiction-publishing process. Ideally, my current literary agent could help, but I didn't want to approach her until I was more educated about the business.

My stomach growled louder than the radio and I realized I hadn't eaten since breakfast. I swung by the deli and selected a mixed greens salad with grilled chicken, contentedly logging it into my calorie-tracker. Maybe this diet thing wasn't so hard after all. Here it was mid-afternoon and I was way below my calorie goal for the day! The salad tasted a little bit like weeds, though, or at least what I imagined weeds tasted like, and I probably had spinach in my teeth now, but it was worth it if it helped bring David back.

I poured the rest of the vinaigrette onto the remaining lettuce and thought about my plan. I felt that I was on track, really. My cooking classes were scheduled to start in less than a week, I had already made David jealous—possibly too jealous—with Nick, and my diet was progressing fabulously. Getting my book polished and sent over to my agent might not be part of the plan, but it felt good, and, frankly, David was being such a jerk at the moment that I didn't care if I embarrassed him by letting people see my "smut" as he called it.

My phone buzzed suddenly. "Speak of the devil," I murmured, blushing quickly and making a mental note to stop talking aloud to myself.

"I was just thinking about you," I said, answering the phone.

"Oh. Uh. Okay. You were?" David clearly hadn't expected me to say that. There was an awkward silence, so I finished the rest of my mango iced tea. "Listen, sorry about waking you last night. I need to get some more documents from the house. From our tax file."

I noted how casually the word "our" flowed. I wondered if he and Traci shared enough to the point where he referred to their stuff as "ours." Certainly not. It hadn't been long enough, right? And it probably never would happen. Any moment now, he'd realize how stupid he had been and would come crawling back to me. He'd beg for forgiveness, on his knees, of course, probably in an expensive designer suit, and he'd fill the house with dozens of roses for days before I'd even talk to him. Maybe he'd even get me one of those diamond anniversary bands

I saw advertised on the massive billboard near the interstate.

"Chelsea? Are you still there?"

"Uh huh," I replied absentmindedly, trying to decide whether I'd prefer diamond earrings or a tennis bracelet as the final apology.

"So is it okay if I come over tomorrow morning?"

I tried to remember if I had plans. Since my calendar was, generally, blank lately, I suspected I was probably available then. "What time?"

"I don't know. Tenish?"

"Should be fine. Look, I've got to go now, so just text me if your plans change." I hung up before he could protest, grinning proudly at being the one to hang up first.

I dumped my napkins and empty dressing packet in the trash and headed out to the library.

By the time I returned home with my new books, I only had time for a quick dinner and a little reading before I needed to change to meet Nick. Since I'd had such a healthy lunch, I popped a frozen pizza in the oven for dinner. It was a reasonably small size, the kind that David and I used to split in one sitting, but according to the label it was actually six servings. I chuckled at the thought, logged the calories, then poured myself a small glass of wine.

Jen called on her way home from work, probably checking that I wasn't too depressed to be alone all evening, but I got off the phone quickly. I needed time to get myself spruced up for the drink. Despite what Jen insisted, it was not a "date." It was two friends getting together for a drink.

And in case Nick had a similar misconception, I kept my outfit casual and stopped on the way to buy a newspaper.

I'd been planning on getting more up-to date about current events anyway, but I wasn't naïve enough to think I'd ever utilize an actual subscription to the newspaper. I already read People magazine cover-to-cover, and for the most part, any other news I needed was readily available on the internet. But for now, the newspaper would work.

I sauntered into the bar, plopped down at a bar stool, then delved into the paper while I waited. As it turns out, the newspaper is gigantic when unfolded. I began a story on a botched execution which was a little gory and clearly designed to garner sympathy for the creepy murderer, but then, just when it got interesting, the page ended and directed me to go to B7. I separated the paper further, finding several other page 7s, but nothing labeled B. I was about to give up when I heard laughter behind me.

I turned to see Nick. He was wearing jeans and a thin long-sleeved shirt that did little to hide the muscle beneath. He looked good, but it was hard to tell if that was just because he's a naturally attractive guy or because he dressed up thinking this was a date.

"What's so funny?"

"You're reading the newspaper," he said, still grinning. "In a bar."

"I like to stay informed," I replied tartly, sensing from his clear bemusement that he didn't buy my explanation. I started to refold the paper, but the more I tried to put it back how it came, the more out-of-shape it was. Finally, flustered, I simply wadded it up, creased it hard along the edge where there should've been a crease anyway if the people who designed newspapers had any brains at all. I set it on the bar beside me, but the stupid paper promptly popped back out of its folded form, knocking my water glass down as it did.

"Fucking news," I mumbled, plucking ice cubes off my lap while Nick grabbed a towel from the bartender. "You'd think someone would come up with a better design for this crap. How do they expect people to have time to read the entire thing at once? That must be what they're thinking, since it's clearly impossible to refold."

Nick, now turning purple from his efforts not to laugh more, lifted up the paper, moved some pages around, then magically reformed it to its original shape.

I narrowed my eyes at him. "Obviously you have an engineering background," I said. "Or perhaps origami."

He grinned and handed me another napkin. "Origami is what most cops study in school, but I went with the more exotic criminal justice degree." He sat beside me, motioned for the bartender, then turned to me for my drink order.

"Riesling," I said, resisting the urge to lean closer to the intoxicating scent of his aftershave. "No, wait, sauvignon blanc," I corrected. I tended to chug sweet wines faster, and I'd hate to get drunk with Nick knowing I was driving home.

Nick raised an eyebrow but ordered a beer.

I stuck the damp paper in my purse, still shaking my head and mumbling under my breath. "Who reads the paper anyway? Don't they care about the environment *at all*? I mean, all that paper, all that ink...this newspaper is single-handedly destroying that ozone layer."

"Which layer is that?" Nick asked with a grin.

"You know, the ozone one."

"I'm pretty sure there's more than one."

I sighed loudly and smiled at the bartender as he handed me the wine. "Stupid paper," I muttered again.

Nick laughed. "You seem a little tense. Crummy day?"

I frowned, considering this, then shook my head. "No, actually it was great. I read this really good book, and I started my new diet. It's going great," I added.

Nick seemed skeptical. "You're on a diet?"

"It never hurts to eat healthier."

"What book did you read?" he asked, swigging his beer.

I hesitated. "It doesn't technically have a title yet. It's one I wrote."

"Oh. About the uh, what was it, a high jumper? No, runner?"

"Runner," I said, "But no, this is the novel I wrote a while back. I think I'm going to polish the manuscript and maybe look into publishing it."

"Wow. That's awesome. What's it about?"

We talked about my book for a while. I was surprised by Nick's genuine intrigue on the topic. He asked pertinent questions about the plot and characters, and then drilled me about my research methods for the sex scenes. While we talked, I slowly sipped my first, then second glass of wine before switching responsibly back to water.

"It's getting late," I said with a sigh. "I should head home before you talk me into something I'll regret."

Nick laughed, flashing his perfect white teeth. "Big plans tomorrow?"

I wrinkled my nose. "David's coming by late morning to get some papers he needs for our taxes, or something."

"You'll be okay?"

I nodded. For some reason, I was certain I could handle David tomorrow. "Thanks for the drinks. You really should let me pay sometime. It's bordering on sexist how often you treat."

He laughed again, and I stood, smoothed my shirt down, and reached for my purse.

"Hey, Chelsea, can I read it sometime?"

"The paper? You can have it," I said, handing it to him. "I'm done with this environmental disaster."

Nick shook his head, chuckling. "No, not the paper. I'll take it and dispose of it for you, though," he said, adding, "In an appropriate recycling receptacle, of course. But what I want to read is your book. Can I?"

I smiled. "When it's finished."

His face fell. "I have to wait until it's published?"

"No, just until I edit it. It's still pretty rough."

Nick flashed his most mischievous grin and leaned closer, so I could feel the warmth of his breath on my cheek. "Sometimes I like it rough."

I turned before he could see me blushing. "Good night, Nick."

8

I went to sleep in an amazing mood, my body still buzzing with excitement over my book and the evening with Nick. But as soon as I woke up and remembered that David was coming over, my mood tanked. I wasn't feeling particularly optimistic about making progress on my efforts to win him back today, and, more importantly, I was still a little mad about his behavior the other night.

I decided to play it cool, although acting nonchalant was not exactly my forte. I spread out my new library materials in the office upstairs, so as soon as I greeted David, I snuck upstairs to work on my book.

After an hour, I needed a coffee refill and decided to check on David. He was clearly not in the mood to chat, so I left him in the basement.

I heard a knock at the door, and when I rounded the corner, Nick was standing in the foyer. "It was unlocked," he said.

I smiled at the welcomed sight. He was wearing dark wash jeans, running shoes, and a fitted tee shirt. As always, he looked ridiculously sexy, but in a way that suggested he wasn't even trying. It was almost irritating, how easy it seemed for Nick to look good.

"David just wanted to go over some tax stuff with me. I think he's leaving soon. Were you in the neighborhood?" I asked, suspecting I was his sole reason to be in the neighborhood.

He nodded and grinned, flashing his perfect white teeth. "I saw your ex's car and thought I'd check that you were okay. I can go now, though." Our eyes locked, and he made no attempt to leave.

David joined us in the foyer, scowling. "Why wouldn't she be okay?"

Nick broke our gaze and turned to David. "Chelsea mentioned you breaking into the house in the middle of the night a little while back.

David flung his hands up. "Christ, Chelsea. I hardly broke in. I used my fricking key." He sighed loudly.

"Oh, please. You waited until I was asleep and snuck into the house. You scared the crap out of me."

"Not intentionally. I can't help that you're afraid of everything. This isn't exactly Harlem. Who did you think was coming in?"

"I don't know, an intruder."

"With a key? God, you're a moron!"

Nick was glaring at David, but his expression softened as he turned to me. "You want me to shoot him?" he offered, reaching his hand to his lower back.

David made an exaggerated eye roll. "Get out of my house," he said.

Nick stood his ground.

"Give us a minute, would you Dave?" I flashed a conciliatory smile in his direction.

David sighed and stomped out.

"Is he always that cranky?" Nick asked.

"Lately, yes. Are you working?"

"I'm on at two."

"Any plans till then?"

"I thought I'd see if you'd eaten yet. But since you have company," he began.

"He's leaving soon," I blurted out.

The corners of Nick's mouth formed the slightest hint of a smile. "I could grab some take out and bring it back here."

"Okay."

Nick hesitated. "Will he be gone by then? I'd hate to actually have to shoot him."

I nodded, then stared unabashedly at Nick's butt as he walked back to his car.

As if on cue, David reappeared in the foyer.

"You didn't have to be so rude to him," I said, brushing past him, eager to finish collecting our tax documents so David could be on his way.

"He threatened to shoot me, Chels. I was hardly the impolite one."

"It was a joke."

David shook his head. "I don't like the way he looks at you. It's like he wants to eat you or something."

I couldn't help but smile. I loved the way Nick looked at me. He always somehow made me feel better about myself with just a simple glance. "He's good at that," I said.

"Good at what?" David wrinkled his nose as he got my joke. "Eating you? Gross, Chelsea." He sighed. "You two are dating, then?"

I shook my head. "No. We're not dating."

Now David's cheeks were bright red. "You know what? I probably have all the documents I need. If you find any other financial things, let me know. Leave a message with my secretary or something."

"Not your paralegal?" I replied in my snarkiest tone.

David ignored me, gathering the papers scattered across the table into his briefcase and stomping out the front door. As soon as his car had left the driveway, I scampered up the stairs, plugged in my hair straightener, and tore off my shirt. I switched into a lacy push up bra, spritzed on some perfume, and found my sexy jeans from the back of the closet.

I toyed with the idea of changing panties, knowing that I'd be more prone to do something I'd regret if I was wearing sexy panties, too, especially since I'd shaved that morning and wouldn't have stubbly legs as a deterrent. In the end, I selected a pair of silk-lace blend hipsters, but only because my current pair didn't match the new bra I was wearing, not because I wanted anything sexier.

I touched up my makeup, straightened my hair, swiped some lip gloss on and ran a dab of yummy smelling finishing gel over the ends of my hair just as the doorbell rang. Smiling, I dashed down the stairs and did my best to act casual as I greeted Nick again.

NICK HADN'T STAYED LONG, but since I was already dressed to go out, I called Jen and we ventured out on an impromptu shopping spree. A new wardrobe was a quintessential component of my plan, and especially now that my diet was going strong, I deserved the new clothes. I hadn't actually lost any weight yet, per se, but I figured my metabolism was just slow to catch on.

The shopping exhausted me, so I went to bed early,

bringing some tortilla chips and salsa with me so I could binge watch a few episodes of *Weeds* on Netflix before going to sleep.

I couldn't have been asleep long when I awoke with a start to a loud crash.

Without thinking, I flew out of bed. Peering over the banister, I immediately noticed a massive hole in one of my front windows. Then I heard thumping and what sounded like a man whispering. My heart pounded. I glanced out the window, praying I'd see David's car and could dismiss this as another visit from him, but I saw no vehicles of any sort outside.

Quickly, I backed into my bedroom, locked the door, and lunged for my cell phone. I dialed Nick. He answered immediately.

"I think someone's in my house," I said. "They broke a window, and now I hear noises. It sounds like he broke something."

"Do you think it's David?" His voice sounded serious, calm, and professional.

"I didn't see his car. And I don't think he'd break a window."

"Alright. Where are you?"

"Locked in my bedroom."

"Okay, good. Stay put. I'll get a patrol car there, and I'm not too far away. Don't leave your bedroom."

I hung up made several failed attempts at deep breathing. I glanced at the clock. It was just shy of two-thirty. I couldn't remember how long ago I'd called Nick, but it had to have been at least a couple minutes, and I still didn't hear any sirens.

My stomach lurched as I realized the exterior doors to my home were locked. The police wouldn't be able to get inside. And if they knocked, what if the intruder panicked and it turned into a hostage situation? I had to devise a plan.

The upstairs hall of my house overlooked the front door, living room, and most of the dining room. If I went into the hall, I could get a visual confirmation that the burglar wasn't in any of those rooms, and I'd also be able to see the cops come to the door. Then, I could rush down the stairs and outside as soon as I saw them. I pressed my ear against the bedroom door, heard nothing, and tentatively opened the door, my heart pounding furiously.

The hall was pitch black, something I hadn't accounted for in my plan. I tiptoed forward a few steps, just past the guest room I used as my office and paused.

Suddenly, there was a figure behind me. His hands quickly covered my mouth and nose before I could scream. I considered trying to kick him in the nuts, but he was holding me too tightly. I inched my mouth open and chomped down, when the man spoke.

"Chelsea, shh, it's me, Nick. Stop biting me."

I froze, and briefly considered that it might be a trap to get me to stop struggling, but that didn't make sense. And there was something familiar about the guy's smell and the feel of his stomach pressed against me. I relaxed slightly and his hands left my mouth.

"Shh," he repeated, pulling me back into the bedroom.

He shut the door quietly and wedged his gun into his waistband.

"I told you to stay in here," he said. "What if I'd been the intruder? You could have been killed."

"I would've bit harder," I replied, sitting on the bed since my whole body was still shaking uncontrollably. "How did you get in? The doors are locked."

"The patrol car beat me here. I told them you probably

had a key hidden under the fake rock by the garage." He eyed me warily and stepped closer. "You're alright now. They're searching downstairs, but it looked like whoever broke in might be gone already."

I nodded, but then there was a loud crash, lots of thumping, and a panicked "oh shit!" from downstairs.

Nick flew to the door, his gun drawn. "Stay here, no matter what," he said, his eyes conveying the seriousness of the order.

I followed him to the door, locking it behind him, and stood there. I felt something damp on my lip and realized I was crying. I wiped the back of my hand across my eyes and strained to listen. There was more thumping downstairs, a struggle of sorts, and then laughter. Lots of laughter.

A moment later, there was a tap at the door. "Chelsea, it's Nick."

I opened the door and peered out tentatively. He was smiling. "We found your intruder. It's an owl."

"What? How did an owl get through my window?" I considered this. "That's not possible. I know I heard a man's voice."

He grinned wider. "Yeah, Eddie said he heard it, too. It's the owl. They called animal control, but they're trying to get it to fly out the back door now."

There was another loud crash.

"You can't just shoot it? It's destroying my house. It broke my window. It scared me half to death!"

He smiled and ran his thumb under my eye. He pressed his lips into my forehead and then pulled me closer, wrapping his arms around me. I buried my face against his chest and breathed in his fresh scent. I never knew what it was— his soap, deodorant, or even cologne, but something about Nick always smelled so tantalizing.

Eventually, he loosened his grip around me. "Better?" he asked.

I nodded, but didn't move.

"Hey Nick, it flew out the back door. We cancelled animal control," a voice called up the stairs.

Nick smiled. "See? Everything's okay. You want to come on down?"

Honestly, I would've preferred to stand there, fully enclosed by Nick's arms, at least until my pulse dropped back below a hundred, but I reluctantly nodded instead.

He backed away, then paused. "Not to be picky, but you might want to throw on a sweatshirt, or at least a bra," he said.

I glanced down. I was wearing pajama pants and a thin, tight fitting tank top. My nipples were probably visible from the next county. I sighed and pulled a bra out of my underwear drawer. I turned my back to him as I fastened the bra and then twisted it back to the front and inched my arms in before pulling the shirt back up.

Nick had a bemused grin on his face. "You can't fasten it without looking?"

I rolled my eyes. Leave it to him to mock my dressing technique at a time like this. "It's hard. You wouldn't know."

"Honey, I could fasten a bra blindfolded with both hands behind my back."

I frowned, trying to envision the logistics of this. He flashed his teeth and clinked them together several times by way of explanation.

"I think you mean you could unfasten a bra that way. Something tells me you aren't often in the position of asking women to put a bra back on," I said, starting down the stairs.

I gazed around at the destruction while Nick introduced me to Officers Eddie Manoso and Marcus Wellington. They both lived up to the high expectations of physical attractiveness I'd developed since meeting several inordinately hot officers from their department.

The owl had taken out the chandelier above the table in the breakfast nook, leaving glass shattered everywhere. A few photo frames had been broken, and many of my possessions had been knocked over, including a chair, a potted plant, and some books, but beyond that, nothing else appeared destroyed.

I must have looked overwhelmed, because Nick tapped my shoulder. "If you get me a trash bag and some duct tape, I'll patch up the window."

Marcus and Eddie exchanged a glance, and I figured it probably wasn't standard police protocol for the cops to clean up after a wild owl, but I wasn't about to complain. I got him the supplies and started a pot of coffee before I began sweeping up the glass. Marcus went out to the car and returned with a laptop, presumably completing his official report.

Nick set the roll of tape on the kitchen counter and jotted some numbers on a post-it note. "This is the size of window you need to replace it. Don't forget a screen. You might take a photo of the other one with you so it matches."

I nodded, hoping windows were sold at the same Lowes I'd visit for my replacement chandelier. Honestly I'd never liked that light much anyway. It was the standard builder-grade light fixture they'd installed when the house was built, and it had zero character. My kitchen needed lighting with personality and zest, more fitting of its owner.

Eddie and Marcus appeared ready to leave. Nick cleared his throat, getting my attention. "Does this rescue merit cookies?"

I smiled. "When do you guys work next?" I filled two

Styrofoam cups with coffee and handed them to Eddie and Marcus before retrieving milk and sugar for them to add.

"Thanks. We're both on Friday," Eddie said.

"I'll bring them by the station then. Thanks for your help. Sorry to have called you for an owl."

Nick motioned that he'd be a minute and they left. He stepped closer and took the broom out of my hand. "What if I don't want cookies?"

"You love my cookies."

"True. But I think you owe me more than cookies this time. You did bite me."

"What did you have in mind?"

He smiled mysteriously, pressed his body against mine and kissed me. My entire body tingled in response. When he ended the kiss, my whole being ached for more.

"I'll think about it and get back to you," he said. He poured himself a cup of coffee and left.

9

———

It took me hours to fall back asleep after the owl incident, so I slept in ridiculously late the next day. Thankfully, my cooking class wasn't until four p.m. I arrived a few minutes early and collected my free apron—a reward for signing up online, apparently. Then I surveyed the classroom.

The room was cavernous, with four tables in the center and four oversized cooking stations along the walls of the room. I took a seat at the table in the front, so I could observe the other students as they arrived. It was a true motley crew. First came two elderly ladies, clearly friends, followed quickly by a middle-aged man who eagerly gravitated towards me. A woman with a cowboy hat and matching boots filed in next, followed by an older man who seemed to be missing some of his teeth.

I was just noticing the extremely pregnant teenager when the man seated near me spoke.

"Just divorced," he said.

"I'm not divorced," I snapped. "It's just a separation."

He frowned. "No, uh, I meant me. I just got divorced. My ex handled all the cooking, so I've never had to learn."

"Oh. Well, this class should be good then," I said politely, turning back to observe the next student to enter.

"I'm Chuck, short for Charles," he said, offering his hand.

I shook his hand, wondering if Chuck was ever short for anything but Charles. Chadwick maybe? Chase?

"And you are?" he asked.

"Chelsea," I replied curtly, hoping he wouldn't want to talk more.

Thankfully, the teacher came in then. She looked to be in her late forties, with uniformly brown hair but slight wrinkles around her eyes that betrayed her efforts to seem younger. She introduced herself, asked the rest of us to do the same, then described the set up for the class. Each week we'd discuss a different cooking technique, then we'd have a chance to try it out in the practice kitchens.

The class went well, and was pretty fun, but I felt a little panicky at the end when she discussed our homework assignments. I hadn't had homework since law school, and that certainly didn't turn out well. Plus it wasn't just one assignment—it was five per week! Maybe Miss Carol thought this was Cooking Boot Camp and not Introduction to Cooking. I took my homework binder and free recipe book and scurried out of the room when we were dismissed, eager to avoid further discussion with Chuck.

I swung by the supermarket on the way home to pick up a few items for my homework recipes, then proudly whipped up my first roux. Once the sauce had thickened, I skimmed the remainder of the recipe.

Crap.

Apparently, the chicken breasts were supposed to have

been boiling the whole time I was working on the sauce. The stupid recipe writer should've said that to start with, really. I considered my options, then went the lazy route, deciding to microwave the chicken. But, by the time the chicken was done, the stupid roux had burned, the flour clumping together and resembling a cottage cheese mixture with blackened specs.

"Ugh," I grumbled. "This is stupid anyway. Why would anyone ever make a chicken pot pie from scratch when they sell them at the store?" I dumped the pot into the sink, disgusted. "And now I'm talking to myself again. Super."

I plopped the microwaved chicken onto a plate, squirted some ketchup over it, then sat down at the counter to eat. While I ate, I glanced over my calendar. There wasn't much coming up, but I did notice one item scrawled in red ink for the following Friday.

It read "Winter formal, 7 p.m."

My breath caught in my throat. I loved David's work formal. Every year, all the lawyers and their spouses got all dressed up and headed to the ballroom of a fancy hotel. I bought a new dress each time, although some wives looked like they rotated a few from year to year. There were always yummy hors d'oeuvres, an open bar, and a sit-down dinner with chicken and steak and some fancy potato concoction. Oh God, and I couldn't forget the delicious dessert buffet.

The best part was always the dancing, though. David had never been a big dancer, but he was a good sport about the slow numbers and then I'd dance the night away with some of the other wives while the guys talked shop. Or sports. Or home maintenance. Who knows what they discussed, actually? Probably Traci's boobs. Their entire conversation probably revolved around her stupid, perky, obviously fake boobs.

I'd already bought my dress for this year's party before David moved out. It was cabernet red with grey beading along the collar. I looked stunning in it, really. I wondered if it still had the tags on it. I fleetingly considered shipping it to Traci and letting her wear it. But the dance was only for the attorneys. None of the paralegals or other support staff were ever invited to this event. They just got the Christmas party. Would David take Traci as his date? Surely the rest of the firm was aware of their fling now.

I shuddered at the thought. How would I ever be able to attend one of these parties again? Everyone would stare at me. Everyone would be whispering about me, saying there is that poor girl whose husband snuck off with the paralegal for a bit.

I swallowed hard, feeling my lunch forcing its way back into my throat. I hoped he did bring Traci. There's no way she'd be as good of a dancer as me. Or as much fun. And she probably wouldn't touch any of the desserts, let alone take one of each to split with David, ranking them each at the end. God, how we had enjoyed those nights! Other couples looked like they felt obligated to attend, barely speaking to each other let alone giggling over inside jokes and whispering to each other in between slow dances.

Two years ago had been the best of all. To kick off our official baby-making mission, we had rented a fancy suite at the hotel hosting the party so we'd only have to stumble upstairs afterwards. David had surprised me with flowers earlier that day, and we were both so giddy and romanced at the dance, reveling in our shared secret. At one point, I'd snuck off to the Ladies' Room and slipped out of my panties, stealthily folding them into David's hand under the table in the ballroom when I returned. The look on his face when he realized what he was holding almost made me want to drag him upstairs right then instead of waiting until after dessert was served.

We had both been so certain that it would work that month—that I would be pregnant the first try. Even a few weeks later when test after test still came out negative, we weren't defeated. David had sensed my disappointment, bought me more flowers and a bottle of fancy red wine I couldn't have drunk while pregnant, and promised me we'd only have more fun trying the next month.

I glanced back at the calendar and the wash of months that the "trying" had continued without success, each month growing more tedious than the last and the arrival of each cycle more disappointing and insulting than the one before. We'd seen a doctor, who confirmed there was no medical reason we couldn't conceive but prescribed birth control pills for me to take for a few months to "reset" my cycle or something like that, and then we could try again. In the month before David left, since I'd started the pills, we hadn't had any sex at all. Why bother, if I couldn't get pregnant anyway? I wondered if that was part of the problem.

I sighed, refocusing my attention on the upcoming formal. I scribbled over the writing on the calendar, but I could still see the lettering. Besides, now that I knew when it was, it wasn't like I'd just forget all about it. Erasing it from the calendar and erasing it from my memory were two completely separate challenges. I needed a distraction. Something even more fun than a stupid winter ball to do that night.

I called Jen, assaulting her with my pleas the second she answered, "please please please tell me you're free Friday night and we can do something fabulously distracting and amazing and spontaneous. Maybe we could go to Vegas for the weekend. Just the two of us. It'll be awesome."

I was already cheered up by this idea. Why hadn't I thought of it sooner? "Hang on, I'm gonna switch you to speaker phone so I can look up ticket prices while we talk," I said, lowering my phone to look at it. I inadvertently disconnected the call instead of pressing the speaker phone button. "Oops," I mumbled, too pleased by my brilliant plan to feel guilty about the accidental hang up. Jen rang back and I answered quickly.

"Don't put me on speaker!" she shouted.

"Okaaaaaaaaaay," I said, drawing my word out slowly.

"What's wrong?"

"Nothing, it's just my phone…"

"No, Chelsea, I mean, what happened? Why do we have to go to Vegas this weekend? Did David do something? Are the cops looking for you?"

"Everything is fine," I replied, in a tone that even I found unconvincing. "And we don't have to go to Las Vegas. We could catch a movie or something instead." I paused. "Although, it'll need to be a really distracting movie."

"Have you been drinking?"

"No!"

Jen sighed loudly into the phone. "I'm sorry, Chels. I'm just really confused. If we had plans tomorrow, I totally spaced it."

"We didn't have plans. I just thought we could make some plans now."

"I have a date tomorrow night. Maybe we could do lunch Sunday?"

"Date with who?"

"A match.com guy. He's a construction manager," she replied. "That sounds hot, right?"

"Sure. And you'll probably have lots in common, seeing as how your careers are so similar," I teased.

"Accountants are boring and definitively un-sexy."

"You're sexy."

She sighed again. "Fine. Male accountants aren't. So back to tomorrow...why is it so important you go out? I can cancel if you need me to."

Now it was my turn to sigh. As much as I wanted her to cancel to baby me, I'd just feel more pathetic knowing she missed a date because of me.

"David's winter work formal is tomorrow," I said glumly.

"You're not going," she replied, more as an order than a question.

"No. I think my invitation got rescinded when David relocated to Traci's apartment."

Jen was unusually quiet.

"I really like that dance," I said.

"I know you do, Chels. I'm sorry."

"I wish I were going, with him, instead of sitting at home thinking about him with Traci."

"Eww. Do you really think he'll bring her?"

"I don't know. I imagine everyone at the office must already know about them anyway." And about me, his rejected wife, I thought.

"Surely she'd never be able to show her face at a work event. No one wants to be The Other Woman."

"It beats being the naïve, oblivious, pathetic woman."

"You are none of those things, Chelsea. You are strong, loving, and optimistic. You always see the best in people. Don't let David's crappy character make you feel bad about that."

"I just don't want to sit at home trying to guess whether he'll go to the dance without me, whether she'll be there, what she'll wear, if they'll dance. What if they kiss in front of everyone?" I grimaced, then tried to remember the last time

David kissed me in front of colleagues. My mind came up blank.

"And you know," I continued, "Even after David and I get back together, will I ever be able to attend one of his work functions with him again? It would be humiliating to go with him next year if he takes Traci this year. God, what if he still works with her after we reconcile things?"

"Chelsea, you're getting way ahead of yourself," Jen said. "Let's just focus on one shitty thing at a time. Right now, that's this stupid dance. I'm not letting you sit at home, drinking and crying over this shitty formal all weekend. If you want me to, I'll cancel my date, but it's tax season. You know I can't go to Vegas now. And I'm afraid if we're together, I'll just join in on the pity party instead of distracting you."

This was true. Although wallowing in self-pity seemed much less pathetic when done with a friend at my side, it still wasn't enough to cheer me up.

"So what do you suggest?"

"I'm thinking," she said. I could hear her tapping her pen against her desk in the background. "It has to be big," she continued.

I was about to remind her that Vegas was pretty big, as far as weekend plans go, but then she interrupted.

"I've got it. You need a booty call."

I rolled my eyes.

"Seriously. You need to meet up with someone for no purpose other than a hook up."

"That sounds like you want me to get a male prostitute."

"Oh please, you'd never have to pay for sex, Chelsea. If you'd just head to a bar alone more often, you'd know that. But really, you don't even have to actually hook up. Just fooling around or even some heavy flirting might do the trick. The point is, you need to focus all of your attention on another guy for the night."

"And I suppose you have a guy in mind?"

"Well, obviously Nick," she said.

"Obviously."

"So you'll do it?"

"Do what?"

"Call him."

I swallowed the nervous lump in my throat. "I've called him before."

"A booty call is totally different."

"How exactly?"

"Because you're not asking him to rescue you from an errant owl."

I considered this. "Okay, even assuming I was okay with a booty call, which I'm clearly not since I'm going to get back together with David, what if he doesn't know that it's a booty call?"

Jen groaned with annoyance. "You really did marry too young, Chelsea, you know that? There are some things you just have to experience and learn for yourself in real life." She sighed. "You call him, last minute, preferably late at night. Tell him you can't sleep, or you're bored, or lonely. Or if you're really daring, be blunt and say you're horn…"

"I'm not daring," I interrupted.

She giggled. "Either way, he'll get the picture. And when he shows up, look sexy. He'll take it from there."

"What if he already has plans?" I asked, and then I stopped myself from going down that path. Somehow I'd gotten caught up in all of Jen's silliness. I did not need to know how to initiate a hook up because it simply wasn't going to happen. I was on a mission—to win back David, not to get laid by someone I'd never talk to again.

"Chelsea, you have to level the playing field," Jen said, interrupting my thoughts.

"What field?"

"Look, let's assume David comes crawling back in a few weeks, begging for forgiveness. He's obviously always going to owe you for being such a colossal dickhead, but regardless, are you ever really going to fully forgive him?"

I didn't answer, because the truth was, I didn't know. On a theoretical level, I reasoned that forgiveness was a quintessential part of marriage. I'd taken vows, and they required me to forgive him, right? So while I didn't know how exactly, or when, it would happen, obviously I'd eventually forgive David, once he was ready to admit fault.

"I know if it were me, I'd always be bitter. Anytime we had an argument, even over stupid stuff like leaving the toilet seat up, it would come back to him having cheated. I would always resent him, unless of course, I'd gotten some revenge," Jen said.

"Like putting Nair in his shampoo?"

"No! Like fucking a sexy off-duty police officer."

"Jen!"

"What? Then David would still be the jerk in the relationship and you'd still have the upper hand, but you'd also have the knowledge—which you could either keep to yourself or share with him—that you got a little something extra out of the separation, too. And then, the field would be leveled."

"You should really just stick to numbers," I told her.

She laughed. "Fine. I'll cancel my date."

"No, don't," I said. "I'll give it a try."

"No you won't. You're going to wear your formal gown, watch Sleepless in Seattle, and eat ice cream till you puke."

"My first booty call could be with Ben AND Jerry," I teased.

There was a pause. "Are you sure you don't want me to cancel?"

I thought about it, and I was sure. I didn't know what exactly I was going to do, but I knew I could do it. "Yes. Now get back to work."

We hung up, and I pulled out my notebook to check my progress on Project Win David Back.

10

———

Friday passed without me reaching a real decision about the night. Determined not to let my emotions get the best of me, I spent the morning working, tried—with mixed success—another recipe from my home-work cookbook, then went for a long walk. I treated myself to a manicure, mostly to remove the stupid acrylic tips and fix my damaged nails beneath, and then poured myself a large glass of wine.

As I refilled my wine glass a few minutes later, I wandered aimlessly around the house. I paused by the digital picture frame in the living room. I had bought it years ago when they first came out, but I hadn't updated the photos since setting it up. To save the batteries, I had switched it off some time ago.

I settled into the armchair by the picture window and flipped the frame switch to "on." I was surprised that it actually still worked, and pictures quickly began appearing as if by magic on the screen. There were several of me in my bridal gown, then more of David and me together on our wedding day. Sipping my wine, I focused on my perfect hair and nails in the photos, rather than the optimistic, peaceful smile on my face.

There were several honeymoon photos next, and I was reminded of my first time snorkeling, swimming with dolphins, and hiking around a waterfall. We were so in love then. It wasn't just a memory—you could feel it in the photos. Even just looking at them, the implicit trust I'd had in David was palpable. The frame switched to more recent photos, David and me before one of his firm's parties, us in front of the house when we just bought it, making faux panicky faces and gesturing at the "sold" sign.

Suddenly, I was mad. No, I was furious. How dare David ruin this? How could he do that to us? How could he do that to me? Did none of this mean anything to him?

I threw the frame angrily onto the floor, and stormed out of the room. Jen was right. I didn't have to sleep with Nick, but I owed it to myself to at least call him. Worst case scenario, he could just watch *Sleepless in Seattle* with me. I changed into my sexiest bra and panties, pulled on tight jeans and a long, flowy sleeveless shirt.

I was not going to sit around the house drinking and crying on my own. I did not break our marriage—David did. And while I might still fix it, I wasn't about to waste another moment today mourning it.

As I dabbed some perfume on the inside of my wrist, I began to get nervous. What would I say to Nick when I called? What if I got his voice mail? Could you even instigate a hook up via voice mail?

I finished my hair and makeup before reaching the obvious solution—text message. I grabbed my phone and typed quickly so as not to lose my nerve: "Can you come over?"

I paced around the bathroom awaiting an instant

response, but none came. And then I panicked more. What if he was on a date? What if he was already in bed with someone else?

Then my cell phone rang. It was Nick.

"What's wrong?" he asked. I could hear loud music in the background.

This threw me. "Nothing."

"But your message... I thought you had another emergency."

"Oh, sorry. There's no one breaking into my house right now, if that's what you mean."

"Oh," he sounded relieved and oddly surprised at this. "I'm working at the club now. I'll be off around one."

I considered that. It was a little later than I'd hoped, and it gave me too much time to lose my nerve. Unless I went to meet him earlier.

"Why did you ask me to come over if you don't have any intruders?"

I paused. "It was a social invitation, not police related."

"How so?"

I took a deep breath. "I'm bored. I thought I could maybe pay off my debt tonight. With the cookies," I clarified.

There was a long silence, and if not for the pounding bass beat in the background, I would've thought he hung up.

"Unless you have plans later," I added, nervously.

He laughed. "No, I am all yours."

"Great. So I'll see you later."

"What are you up to now?"

"Nothing." I had just over two full hours of free time to panic and come up with ways to get out of this.

"I could use some company before then," he said. "You could bring your friend and come hang out."

I smiled. That was exactly what I needed to stop panicking, two martinis in a club. "Yeah, I like that idea. See you soon." Of course, since Jen was busy, that left me on my own. I called for a car before I could change my mind, then switched out the jeans for a cute black skirt and paced around until my ride arrived.

Dusk was packed when I arrived shortly before midnight. I spotted Nick immediately as I entered, but he was talking with someone, so I made my way up to the bar. Most people in the club were dancing by this point, or at least gathered around the tables in small groups, so I was able to snag a free stool at the bar.

I was debating my cocktail options when I felt a tickle on my neck.

"You look hot," Nick whispered in my ear.

"Thanks," I said. "You look busy."

"Ouch."

"Oh, no! I mean, you look hot, too, it just seems like you're really busy now."

He glanced around and smiled before leaning in again. "That was your first booty call wasn't it?"

"It was a text," I said, avoiding the question.

"You invited me over solely for sex. That's a booty call."

I knew I was blushing. "I invited you over for cookies. We could watch a movie. I have every Meg Ryan movie from the late 80s to mid 90s."

Nick shook his head. "Tempting, but that wouldn't work off your debt." He kissed behind my ear and disappeared into the crowd. My pulse was racing just from a simple kiss from Nick. If I actually saw him naked, I'd probably have a heart attack.

"You're back," the bartender said, interrupting my panic.

"You remember me?"

"I saw you talking to Nick. You're the married one, right?"

"Separated," I clarified. "My husband's screwing his secretary. I need a drink." Okay, technically Traci was a para-legal, but why attribute to her additional skills I wasn't sure she merited?

He chuckled. A moment later, he placed a highball glass with ice and a caramel colored liquid on a napkin in front of me before turning to another patron.

I sniffed the mystery drink, then took a tentative sip. It smelled and tasted like sugary alcohol. Good enough for me. I chugged it and motioned for another. If I was going to follow through with my plan tonight, I needed liquid courage.

I was a few sips into my second drink when a man approached me. He was probably pushing forty-five, but he still had all his hair and was attractive in a predictable sort of way.

"Care to dance?" he asked.

I glanced around to confirm he was talking to me before answering. "Sorry, I'm meeting someone later."

The man leaned in, smiled, and said, "He's not with you now."

I considered this. Although I was enjoying my bever-age, I didn't want to be too drunk to walk out the door with Nick later, and sitting there all alone was leaving me too much leeway to consider how long it had been since I'd had sex with a man who wasn't David. I knew I wasn't alto-gether ready to be with someone else in that way, but I didn't feel he'd left me much choice. David was the one who moved out and started sleeping with Traci. So there was no problem if I had sex with someone else too, was there?

I realized the man was awaiting a response. I gulped one last drink and stood up. "You're right," I said. "I'm Chelsea."

"Ben."

I made my way to the dance floor with Ben and tried to look cool shaking my booty to Rihanna. Towards the end of the song, I caught Nick watching and gave him a flirty stare. He laughed in response. After two more songs, I noticed a blonde in the corner giving Ben the look. I figured the nice thing to do would be to set him free so he could meet up with someone that might head home with him later.

"Thanks for the dance," I said, "but I really do need to meet someone. And I think she's in line next." I pointed the blonde out to him and returned to my bar stool.

I finished my drink, alternating between watching Ben and Blondie dance and spying on Nick. Then I caught the bartender's attention and motioned for a refill.

"No can do," he said, handing me a cup of ice water. "Nick said not to give you more."

"That's not fair. He just wants me sober so he can…" I opted against finishing that sentence. "I can make my own drink decisions. I've only had two."

He shook his head. "Sorry, but if security says you've had enough, I can't serve you anymore. Liability issues. It's on the house, though, on account of your husband sounding like an asshole."

"Thanks," I mumbled. I stumbled up to head to the restroom. There were two people in line, so I pulled out my phone. I had a text message from Nick. I clicked it quickly, praying he hadn't ditched me in the past few minutes.

It read: "Sorry about the drink, but you're a sleepy drunk."

I typed a quick response: "If you're worried I won't stay awake, you must not be as good as you promised."

It was my turn to pee, and then I washed my hands, dried them by waving them about like a lunatic since they were out of paper towels, and stepped out of the bathroom. I had nearly rounded the corner of the hall when I bumped into Nick. My stomach fluttered as I recalled the last time I ran into him in this hall.

We eyed one another warily for a moment. "I think you're bluffing," he finally said. "I don't think you'll follow through with this."

I narrowed my eyes. "Oh yeah? Well, I think you're hoping I lose my nerve so I don't find out you're not the Casanova you claim to be."

His lips curled up into a slight grin. "Why don't we get out of here and settle this dispute at your place?"

I tried to swallow the lump in my throat while maintaining a cool demeanor. "Fine."

"Fine," he said. He took me by the hand and led me out of the bar, nodding to a few coworkers on the way out.

Nick was quiet during the drive, giving me more than enough time to panic. I wasn't good with silence. I needed meaningless banter.

"That was pretty low, cutting me off at the bar."

"A man's gotta do what a man's gotta do."

"I hate clichés."

"Well, desperate times call for desperate measures," he said, grinning.

"You better be nice or I'll change my mind."

He turned to me. "So you admit you were bluffing?"

"I admit nothing."

He reached his hand out to my thigh then shifted it northward. My entire body tensed at the sensation of his fingers pressing against me through my panties.

"I like the boots," he said calmly.

I would've responded, but I could barely breathe, let alone speak, with his hand resting there.

"And the skirt is hot, too, although I would've preferred it without the undergarments."

He turned into my driveway, killed the engine, and opened my car door before I had even registered that his hand had left my body. I dawdled unlocking the front door, and then paused in the kitchen.

"Can I get you a drink?"

"No," he said. And he leaned in and kissed me. The kiss began innocently, with a fair amount of space between our bodies, and with Nick's hands resting politely on my hips. Within moments though, his tongue was in my mouth and his hands had slid to my butt. I tried to focus on deciding once and for all if I could really go through with this, but instead all I could think about was how soft his tongue was, how perfect he smelled, and how firm his ass was. That's when I realized I was groping him.

I pulled away suddenly, and I must have looked startled, because Nick laughed. "Cupcake," he said, shaking his head. He grabbed my hand and led me towards the stairs.

I held back. "Don't you want to watch a movie or something first?"

He ignored me, pulling his shirt off over his head as he made his way up the stairs. He tossed his shirt back towards me and I gasped, having forgotten how good he looked without a shirt. His back was lightly tanned, smooth, and muscled. I licked my lips eagerly. He kicked his shoes off in the hall and then I heard a clanking in my bedroom, presumably him placing his gun on the dresser.

I took a deep breath and started up the stairs. Nick stood in the entry to the bedroom, wearing nothing but his jeans and a big grin. I hesitantly approached and flipped off the light.

"That's cheating," he mumbled, but he left it off. He slipped my shirt up over my head and ran his lips along my neck, sucking at the delicate flesh before running his tongue along my collar bone.

He paused, and glanced to my boots. Certain he could hear my heartbeat, I walked away from him, propped my foot up on the bed, and slowly unzipped one boot and slipped out of it before moving to the next.

Nick stood his ground, watching me expectantly as though he expected me to fold any moment. I took a deep breath and unzipped my skirt, letting it fall to the ground.

He grinned and came closer, and we kissed again. This time my hands explored his back, eager to have bare skin to knead as the tension in my body increased. His hands followed suit, gently caressing my back, and then venturing to my sides, tracing stealthily along the outer edge of my breasts.

Suddenly, his hands left my body, and I realized he had unzipped his pants. He pulled back from the kiss and stared at me. "Your move," he whispered.

Apparently, he wasn't just expecting me to change my mind—he was actively seeking confirmation each step of the way that I was still ready to do it. My head hadn't quite resolved its uncertainty about the situation, but my body had no remaining reservations. I felt powerless to resist the temptation Nick offered any longer. I kissed him again, thrusting my hands into the sides of his jeans and nudging them downwards.

Apparently, that was all the reassurance he needed. Within a moment, we were both in just our underwear and he was laying me back onto the bed, collapsing on top of me. The kissing grew hungrier, and by the time his mouth reached my hardened nipple, I thought I was going to hyperventilate. He inched his way lower, kissing my stomach before tugging at my panties. I lifted my hips slightly, helping him to undress me, and then realized what he was intending to do.

I'd never been a fan of oral sex, either giving or receiving, and I knew I wouldn't enjoy it with someone the first time we were intimate. I opened my mouth to protest, but before any words came out, his tongue reached its destination and my entire body went limp. Within minutes, I was seeing stars and it took all the self-control I could muster not to scream out with ecstasy.

Nick worked his way back up my body, grinning proudly. "I told you," he whispered, kissing my neck again before returning to my lips. I kissed him back eagerly, shocked that I'd actually had an orgasm from that and even more shocked that I still wanted more. I slipped my hands under his boxer briefs and smiled as my fingers touched his bare flesh.

He pulled away suddenly, leaving me cold and vulnerable, lying naked on my bed. I was too breathless to question him, but it didn't matter, because he retrieved a condom from his wallet and returned quickly. He tore the wrapper, kissed me again, and rolled onto his side to put it on.

"Last chance to bail," he said, pausing. "You sure?"

I'd have to be insane to change my mind now. I wrapped my arms around his waist and pulled him to me. We made love feverishly, with both of us climaxing within moments of one another. There was a long silence after, as we lay, still entwined, on the bed.

I couldn't figure it out. I'd glanced at Nick's goods when he slipped on the condom, and frankly, his manhood looked about the same as David's. But I was positive that David's had never done that. And even before David, I'd never had two orgasms in the same night, let alone the same hour.

"I'm impressed," Nick finally said, cutting into my thoughts.

"Huh?"

"Not only did you actually go through with it, but you were amazing. I'd figured the sex would be good, but not that good."

I supposed that was a compliment. "You probably say that to all your women," I finally said, sounding more drunk than I was at this point.

"Babe, there are no other women in the world as hot as you," he said, climbing off of me and heading into the bathroom.

He returned before I had a chance to panic. I had no idea what was supposed to happen next, but I didn't have long to consider it. Nick climbed back into bed, kissed me on the forehead, and was asleep.

When I awoke the next morning, light was already peeking in between the curtains, but I still didn't feel rested. I was acutely aware of Nick's presence in my bed, even before I turned to face him. He was still asleep, sprawled out on his stomach. I was immediately envious. Not just of Nick, but of every male in the universe. Somehow, women lay awake at night, tossing and turning, but men manage to sleep like overgrown babies, without a care in the world.

I inched out of bed, snuck into the bathroom, then returned. I wasn't sure what the protocol for this situation was. Did I go make breakfast? Wake him up? Climb back into bed and pretend I'm still sleeping until he awakens? I finally decided just to slip back under the covers.

The movement woke him. He smiled before slowly peeling his eyes open.

"Hi," Nick mumbled, scooting closer. I felt his hand on my hips. "Hey," he said, snapping the band of my panties. "Where did these come from?"

"I don't sleep naked. Anyway, you put your underwear back on, too."

"Only because your sheets are too soft. Every time they brush against me I think it's your hand and get all worked up."

I did have soft sheets. I'd bought them as a part of my big bedroom renewal project. They were 800-thread count Egyptian Cotton and pure heaven against my skin. "I'm surprised you stayed. I didn't think that was proper booty call procedure."

"Like you'd know." He rubbed his eyes and strained to see the clock. "I make it a point not to leave a beautiful woman's bed until I'm asked to. And besides, I was exhausted."

"So what happens now?"

"I wouldn't mind a shower," he said. "You're welcome to join me."

I took a deep breath. "I mean with us."

He froze, like a deer in headlights, and then crawled out of bed. "We should do this again sometime. I had fun last night, didn't you?"

I noticed the lack of eye contact, but decided I needed further explanation. "So you just want to have sex with me on occasion?"

He shrugged. "I suck at this game. Can you just tell me what you're really thinking?"

"I'm just trying to figure out if this is just sex for you or if you want like a relationship or something."

"Oh."

I could hear him gulp from across the room.

"Well, um, I guess I thought we were both thinking more of the first option."

I nodded. He waited a moment, and then started the shower.

I dressed in my gym clothes while he showered. I hadn't exactly planned on working out, but all my other clothes were in the closet, and I didn't want to trot through the bathroom where Nick was showering to get to the closet.

By the time I had my cute zip-up hoodie pulled on over my hot pink tank top, I burst into tears. It caught me by surprise, since I felt I'd been avoiding my thoughts pretty well.

And just then, Nick emerged from the bathroom, looking like the model from a shower gel commercial, with his perfectly toned torso glistening with droplets of water. I, on the other hand, looked like a deranged workout Barbie, sobbing on the bed in clothes which, based on my fitness track record, I had no business owning.

Nick saw me and clearly wished he'd stayed in the shower. He took a moment before joining me on the bed.

"Are you okay?" he asked.

I rolled my eyes. "Do I look okay? No. I'm not okay. I'm a mess. My whole life is a big fucking mess."

There was another lengthy silence.

"Is this about what I said earlier?"

"No. Yes. I don't know."

He rubbed my back gently. "Hey, Chelsea, maybe you could stop crying. I don't want to be a jerk, but I'm not great with crying women."

"You could leave," I muttered.

He sighed, but stayed.

"Do you realize you're the first man I've slept with since my husband? I mean, we're still technically married, and I broke my wedding vows to spend a night with you, and you apparently, are just using me for sex. I know I'm supposed to wait until you leave and don't call to start crying, but what's the friggin point?"

"Look, Chels. It's not just about the sex. I like hanging out with you. You're fun to be around and you make me laugh. And I didn't mean to use you. I thought it was more of a mutual thing."

"What?"

"You wanted to have sex either to even the playing field with your husband or to help you get over him, right? So it's not like you didn't get something out of it, too. If you think about it, we've got the perfect arrangement."

I sighed and wiped my eyes on my sleeve. "How so?"

"I'm not a relationship guy. I'm not at a place where I want to get involved in something serious. You're not sure what you want to do about your marriage, so you have no business getting involved in a relationship. In the meantime, we can have each other."

I knew I must be sleep deprived, because that almost made sense. "Why don't you want a relationship with someone?"

"Why would you even consider taking your husband back?"

"I asked you first."

"I had a relationship for a while. It didn't end well. Now I know that people change and that relationships aren't meant to last forever. And I like being single."

"She broke your heart," I said, turning to face him. He dodged my stare. "Were you married?"

"Engaged," he said. "Your turn to explain. Your husband

is a dickhead. You could do way better than him. It's baffling enough that you even consider getting back together with him, but why would you ever go through the effort of changing yourself for him?"

As a self-professed non-relationship guy, Nick wouldn't understand. But I knew that no marriage was perfect. Obviously, mine hadn't been going according to plan lately, but that didn't mean it was doomed. "David's a good man. He's made some lousy decisions and yes, he's being a jerk now, but that's not who he really is."

I paused, debating whether to admit the rest. "It's not like I think we'll get back together and have a fairy tale romance, but we had a life together that for the most part worked. He made good money, we have a house together, cars. We took vacations. I could spend my days writing. And we were going to have a baby. The whole baby thing is what started us fighting in the first place, and I'm sure that's what drove him to Traci. If we just would've conceived right off the bat..."

"Wait a minute. You're telling me you want to have kids with that guy?" Nick looked disgusted.

"You wouldn't understand. I've always wanted to have kids, and I was supposed to have a baby by the time I'm thirty. It was in my plan, and I still want that. Without David, I'm back to square one."

"You're insane. You'd be better off using a sperm donor."

For some reason, I smiled at this. At least Nick was honest with me, which was more than I could say for anyone else in my life. All my married friends were avoiding me like the plague, and treating me like a cancer patient when they did see me. Jen, on the other hand, was going above and beyond trying to show me how awesome the single life was. And my mom acted like every marriage sucked and I was required to make it work.

"Sorry for crying," I mumbled.

"Sorry for upsetting you."

I paused. "Now that you know I'm crazy, does this mean I won't hear from you anymore?"

He grinned. "I've never thought you were mentally stable."

I mustered a smile. And then the doorbell rang.

I popped up. "Shit!"

"What? Are you expecting someone?"

"No. I'm not expecting anyone," I said, rushing to the window in my office where I could peek out to the driveway. "And the only person who just drops by is my mother." I grimaced at the sight of her green Mazda Protégé. "Quick, hide!"

Nick didn't budge. "How will you explain the car in the driveway?"

Crap. "Well, at least get dressed then."

"I can do that," he said, pulling on his clothes in record speed.

"Your hair is wet. Do you have a hat?"

He shook his head, then rubbed the towel through his hair. His biceps flexed visibly as he moved and I got goose bumps, my mind wandering uncontrollably to recent memories.

The doorbell rang again.

I rushed down the stairs and opened the door. Nick followed closely behind.

My mother immediately gazed past me at Nick. "I was wondering about that car in the driveway," she said.

"Hi, Mom. This is Officer Gyllenhaal," I said. "I was

interviewing him about some police business in my next book," I added, thinking quickly.

"Nice to meet you," she said calmly.

"The pleasure is all mine," he replied smoothly. Then he turned to me. "Feel free to email or call if you need anything else."

I nodded, my cheeks flushed, and shut the door behind him.

THE MOMENT MY MOM LEFT, I called Jen. I desperately needed her expert opinions on the happenings of my last twelve hours. As the phone started to ring, though, I hesitated. Until I told Jen about sleeping with Nick, it was almost like it hadn't happened. Maybe I should just keep it to myself and pretend I was still the faithful wife grieving for her lost marriage.

"Well?" Jen asked as she answered the phone.

"How was your date?" I asked, deciding to keep my transgression to myself for now.

"I want to hear about your night first."

"I asked you first," I said, childishly.

"Fine," she said. "My date was fine. He was cute enough and nice enough and surprisingly smart, but..."

"I had sex with Nick." I blurted out, interrupting. Lord knows I couldn't have kept information that critical from Jen for long.

"What?" Jen's shout pierced my eardrums. "Oh my God. Are you serious? How was it?"

"You're shouting."

"I'm in shock!" she said, still at a volume more appropriate for a concert than an intimate phone call. "How was it?"

I felt my cheeks flush as I remembered. "Good. Very good, actually." Two orgasms definitely merited two "good"s, I reasoned.

"Oh my God!"

"I'm going to hang up if you can't keep your voice down."

"I can't believe it," she said in a hushed whisper.

"He spent the night after," I added.

"Yeah? That's a good sign. Did you do it again this morning?"

"No. I started crying and then my mom came over and he left."

"Huh?"

"I might have scared him off."

"Yeah, I'd say that's a possibility."

"I'm just so confused."

"Understandable," she replied. "You need a few days to process everything and then see how you feel. It might be that one night was enough to cure you of your misery over David, but it might be that you need a repeat dose—or two or three—to get the full benefit of the therapy."

"So what do I do?"

"I need more details to give my expert advice," Jen said.

I relayed the events of the last night in detail, starting with my text, and finishing with the arrival of my mother. Jen mulled it over for a few minutes, then suggested I text him, and outlined exactly what I should say.

I took a deep breath and counted to five before exhaling, then typed out the text. "Sorry again for crying. I had fun last night but I'm really confused and not sure I'm in a place where I can do that again. Also, very busy week coming up-can we talk next week?"

I hit send, then asked Jen for more details about her date.

My phone buzzed right as she admitted she liked her date enough to not sleep with him on the first date.

"He wrote back," I interrupted.

"Read it!"

I switched to speaker phone and glanced at the message. "Last night was fun. I can do friends or friends with benefits. No pressure, no worries, no need to avoid me for a week. Call whenever."

"Well?" I prompted when Jen didn't comment instantly.

"I think he sounds sincere," she said.

"About what?"

"About the friends part. I think he means you guys can go back to just hanging out and not having sex."

"Really?"

"Well, no. Probably not. I mean, that's what he says and I bet he thinks he means it, but deep down I'm sure he still really wants the sex."

Hmm. Deep down I still really wanted the sex, too, but without the accompanying moral dilemma and complex emotions.

"Chelsea? Are you still there?"

"Yeah," I said, squeezing my eyes shut to block out the delicious memories of the sex I pledged never to repeat.

"So, what's your plan?"

I needed a plan now? Geesh. Being sort of single was complicated. "I'm going to play it cool," I said authoritatively, making up the plan as I spoke. "I'll text him in a day or two and tell him I'm experimenting with some new cookie recipes and need a taster, and then I'll drop them by the station later this week while he's working. Then he knows I'm not avoiding him and that we can keep hanging out without me sobbing, and I won't be in a situation where there's any possibility of sex."

"Good thinking. That buys you some time to get your shit together."

I started brainstorming new ways I could tweak some of my classic cookie recipes while asking Jen if she anticipated a second date with the construction guy. When we hung up, I kept myself busy with work and with tracking down someone who could mow the lawn. As for Nick, I did exactly what I told Jen I would do, and it worked perfectly.

11

The next week passed uneventfully, a fact which I clearly should have interpreted as a bad omen. With the way my life had been going as of late, things just didn't go smoothly for two days without consequence. But instead of realizing that and being cautious, I got cocky and assumed I was no longer cursed.

I was in such a good mood that morning that I was literally whistling as I dried off from the shower. My plan was to try out a recipe from the beginner's section of my cooking class workbook—a classic fried chicken—then to tour a few nearby fitness centers to find the best match for me.

I remembered the first tip from my cooking class and read the *entire* recipe before beginning, and then I even set all of the ingredients and utensils on the counter in a row. That way, Carole had said, I'd never have to run around to gather or prep items once I began cooking. I had to admit that made a lot of sense. There had been countless times when I'd had to abort the mission halfway through a batch of cookies because I realized too late that I was lacking a key ingredient.

I dredged all the chicken pieces in flour, scrubbed my hands, then turned the burner on to medium-low and measured out the oil. The recipe cautioned against turning the heat up too high. It warned that the pieces would take longer on a lower heat to cook, but said the meat would be more tender and evenly crisped.

That may have been true, but the first batch took *forever* to cook. And with everything already prepared for the second batch, I had nothing to do while they fried except turn them with my metal tongs every few minutes. Cooking was boring, I quickly decided. Obviously, I should have selected a more advanced class that would have challenged me rather than putting me to sleep.

I carefully removed the first batch from the frying pan, placing it on my prepared baking sheet, refilled the oil, then plopped the next batch of chicken in. I didn't measure the oil this time, so it looked like a bit more, but now that I was experienced, I could fiddle with the recipe a bit and still have success. The chicken barely even sizzled when I plopped it in, so I turned the dial on the burner up just a smidge higher.

Then I glanced around for my magazine, but realized I had left it upstairs. I poked at the chicken—still eons away from being finished—and dashed up the stairs to grab it. There was an ad on the first page of the magazine for a new lip gloss, so I went into the bathroom and rummaged through my makeup drawer until I found my current lip gloss, which was decidedly not the same color. I decided I'd buy that new kind at the store the next time I went. I pulled out my phone to add it to my grocery list, then noticed my hair was almost dry.

My hair had always been pretty low maintenance, but on high humidity days, it would frizz if I let it air dry. Even if

I just used the blow dryer for a couple of minutes at the very end of the drying process, it would tame my locks. I plugged in my dryer and flipped my head upside down to dry. After a minute, I brushed my hair smooth while blasting the top layers with the dryer set on cool. It may not have been the most typical hair routine, but it was quick and effective.

As I switched the power to low, I heard a strange beeping sound over the hum of the dryer. I turned it off, paused to listen, then realized I was hearing the smoke detectors.

"Shit!" I screamed, dashing down the stairs. "I burned the chicken!"

When I reached the kitchen, I first noticed the platter of perfect chicken legs on the counter beside the stove and felt immensely proud of my successes. The feeling was fleeting, though, as I observed that the chicken still in the skillet was not only burnt, but actively on fire. Thinking fast, I grabbed some baking soda from my pantry and dumped it over the pan. It simply sizzled louder.

I looked for a towel to smother the flames with, but it was pretty hot, and I wasn't sure how accidentally setting a hand towel on fire would help the situation. I remembered my instructor saying something about using the lid, but the pounding in my chest told me I was definitely out of my league.

I cut my losses and dialed 9-1-1. After explaining the emergency to the dispatcher and being instructed to immediately leave the house, I ran to the front door, unlocked it, then returned to the kitchen. I couldn't find the correct size lid, so I grabbed a plate which seemed to be about the same size as the skillet. I stepped closer to place the plate tightly over the top of the skillet, but the heat startled me, and I ended up tossing the plate the last few inches, which of course shattered it everywhere.

"Stupid cheap plates," I mumbled, warily watching the flames jump higher. I felt I should do something, anything, but was unable to even move, the sight of my stove going up in flames too mesmerizing and terrifying. A moment later, I heard sirens, and I rushed to the front lawn, determined at least to avoid a lecture from the firemen about having stayed inside.

The next few minutes were a scurry of activity, with two fire trucks pulling up and a handful of fully uniformed men dashing into my house with an array of heavy and expensive-looking equipment. I felt silly then for having called them, since it wasn't like the whole house was on fire, but the firefighter who stayed outside with me assured me that I had done the right thing, and that no fire was too small for their skilled hands.

I glanced around warily, praying none of the neighbors who knew David were home, feeling deathly embarrassed when passing cars slowed to watch the bedlam. Honestly, I hadn't expected such a commotion from a silly little stove fire.

"Could you at least turn off the lights?" I asked, eying the silent, but flashing fire truck. The firefighter hesitated, then nodded and ducked into the truck for a moment, thankfully stilling its lights.

Once the flames disappeared, things calmed down pretty quickly. I was allowed to re-enter the premises and survey the remnants of the pandemonium. There were still three firefighters in my cramped kitchen, all hunched around my poor dead stove.

While they discussed the possibility of smoke damage inside the wall behind the stove, I tried to ascertain what the correct protocol was in this situation. Since my house was still standing, it seemed the easiest fix would be to repaint the wall behind the stove and buy a new stove. I knew I could get that done for cheaper than my property insurance deductible, and I wasn't too eager for David or my insurance agent to learn the exact parameters of my crappy cooking skills. But, it seemed logical that once the fire department got involved, I was probably supposed to report the incident. After all, there was still one giant red truck parked in front of my house.

I poured some lemonade for the firefighters and offered them scones I'd baked the night before, hoping to butter them up and then ask my question. But before I got the chance, the door leading into the house from the garage opened.

We all turned, and I, at least, was expecting another fireman. Instead, there stood Nick. A bemused grin quickly replaced the look of panic on his face as he looked at me. He turned to the firefighters and quickly introduced himself before approaching me. He was in light uniform that day, meaning his cargo work pants and a tee shirt bearing the department name.

"Babe," he said, shaking his head. "Are you alright?"

I nodded meekly and lifted up the platter in my hands to cover my crimson face. "Scone?"

"No thanks," he said. He placed his hands on my forearms and pulled me closer before rubbing his hands up and down my arms, as if he were trying to warm me up. "What happened?"

"I was trying to make fried chicken."

"At ten in the morning?"

I shrugged. "Not to eat. It's for my cooking class."

I could tell Nick was struggling not to laugh. "You're taking a cooking class?"

"Yes." And now I was going to flunk. I wasn't completely

sure it was possible to fail a class at the community learning annex, but clearly this would justify an exception to the policy. "I'm a horrible cook. I wanted to be able to cook dinner for David sometime."

"But you're so good at baking."

"I know. Apparently, talent with the oven doesn't translate to competence with the stove. Who knew grease could be so flammable?" I sighed, wistfully realizing it was time to give up on the visions of a domesticized me cheerfully placing platters of roast chicken and sautéed root vegetables on the table in front of my loyal husband.

"Did you put water on it?" Nick asked, his eyes scanning the charred wall behind the stove.

"No, I'm not an idiot. As soon as I came in the room and saw the flames, I dumped baking soda on it, but it was already pretty bad by that time."

"You left the room while you were frying chicken?" His eyes grew wide.

I redirected my stare to my feet. "I had to dry my hair." And had I known I was going to have half of the town's public servants in my kitchen, I probably would've taken the time to swipe on some of my crappy old lip gloss, too.

He shook his head and then wrapped his arms around me for a quick hug. "No more cooking, okay?"

I solemnly nodded. "Baking is still okay, though, right?"

Nick smiled. "Yes, I expect cookies to magically appear at the station tomorrow as a thank you for me coming by to check on you."

I sighed, still shaking my head at the mess in my kitchen.

"What's the deal with the plate?" he asked, pointing to the shards of porcelain beside the stove.

"I don't want to talk about it."

He chuckled again.

"This is a disaster," I moaned.

"We can fix your house," he assured me, patting my arm.

"Not that. Me. My whole plan is going down the drain. I was going to wow David with a home cooked meal and he'd see how much I've changed and come back." I omitted the other part, how I'd already humiliated myself with Nick by crying after sex and now, the next time he was seeing me, it was because I started a grease fire in my kitchen.

Nick groaned. "Any guy that thinks you need to change is nuts and not worth taking back."

I rolled my eyes. "Thanks."

"Chels, I'm serious. You could've hurt yourself today, or burned the whole damn house down. He's not worth that. Besides, your cookies are worth a million fried chickens."

I smiled and we were quiet for a moment, watching the firefighters continue their cleanup. "Hey, how did you know there was a fire?"

"I heard it on the dispatch radio."

"Oh." That probably meant I had to report it to insurance. Or did it? I rose to my toes and whispered my question in Nick's ear.

He laughed. "Why, are you on your third strike for random property accidents?"

"No, I just don't want David to find out."

Nick nodded, then turned to the fireman to inquire about the extent of the damage. I tuned out while they spoke, barely noticing Nick ducking his head into the laundry room which shared a wall with my kitchen. A moment later, I heard him scooting my washing machine away from the wall, and then one of the firefighters drove a small axe through the wall.

I screamed reflexively as they chopped a hole the size of

a small dog in my poor wall. Nick returned to my side, wrapping an arm around me.

"Sorry babe, but they need to make sure there's no structural damage or any fire or smoke remaining in the wall."

"But there's a h-h-hole in my wall now," I stuttered.

"I'll come by this weekend and help you patch it. In the meantime, maybe this will help it air out."

Luckily, the damage was minimal, and Nick agreed I'd be better off just paying out of pocket to have the damage repaired.

THE NEXT MORNING, Nick arrived, supplies in hand, to patch my wall. I offered him some coffee and muffins, then perched on my counter across the room and chatted lightly with him while he worked.

"What do I owe you for the drywall?" I asked as he finished, realizing I had no idea how much drywall cost.

Nick smiled. "Interesting that you should phrase it that way."

I raised an eyebrow. He wiped his hands on his pants and approached me.

"Not, how much should I pay you, but what do I owe you," he said. "Well, I can think of several things you could do to compensate me, but the ones that offer you the most benefits all require your clothes to come off."

I planted my hands on my hips. "And the other things?"

He shrugged. "Those mostly just require my pants to come off, but it would probably help if you were at least topless."

I shook my head. "I told you, we're not doing that again."

"Again? When did we ever do *that*?"

"I can't keep having sex with you while I'm trying to win my husband back."

"Why not? You've got needs, and he's not back yet. No sense in turning away someone who's perfectly willing to satisfy those needs."

I inhaled calmly through my nose, desperately pushing away mental images of all the many ways he knew to satisfy my needs.

Nick laughed and slipped his hand under the bottom edge of my shirt, his cool fingers barely touching my bare stomach. "You're considering it, aren't you?"

I stepped backwards. "That doesn't make any sense. Why would you want to get involved with me if you know I'm just going to go back to David?"

"I don't want to get involved," he said. "What I was offering was just sex."

"You're already involved."

His eyes conceded the point. "I like you, I like sex, and I really like sex with you. And I don't want a relationship. The fact that you're only using me to fill a void till David returns makes you perfect for me."

"You're insane," I replied, turning to inspect the wall. I'd need to paint it to match the rest of the room once the drywall goo dried, but other than that, he'd done a pretty good job. And once my new stove was delivered in a few days, my kitchen would be as good as new. "How about I buy you a pizza?"

He shook his head. "I have plans tonight, and besides, I thought you were on a diet."

"Diet's not going so well. I was thinking about joining a gym instead, you know, maybe just tone up instead of actually cutting back on food."

He nodded.

"You're not going to make fun of me?"

"No, that actually makes sense. You don't need to lose weight, and I'm not saying you need to tone up either, but a little exercise never hurts." He glanced at his watch. "Why don't I take you out for dinner on Tuesday instead?"

"Then I'd owe you for dinner and the drywall."

"Not if you put out after the date."

"It wouldn't be a date. And why don't I buy dinner to pay you for the drywall work."

"Fine. And I'll buy you dessert to pay you back for the lap dance after dinner."

"I'll just make dessert myself."

He laughed and started towards the door, his tools all wedged into one jumbled oversized toolbox. "You pick the restaurant."

"What sounds good?" I opened the front door for him and he started out.

"Fried chicken," he replied with a grin.

I slammed the door and went to go research gym memberships.

ON TUESDAY NIGHT, Nick glanced around the restaurant skeptically. "When I asked for fried chicken, I wasn't expecting Cajun food."

"It's good to try new things," I replied, holding up two fingers for the hostess.

Nick placed his hand on the small of my back as we made our way to the table. "I couldn't agree more," he said. Then he leaned closer, his warm breath tickling my ear. "How about I try something new at dinner, and you try something new after."

I turned to face him and he wiggled his eyebrows suggestively. "There's nothing new about that," I said.

"You'd be surprised," he replied, pulling my chair out for me.

We were both quiet while we perused the menu, but as soon as our drinks arrived and we ordered, I decided it was time for answers.

"Why don't you like commitment?" I asked.

He stared back at me for a moment, presumably trying to decide how easily I'd let the topic drop if he dodged the question. "When people get attached, someone inevitably gets hurt. If there's no commitment, no one gets hurt. You get the benefit of a relationship without the downside."

I opened my mouth to speak, then shut it. I was certain there was a logical retort for his assertion, but I couldn't think of it.

"So you don't ever date single girls?" I finally asked.

He shrugged. "Of course I do. There is a serious shortage of hot recently-separated women in town."

"How do you justify doing that? At some point in dating, a woman is going to expect a commitment. When you don't take that next step, she'll be hurt anyway. Or she'll dump you and you'll get hurt." I added, suspecting no rational woman would ever dump Nick.

"True, but that is different. All breakups suck, but when you're just dating and it ends abruptly, that's the sort of thing you can get over in a matter of days with a few stiff drinks. When serious relationships end, you can't just shake it off. That's the sort of break up that has you doing all sorts of crazy stuff."

"Like learning to cook," I added softly.

He nodded.

"I will say that your theory makes sense. But I think a lot

of experts would argue that it's not healthy to isolate yourself, that there is some value to putting yourself out there and taking a risk."

Nick shrugged again and motioned for another drink. "Been there, done that, didn't like it," he mumbled.

I'd never seen him look so thoughtful before. I was dying to know what had happened to make him so jaded, so I took a risk. "You said you were engaged before."

He nodded.

"How long ago?"

"Four years."

I felt my eyes widen. "And you're still not over her?"

Nick snorted. "I'm completely over her. I'm just not going to make the same mistakes again."

"What mistakes?"

The waitress brought our drink refills. He sipped his before answering. "Making plans."

I frowned. "What happened?"

Nick paused a beat, probably deciding if he would answer. "She left me on our wedding day."

"Ouch. I guess that would be traumatic."

He smiled.

"I'm sorry," I added, just as our food arrived.

Nick picked at his meal warily before testing a small bite, chewing cautiously, then spearing a larger bite with his fork.

"In retrospect, I should have seen it coming," he said after swallowing. "Katelyn—my fiancée that is—started acting strangely months before the wedding. I just chalked it up to pre-wedding jitters and that typical bridezilla crap you hear about, but deep down I knew it was something more. She stopped sleeping over, started talking about going on to grad school or traveling abroad, and she took up yoga."

"Oh, God, she didn't leave you for the yoga instructor, did she?" I asked, cringing. That would have made us the two biggest clichés out there.

He laughed and shook his head. "No. She didn't leave me for anybody. That was maybe the hardest part. It wasn't that there was someone else she wanted to be with more, she just didn't want to be with me."

"Well, she sounds insane. Any woman would have to be crazy to walk away from you."

"Thanks. But I get it now. We were so young then, and she just didn't know what she wanted. We started dating early in college and by the time we were graduating, I'm not sure it occurred to us that we even had options. It just seemed like we were supposed to get married, buy a house, and have kids." He paused, chewing another bite. "I don't think Katelyn liked my job either. The idea of life with a cop must have seemed exciting to her at some point, but the reality of it, with the unpredictable hours, crappy pay, and constant stress, just wasn't her cup of tea."

I chewed thoughtfully, uncertain of what to say. "Sounds like you dodged a bullet then. Better to find out she's not cut out for the life before you tie the knot, right?"

He nodded, and I realized I'd unintentionally just endorsed his whole theory of bailing on relationships before you get too invested. I grimaced and chugged my drink.

"She moved to Colorado a month later, married an engineer eighteen months after that, and now they're expecting their first kid. A boy," he added.

"Facebook?" I guessed.

He nodded. "Fucking Facebook. I mean, you can't *not* be

friends with them. It's natural to be curious, right? But then you realize you didn't really want to know."

I laughed. "Thankfully David isn't on Facebook, so the issue never came up. And I haven't searched for Traci," I said, making a mental note to do that the second I got home. Or maybe as soon as I had a moment alone with my phone. Actually, the restaurant had long tablecloths, I decided, discretely slipping my phone out of my purse and searching for my Facebook app.

"Don't even think about it," Nick said, reaching over the table and snatching my phone away. "If there's any secret action going on under this table, it had better involve your panties and not your damn phone."

I smiled sheepishly. It was a little creepy how well he knew me.

"Anyway, now that you know all my dirty laundry, it's your turn. Tell me what's so great about David? Why is he worth nearly burning down your house?"

I rolled my eyes. "Obviously, that was unintentional," I began, pausing to think about the old days with David. "For starters, he's smart. David is one of those guys that can shout out the answers to Jeopardy before the contestants. He's a good singer too. When we drove places, he'd blast his Rat Pack CDs and croon right along with Sinatra. And he's funny. He had this way of telling me stories from work that made even boring legal stuff sound amusing."

I paused again. "He was dependable, too. He took care of the lawn, changed the batteries in the smoke detector, and made sure my car always had gas in it. He dealt with taxes and insurance and all of our customer service complaints. And we had a routine, you know? He made the coffee in the morning, he called me at lunch, and after work, we'd take a walk through the neighborhood together and spy on all the weird neighbors. Then we'd eat dinner on the couch watching TV."

"Sounds exotic," Nick teased.

"I really wanted a baby," I confessed suddenly. "And he did too, at first, but I guess maybe when it didn't happen right away, I became a little obsessed with it. And then I started to resent him because he wasn't reading all the books or following the right diets. One night, I caught him taking a really hot bath. Can you believe that?"

"The bastard!" Nick exclaimed, oozing with sarcasm.

"Prolonged heat exposure lowers sperm count," I explained. "David knew that. Or at least he would have if he'd bothered to read any of the books."

Nick nodded with understanding now, although I sensed he didn't really get how offensive David's transgression had been at the time.

"In the month before he moved out, he stopped calling me at lunch, and started working late a lot. A couple times he ended up going out of town for depositions, but once he didn't answer his cell phone, and so I called the office to find out what hotel he was staying at and they had no idea what I was talking about. I should've known then that he was cheating. I guess deep down, I did know, but I didn't really accept it." I shook my head. "Never in a million years would I have guessed he'd stoop so low as to shtup his paralegal."

I could tell Nick was struggling not to laugh.

"It's fine. Go ahead and laugh. It is funny, when you think about it, the lawyer and his paralegal."

Nick shook his head. "I was laughing at your Yiddish, not your jerky ex."

I smiled and chewed thoughtfully, enjoying a peacefulness that accompanied the rare feeling that I didn't have to try to fill every silence with meaningful chatter.

After a moment, Nick interrupted the quiet. "Can I ask you something? Have you considered the possibility that David won't come back?"

I set my fork on my plate with a clank and turned to face him. "Of course I have. I'm not a complete idiot. I realize I can't control what he does or force him back, but that doesn't mean I'm not going to fight to save my marriage."

Nick nodded complacently as though he agreed with me, even though his words revealed he didn't. "I mean on a practical level, Chels. Have you thought about what you'll do if you get divorced? Like where you'll live—if you'll keep the house, how you'll pay bills, that stuff?"

All the serenity I had been feeling whooshed out of me like air from a punctured balloon. Of course I wasn't getting rid of the house. It was our house. It was bad enough living there without David; I certainly couldn't *not* live there without David. "I set up automatic bill pay," I finally said, realizing Nick expected a verbal answer.

He raised an eyebrow but didn't press for details. "You have your own income from your writing, right?"

I nodded.

"Where does it go? Do you have your own bank account?"

I shook my head. "Joint checking."

Nick frowned. "Chelsea, you need to set up your own checking account as soon as possible. With just your name on it. Withdraw some funds from your joint account to fund your new account, then make sure your paychecks get deposited directly into your new account."

I considered this suggestion. It did make sense, actually, aside from the part where I took David's money and put it in an account he couldn't reach. "I think that would piss off David," I said.

"Do you think he'd hurt you?" Nick asked, leaning forward and lowering his voice.

I rolled my eyes. "No! Geez, not every husband beats his wife!"

"A lot do," Nick retorted. "More than you'd expect."

"I just think it wouldn't be fair for me to take our money and make it my money."

Nick shrugged. "There's nothing stopping him from doing the same thing, and you need a safety net more than he does. If you get back together you can always merge accounts again."

"Fine," I said, although secretly I was still undecided.

We finished eating and Nick asked for the check. As soon as it arrived, I snatched it from the waitress, knocking her leather-bound notepad out of her hand.

"Sorry," I mumbled to the waitress, figuring now at least I could just tip 20% to compensate for my folly and save myself the hassle of trying to calculate 18%. I handed my credit card to the waitress then turned back to Nick.

"When you always pay, it feels like a relationship, which it's not, right?"

"Right," he said skeptically.

"When you go out with your other friends, do you insist on always paying?"

"No, but my other friends are all guys. It's not so much a relationship versus friendship thing as an old-fashioned and sexist thing."

"Were you serious when you said you wanted to be friends even if we're the kind of friends that don't have sex?"

Nick raised his hand to his eyebrow, embarrassed, as the waitress returned to the table right as I spoke. When she left, he laughed.

"Yes, I was serious," he said. "I have my preference between the two, but I'll take either."

"Just no relationship," I said.

He nodded.

The more I thought about this, the less it made sense. "If you have a friend of the opposite sex who you have sex with, how is that not a relationship?"

"It all hinges on the future. If it's friendship and sex with the assumption that it will lead to a happily-ever-after, meeting the parents, buying houses, white picket fence and shared pets, that's a relationship." He paused. "Besides, I think the friendship without the sex has a lot more in common with long-term relationships than the friendship with the sex."

We stood to leave the restaurant. "I don't know how you do that," I said. "I know deep down that your logic is completely flawed, but I can't figure out exactly how."

Nick raised his eyebrows suggestively.

"You're dropping me off at my house,' I said. "I still haven't wrapped my head around all this and I can't do that with you seducing me. Besides, I have an early morning at the gym tomorrow."

"I wouldn't dream of interfering with that," he said. "Good thing you paid, then."

I shoved him playfully, but secretly agreed. Right or wrong, I felt much less pressure when I paid. If only I could find a similarly easy solution to make myself less distracted by Nick's dreamy eyes or his soft, welcoming lips.

12

———

True to my word, I headed to the gym in the morning. Well, first I stopped at the bakery to pick up a sesame seed bagel and vanilla latte, and then I went to the gym. I flipped down the mirror on my car visor to check my appearance before exiting the car. The last thing I wanted was to draw attention to myself during my workout by looking out of place.

My hair was pulled into a tight, high ponytail, and, like all serious athletes, I hadn't wasted time applying makeup. Okay, maybe I had on a negligible amount of lip gloss and a single swipe of mascara, but that was all. I had selected black spandex-blend pants that fell just below my knees and were both functional and flattering, and I'd paired it with a sports bra and a fitted hot pink tank top that advertised its moisture-wicking ability on the tag. Yep, I definitely looked like I belonged at the gym.

I retrieved my free two-week trial pass from my purse, tightened the shoelaces on my brand new trainers and confidently strode in the door. Just inside the main entrance, there was a turnstile. The two women ahead of me pushed through it with ease, barely even pausing, so I stepped in line to do the same, but as I nudged the metal bars, they didn't move. I pushed harder, but the turnstile didn't budge.

A hand reached around me and gave it an extra nudge and it rotated easily, nearly knocking me forward. I stumbled through then turned to smile politely at the elderly gentleman who had helped me.

"Thanks. Hard to shove that, huh," I murmured.

He eyed me curiously, but didn't say anything, so I made my way to the aptly labeled Information Desk. The woman seated at the desk didn't appear particularly friendly, and as I approached, I could hear her engaging in a phone conversation. I waited patiently for her to acknowledge me, and, finally, she hung up and turned her glance to me.

"Hi. I have this two week pass and I was interested in touring the gym and possibly joining," I said.

I must have said the magic words, because the woman's face instantly transformed into a broad, welcoming smile. "I'm Shelby. I would love for you to fill out this quick little form here and while you get that done, I'll page one of our trainers to meet you down here, give you a tour of our facilities, and even squeeze in a short personal training session if you like."

Her thick southern accent reminded me of the syrupy pecan pie I ate as a child while visiting relatives in Georgia. I licked my lips hungrily and nodded politely, accepting the form. I scribbled my address, phone, and generic personal information on the paper and slid it back across the desk to her.

"I do thank you for this information," Shelby said sweetly. "And this here is Kenya. She'll give you a tour and get you set up with a trainer, free of charge. When you're all done today, we'll just scan your credit card information but you won't be charged a thing until after your two week trial period."

"Um, what if I decide I don't want to join?"

She shook her head dismissively. "That won't happen, hon, but if it did, that would be A-okay. You just let us know at any time before the end of the trial period and we'll cancel it, and after that, we'll just stop chargin' your card whenever you tell us to."

I nodded with confusion and turned towards Kenya. She appeared to be fresh out of high school, but thankfully had a more even-keeled amount of enthusiasm. She showed me the locker rooms, the pool, the group class rooms, the daycare, and, finally, the cardio room and weight rooms. There, she introduced me to my trainer for the day, Kristin.

I was relieved that my trainer was a female, and that she didn't resemble a steroid-laden heavyweight. She led me back to the locker room and told me she'd wait for me in the weight room.

Since I'd already donned my full workout gear, there wasn't much for me to do except to shove my purse in a locker. Once that was done, I went to meet Kristin. She asked me a lot about my current fitness level and workout regime, and I offered vague responses that sounded plausible enough.

"So you're definitely consistent with your exercise," she summarized for me. "What about strength training? How often do you incorporate that?"

"Oh daily," I replied. Nearly everything I did required some form of strength.

Kristin appeared alarmed. "You mean you work out different muscle groups each day, right? Not that you work the same ones every day?"

"Of course," I said, as though the latter option was the most absurd thing I'd heard all week.

"Okay, well let's get a base assessment on your strength so you can monitor your progress," she said. "You're probably pretty familiar with the strength machines already, and the great thing about these is you just type in your user number on the keypad by each piece of equipment and it will tell you the weight and reps you did last."

"Cool!"

She nodded in agreement. "Let's start with quads," she said, leading me to a leather-padded metal thingy.

I eyed the machine warily, trying to decide how it worked or what exactly comprised my "quads." I was pretty sure that was something in my legs, so I must be supposed to lay down on the machine. I stepped closer and started to crouch over it when I caught the curious look in Kristin's eyes.

"You know, I actually do my strength training without the machines most days, so maybe you want to just do a quick review of how they all work," I said casually.

Kristin appeared relieved. She stepped past me, sat on the machine, wedged her calves under the padded bar and lifted it upright. The exercise seemed about as hard as straightening a leg, so I really didn't think it was going to do much toning, but I wanted to at least give it a fair chance.

I sat on the machine, mirroring her position, then pointed my feet upward, expecting the bar to raise with it, but it didn't move. I pushed harder still, but nothing. I frowned at Kristin. "I think it's stuck."

She reached out with her hand and lifted upwards. The bar moved easily.

"Er...right," I said. I held my breath and forced my legs upwards with all my strength and managed to eek out two reps on my own. "Let's move on to the next one," I said, sweating profusely. "I don't want to run out of time."

She set the weight more reasonably on the remaining machines, so there weren't any other issues. When we finished with those, Kristin quickly showed me each of the cardio machines and told me briefly how they worked. I thanked her for her time, proudly wiped my sweaty brow on a clean gym towel before tossing it into the laundry bin, and made a mental note to bring my swimsuit the next time so I could check out the hot tub. I mean, after swimming laps, of course.

I stretched slowly in the Relaxation Room, careful not to violate the "no talking, no electronic devices" sign on the wall. Then I retrieved my purse from the locker room and drove home, proud of my success. I had joined a gym. I was officially a gym rat, soon to be a total health nut.

I was grinning widely as I hopped into my steamy shower. As soon as I hopped out and dried off, I called Nick to brag.

"Is this another booty call?" Nick asked without any greeting. "Because I have plans later tonight, but I could totally reschedule for that."

I groaned. "No. And don't hold your breath on that one. It was a one-time thing."

"You keep saying that, but I'm not convinced."

"What are your plans anyway?"

"Meeting some guys to watch the playoff game later."

"Oh," I replied, absentmindedly trying to decide which sport would be playing off in March. I settled on basketball, in the end, but didn't say anything further in case I was wrong.

"Chelsea?"

"Yeah?"

"Why did you call, if not for mind blowing sex?"

I panicked, not immediately remembering my initial reason. "Can't I just call to chat?"

"You could, but I don't think you did."

"Oh, all right. I just wanted to tell you that I started my new hobby today, and it's going great."

There was a lengthy silence. "This hobby doesn't involve flammable materials, does it?"

"No, smartass, it's the gym. Remember? I told you I was going to join one."

"Oh. Right. Does that count as a hobby?"

"Going to the gym? Of course it does."

"Huh," he replied, sounding distracted.

"What's your idea of a hobby then?" I demanded.

"I don't know. Golf."

"You golf?"

"Hell no, but I think it constitutes a hobby."

"What do you have against golf?"

He laughed. "Nothing, I'm just not a golfer. There's two kinds of men in this world—guys who golf and guys who don't golf. I'm in the second group."

This made absolutely no sense to me. "David golfs," I replied.

"My point exactly."

"What?"

Nick chuckled again. "Look, Chelsea, I'm very glad your trip to the gym was successful and that nothing burned down, but I'm actually at work now."

I grimaced. That hadn't occurred to me. "Wait- you were talking about booty calls at work?"

"I'm a cop, not a preschool teacher. Ain't nothing unlawful about two consenting adults dancing in the sheets," he teased.

"Jeez. I'm hanging up now," I said, pausing a beat before actually hanging up.

I still had so much energy buzzing through me after my successful workout that I decided to drive to the bank after lunch. I did just what Nick had suggested, withdrawing some money from our joint savings account, then establishing my own checking account and arranging for my paychecks to be directly deposited there. I felt an odd sense of both accomplishment and betrayal as I drove home, but when I called Jen and told her, she assured me I'd done the right thing, so I dismissed my negative feelings.

THE NEXT DAY, after wandering around aimlessly for the better part of an hour trying to figure out how any of the cardio machines worked, I decided to try the Turbo Step Aerobics class. I was great at following instructions, so a group fitness class would be a more productive use of my time than boring equipment. The sign posted to the door said the class didn't start until 11 a.m., but since the room appeared to be filling up already at 10:45, I made my way into the classroom.

There were a few men in the room, but ninety percent of the students were women, all approximately my age. They seemed to be dressed alike, from their colorful shoelaces to the thick headbands that appeared to uniformly coordinate with their tank top colors. I touched my own sweaty forehead and decided I should probably invest in one of those headbands, although I was certain the reason no one else had visible perspiration yet was because no one else had hit the weight room already like I did.

Each person had staked out a little spot in the room and

marked it with a step. The class was divided, with about half the students having one riser under each end of their step, another quarter with no risers under, and another quarter with two risers on each end. I located the steps along the side wall of the gymnasium and decided to set mine up with one riser on each end. Probably I could handle two like the other experienced exercisers, but since I'd already done some weight lifting, I didn't want to push it.

I carried my step and risers to the back of the room, near a mirrored wall with a ballet barre. Thanks to mirrors on every wall, I was reasonably confident I could see the instructor from the back, without the risk of having all eyes in the class on me. The last thing I wanted at my first group fitness class was to draw attention to myself. I stretched a bit, tightened my shoelaces, and sipped from my water bottle until the instructor, Jade, arrived.

She greeted the class, introduced herself, and asked the new students to come to the front so she could help them with form. I froze, turning my glance to the ground in hopes she wouldn't call me out. A moment later, Jade turned the music on, and I breathed a sigh of relief. It was a hip hop song I recognized, although I'd never heard it played this loudly before, and it seemed to be remixed to twice its normal speed. I could definitely exercise to this, though, I thought. It was upbeat and fun, and the enthusiastic energy buzzed throughout the room nearly as loud as the bass from the stereo system.

I followed Jade, marching in place to the beat, and then hesitated while the class began stepping up onto the step then back down again. It seemed simple enough, I decided. I watched my feet as I stepped until I grew comfortable with the movement. When I looked up, the class was already doing a kick while up on the step.

I grunted with frustration but caught on quickly enough. But right as I started to kick and step back without feeling clumsy, Jade added a backwards lunge into the move. I stumbled on the first one, then figured it out. Clearly, I was a natural. We continued this process, with Jade introducing a new move as soon as I seemed to master the previous one, for a few more minutes and then the music slowed.

"Good warm up guys, let's stretch it out and then get started!" Jade shouted.

I paled. Started? That was the warm up? I reached under my step for my towel, burying my face in the rough cotton blend so no one could see my frustration. I was already sweating, shaking, and more than a little stressed over the challenge of keeping up. Surely she didn't mean it would get even harder?

Stretching calmed me down, mostly because it was slow and I could easily follow along with the moves. As soon as the music picked up again, I winced, knowing it was about to get harder. I took a deep breath and braced myself.

"Let's start our first combo with an L-step," Jade shouted. The rest of the class delved seamlessly into an unpredictable pattern using the sides of the bench. I managed to at least get to the right end at the right time once before Jade called out the next step. "Repeater knees!"

This move I figured out by the second try. And then, thankfully, we started "from the top," which is an expression that really never made any sense to me since it involved going back to the start, but, in this instance, I was grateful for any repetition I could get. I still couldn't quite figure out this L-step crap, but I was moving right with the group on the repeater knees.

"Over the top!" Jade shouted, and I watched as the class

moved in unison over their step and then back, swinging their arms over their heads.

I followed along, albeit considerably slower, then pledged to actually be with the class by the next time through. Sure enough, Jade ordered us to take it from the top again, and this time, I was determined to keep up. I hopped from one end of the bench to the other, popped my knees up when everyone else did, and even managed to get over the bench at the right time.

As I went to hop back over my step, though, the tip of my shoe caught on the edge of the step. I slipped right off it and felt my body catapulting forward, so I quickly pulled my leg back. This, unfortunately, caused my entire step to rock backwards, sending me sailing back with it.

I heard shrieks from the steppers around me, a loud thump, and then the room went black.

When I came to a moment later, I heard a distant thumping of music. I opened my eyes slowly and saw a hoard of unfamiliar faces hovering right above me. I squeezed my eyes shut tightly, praying they couldn't see me as long as I couldn't see them, but then someone shook me.

"Ma'am? It's Jade, the instructor. We've called the paramedics. Stay still and try to relax. You might have a concussion."

I groaned, then slowly peeked my eyes open again. Stupid Jade was still positioned directly over my face, with her stupid sweat-free forehead and her stupid perky boobs way too close for comfort. I swatted her away and tried to sit up but got too dizzy.

An eternity later, she finally backed away and the crowd parted, only to be replaced by two uniformed paramedics with a gurney. One of them took my blood pressure while the other shined a flashlight in my eyes.

"Can you stand?" one of them asked.

"Of course," I snarled, starting to stand. I got woozy and slipped backwards, though, so then the two paramedics loaded me onto the gurney. That probably was the low point of the class, being wheeled through the room on a raised bed for all my classmates to see. It didn't help that the gurney had to go ridiculously slowly so as to be steered between the assembled steps.

When we reached the hall, they helped me sit slowly and then said we would take an ambulance to the emergency room.

"No!" I shouted, possibly louder than necessary.

"Ma'am is there someone else here with you who can drive you to the hospital?"

I shook my head slowly, debating whether it was worse to call Nick or to be humiliated during an entire ambulance ride. In the end, I opted for Nick. He already thought I was a mess, and besides, it shouldn't matter what he thought of me anyway. The paramedics handed me an ice pack but insisted on waiting with me until my ride arrived.

I held the ice pack to the back of my head, wishing I could blend into the wall so people would stop staring as they passed by. I kept my eyes glued to the floor, in part because I was still dizzy, but mostly because I didn't want to see the judgment on people's faces.

I glanced up when I heard a familiar sigh.

There stood Nick, in full uniform. He looked unbelievably sexy, but he didn't exactly blend in with the rest of the gym-goers, thanks to the multiple weapons and badges secured to his person.

I groaned. "Why are you wearing that?"

"I'm on duty," he said, crouching down. "And what

happened to, thank you Nick, for coming to my rescue yet again?"

"Sorry. I was hoping to not make more of a scene. Now people are going to think I'm under arrest."

I saw him glance at the two paramedics standing beside me. "What, no fire department today?" he teased.

"Can you just take me home? They're saying I can't drive and that I should go to the hospital to get checked out. Some liability thing."

"What happened?" he asked.

I shrugged, so he turned to the paramedics.

"Witnesses said she tripped over her step and hit her head on a ballet barre. She was unconscious for more than a minute. Probably a concussion," the older paramedic replied.

"It was a really big step," I said. "That turbo step class should have a warning on it."

Nick ignored me and turned to the paramedics. "I can drive her to the hospital. Do you have everything you need?"

The paramedics nodded and backed away.

"Have a nice day, ma'am," the younger one said.

"Ma'am," I repeated with disgust.

Nick chuckled. "You sure aren't too grateful to people trying to help you today. Do you think you can stand?"

I nodded and let him pull me to my feet. He wrapped an arm around me and helped me to the door. His car was parked at the end of the fire lane, lights flashing, but at least the siren was off. I made a mental note to cancel the gym membership in the morning. Surely my dignity was worth more than the ridiculous new member fee I'd forked over the day before, when my free trial was going so well.

"You're not really driving me to the hospital, are you? I'd rather just go home."

"Babe, you have a head injury. I'm taking you to the hospital, and then I'm leaving you there because I'm still on duty. I'll pick you up in a couple of hours when I'm off and we can get your car then."

Nick walked me into the emergency room, deposited me in the waiting room, and left. I checked in and began filling out paperwork, ignoring the grimaces from patients seated around me who apparently hadn't just completed a hardcore, sweat-inducing workout. I read two magazines from cover to cover before I saw the doctor, and polished off another while waiting for my CT scan. By the time I was ready for discharge, I was starving and had nearly killed my phone battery.

Fortunately, I didn't have to wait long for Nick to return to the hospital.

"I thought we were going to pick up my car," I said, certain he was not taking the shortest route.

"We're picking up food first."

"Oh." I glimpsed over at Nick as he drove. He seemed calm and alarmingly chipper for having just gotten off work then driven to the hospital to collect me.

"Yes?" He noticed me eying him.

"Thanks for rescuing me. Again."

He laughed. "On a day where the second most important thing I did was write a speeding ticket, I honestly didn't mind swinging by the gym for you."

"No fair. You changed clothes." I was still in sweaty gym clothes, but Nick's uniform had been replaced with dark worn jeans and a long-sleeved tee shirt. He looked sexy, and I was frumpy. Plus, I was pretty sure the faint odor in the car was me.

Stupid Turbo Step.

"I changed cars, too," he said, parking in front of a Chinese restaurant. "Be right back."

He returned a minute later with a large paper sack full of steaming hot, fragrant foods. He plopped the bag on my lap and started off towards the gym. "You're sure you can drive okay?"

I nodded, peering into the bag. "Awful lot of food here for one person."

"Babe, do you want some food?"

I was determined not to put myself in a position where I'd owe him more than I already did. "No, I'll just whip something up when I get home."

"On your new stove?"

"Maybe," I retorted. "Or maybe I'll just shower and go to bed. Today was exhausting and I'd really just like to put it behind me."

"Chels, you have a concussion. You can't sleep for at least another five hours." He stopped the car next to my car and unlocked the doors before lifting the food off my lap. "I'll follow you back to your place."

"And then what?"

"And then you can split the food with me." He wrinkled his nose. "After you shower."

The drive home was unduly stressful. Anyone who has noticed a cop in the rearview mirror knows the feeling, but this was almost worse because I knew even if I turned down a random street, he'd keep following. And while I was also pretty sure he wasn't going to ticket me, I never could be positive with Nick.

I plopped my gym bag and car keys on the counter, leaving the garage door open for Nick. I waited for the water to steam up and then climbed in. I shaved first, before I lost my motivation, then shampooed and conditioned my hair, and finished up by scrubbing my face and rubbing my entire body with a soapy loofah. I was just at the point of the shower where I stand there for several minutes enjoying the steam and feeling guilty about the environmental hazards caused by my excessively long showers, when there was a knock at the door.

"Still alive?" Nick asked.

"I'll be out in a minute," I hollered.

Suddenly, the bathroom door opened. Why my house was built without a lock on the master bathroom door, I'd never know.

"What?" he asked.

"Get out!" I shrieked. "I said I'll be out in a minute."

He stayed in the room, but averted his eyes. "What? I've seen it all before."

"Get out," I repeated, my voice firmer this time.

"Food's getting cold," he said, leaving.

I shut the water off and wrapped the thick towel around my body before he could barge in on me again. I put on clean underpants and my new bra, followed by sweatpants and a comfy tee shirt. I combed my hair and applied the minimal amount of makeup possible, but left my hair wet. I was hungry.

Nick had already arranged the takeout cartons on my coffee table, turned on the TV to a football game, and helped himself to a beer. He offered me chopsticks or a fork. I took the fork and sat beside him, eagerly grabbing the carton closest to me.

"So, I see you went all out on the wardrobe tonight," he said, trying to hide a smile.

"I just keeled over in front of twenty women at the gym and then rode to the hospital in your squad car, where I got to spend the next three hours rotting in my sweaty gym clothes. Trust me, this is an improvement."

We ate in silence for a few minutes, and then he spoke again. "I should have picked up some movies, too. I don't know what I'm going to do to keep you awake for the next four hours."

I turned and our eyes met, the sparkle in his eyes telling me he knew exactly how he'd like to pass the time.

"Not a chance," I said.

By the time we'd eaten enough food to comfortably feed a small Chinese village, the game was over. Nick flipped through the channels and then frowned.

"How do you get your cable to work?"

"Um, you call the company and pay the bill," I said. "I just have basic cable." Which basically is just the networks.

Before I even noticed he'd turned the TV off, Nick had scooted closer and his lips were on mine. His mouth felt warm and welcoming, and I couldn't resist kissing him back. His hand rose to my head, pressing into my damp hair. I tried to focus on my breathing, my heart racing as a warm, tingling sensation rushed through my limbs. Nick's hand grazed the side of my breast and I snapped out of my trance, pushing him away.

He smiled at me mischievously. I took a deep breath and realized the room was spinning.

"Whoa."

"You okay?" he asked.

"Just dizzy," I said.

Then, noticing his proud smile, I added, "I'm sure it's the head injury."

He shrugged.

"I can't do this with you," I said, once I'd caught my breath.

"Then you should pay for cable so I have something else to do while I babysit you."

"I don't need a babysitter."

He was skeptical. "What will you do if I leave?"

My eyes drooped shut. "Sleep," I whispered.

"Then you need a babysitter."

I didn't answer.

"Chelsea," I heard him say in the distance. "Chelsea!"

My eyes snapped open at the louder call.

"Two more hours, babe. You can do it." He handed me the remote. "I'll even let you pick what we watch. As long as it isn't *Grey's Anatomy*."

"I like that show."

"I know. All girls do. And all girls cry when they watch it. So, no deal."

I shrugged and we settled on a different show. I muddled through the first half okay, but at some point near the end, my eyes slipped shut again, the gentle hum and buzz of the television growing softer and softer.

I knew I was sleeping when I felt a hand brush across my breast, tickling my nipple through my bra. A delicious sensation rushed through my body and I moaned, delighted to be having a dream that didn't involve flying monkeys or items on my to-do list. My bra was off instantly, in that delightful magic way things happen in dreams, and my shirt quickly followed. Then there were lips on mine—juicy warm lips, that I eagerly kissed with reckless abandon.

I was aware of my hands reaching out, exploring a man's body, first his broad shoulders and then slipping under his shirt and pressing along each muscular ridge of his stomach and chest. The kissing paused as his shirt came off. I heard another groan, and I wasn't even embarrassed by the knowledge that the carnal noises were coming from me because, well, a girl could get away with anything in a dream.

A hand slipped under the band of my pants and slowly tugged them over my bottom and down to my ankles. I reached forward until I felt denim between my fingers, fumbling with the button and zipper before letting my hands fall to his hips as he wriggled out of his own jeans. My hands brushed across something cold and hard, metallic. A gun.

"Nick," I moaned, realizing it must be him that I was dreaming about.

"Chelsea," he groaned back, guiding me down on the couch and gently crawling on top of me.

The intensity of the kissing increased and then stopped, suddenly, with a pause that seemed to go on forever until finally, the lips reached my body again, his tongue lapping across my breasts as his hand reached lower and lower on my body. I wriggled against his hand, pressing his fingers against my flesh harder until I knew I wasn't going to get what I wanted from his hand.

I reached for his hand, clasped it in mine, and pulled him back up my body. There was another pause, and I felt my panties slip down my legs, then his lips met mine and our bodies pressed together. I moaned louder as he pushed into me, the warmth of the movement in our hips sending dizzying tingling sensations throughout my entire body that grew stronger and stronger until finally, I heard myself cry out loudly. There was a deep male groan a moment later and then our bodies stilled.

There was silence, and I would've thought the dream over then, except I felt myself smiling and breathing hard. And then the lips brushed across my forehead again.

"Hey, don't get too comfy now, you've still got an hour," I heard Nick say in the distance.

My eyes popped open with a panic. I sat up, then winced and reached my hand to my pounding head. I looked around. I was naked on the couch. Nick was just emerging from the bathroom, buttoning his jeans and grinning widely. His gun was on the coffee table, almost within reach of my fingertips.

I instantly realized my mistake.

"Why are you staring at my gun like that?" he asked.

"I'm deciding whether to shoot you."

He leaned forward and grabbed the gun, quickly tucking it into the back waistband of his jeans. "And you wonder why I leave it on when I'm with you," he mumbled.

I stared at him and suddenly noticed the calm oblivious expression on his face. "Nick!" I shrieked, quickly jumping into my sweatpants and tee shirt, omitting the underwear.

He laughed and sat beside me. "Yes, Pumpkin?"

"What just happened?"

His eyebrows narrowed to a point but he kept smiling.

"Nick, you can't keep taking advantage of me like that."

"I think you were more the ringleader there, Sugar."

"I thought I was dreaming!"

He gazed towards the ceiling and nodded slowly. "That does explain some things. I'm pretty sure you were drunk the last time and you were still more reserved then." He shook his head. "You were an animal tonight, Chelsea. I'm impressed."

"Nick, you just took advantage of a woman with a head injury. What is wrong with you?"

He grimaced. "So now probably isn't the best time to tell you we didn't use protection?"

I rolled my eyes. I was on the pill, so that wasn't an issue, but a single guy like Nick who moves through women like they're tissues could have any number of sexually transmitted diseases.

"Don't look at me like that. I'm clean," he said, reading my mind.

"Aren't you worried about me?"

He shrugged. "Chelsea, you married freakishly young and never cheated on your husband. I'm pretty sure you're safe." He paused. "As long as you're not pregnant."

"Pill," I mumbled, tugging a pillow over my face.

"Got any cookies?" he asked.

I threw the pillow at him and stormed upstairs.

13

―――

Nick stayed the night to babysit, but he kept his hands to himself the rest of the night and finally did let me sleep. Still, when he left in the morning, I had what felt like a brutal hangover, even though I hadn't consumed any alcohol. I brewed a full pot of coffee and swallowed some ibuprofen while I waited.

Suddenly, my phone rang, its shrill ringtone inciting a painful pinging sensation between my ears.

"Hello?" I grunted into the phone without checking the caller ID.

"Chelsea? It's me," the voice said.

I was so groggy that it took me a moment to realize it was David.

"Hi. How are you?" I said, trying to sound more chipper.

"Fine, thanks. So listen, I'm in the neighborhood and had a few questions. Do you have a moment to chat?"

"Here?"

"Uh, yeah. Are you at the house?"

"Yes. Sure. Of course. I'm at *our* house," I said, overemphasizing the joint ownership.

"So it's okay if I drop by?"

"Yep."

"Okay. Great. See you shortly."

He hung up before I got clarification on how soon "shortly" meant. I set down my phone, flew out of my chair, and quickly rearranged the couch cushions and pillows, carefully inspecting to ensure that all signs of Nick had been erased. I zipped upstairs and made the bed, then checked that both bathrooms showed no indication that I'd had company the previous night. I dressed quickly, swept my hair into a casual ponytail, and was about to apply makeup when the doorbell rang.

I winced, but hurried to the door just as my coffee pot beeped, signaling it was done brewing. I smiled as I opened the door for David, and he smiled back politely, but his eyes showed a look of horror.

"Come on in, I was just getting some coffee," I said, making a beeline for the kitchen. I poured myself a cup, then realized he hadn't followed me. I made my way back to the entry, where David was still standing, awkwardly.

"You can come in," I said. "It is your house too. Do you want any coffee?"

He shook his head. "No thanks. I just have a minute."

"Okay." I sipped my coffee, wishing it were cooler so I could just chug it.

"Are you okay? You look really tired."

If only I'd had time for makeup, I thought. I wasn't about to fess up to the real reason for my fatigue—that I was clumsy and got a concussion or that I cheated on him with a sexy public servant, so I went a different direction. "Yeah, I haven't been sleeping well." It was the truth, generally.

"I know you traveled some since we've been married, but I'm really not used to sleeping alone. It's been an adjustment, that's all," I said, wishing he'd interrupt my rambling before it got really pathetic. "It's sort of creepy being alone in this big house all night," I added.

"Is this about the night I came over?" he asked, his voice filled with irritation.

"No! It's just different, that's all. I haven't lived alone since college. I wake up with every little noise and I'm just tired, okay?"

He nodded and his expression softened. "Maybe we should get an alarm system installed," he suggested. "Would that make you feel more secure?"

His idea caught me off guard, but I nodded, surprised that he'd even suggest it.

"It would help resale value for the house anyway," he added, as though he worried he was coming off as too nice.

"Well, um, yeah. Thanks. I think I will have an alarm system installed."

David nodded curtly. "How will you pay?"

"I'd probably put it on one of our credit cards, if that's okay."

"You've been paying all those bills still, right?" It was clearly a question, but he phrased it like a statement.

"Yes."

He gazed down at his feet, shuffling them awkwardly. "I got an alert on my phone yesterday that a large withdrawal was made from our bank account. Do you know anything about that?"

"Yes. I withdrew some money."

"For what?"

I hesitated, but was too sleepy to even decide if lying was the way to go here, let alone to actually create a plausible fiction. "I started a checking account in my name. I thought it was a good idea in case you don't move back in soon."

My explanation clearly surprised David. He was rarely at a loss for words, and he wasn't one to think before speaking, yet that was precisely what he appeared to be doing here.

"You didn't spend it?"

"No."

"Well, okay. I guess that's not a bad idea. But you won't take any more out without talking to me?"

"The credit card payments come from the joint checking," I said.

He nodded, as though he were considering this. "You know, we'll get all of this settled up and divided after the mandatory waiting period. I don't want you to be without something you need in the interim."

"Thank you?" I said, except I phrased it like a question. David had me confused after all his statement-questions.

"I'd appreciate if you'd let me know if you need more money for something, though. It worried me when I saw the large withdrawal."

"No problem," I said, proud of how civil we were being. An awkward silence ensued.

"So you're doing okay, otherwise?" he finally asked.

I pursed my lips to avoid speaking the whole truth. "Honestly, David, the past several weeks have been really hard on me. I wasn't expecting you to move out and I certainly never asked for it. I thought our marriage vows meant the same things to you as they did to me."

David opened his mouth to speak, then shut it. After another lengthy pause, he spoke again. "I'm sorry," he mumbled. "I should be on my way."

He left wordlessly and I shut and locked the door behind him before sinking to the floor, crying. I was so confused.

My hair appointment was at noon, so I didn't have long to wallow in self-pity. I chugged the rest of my coffee, put on some makeup, and trudged out the door.

When I returned home two hours later, my mood had completely altered. With my new highlighted hair, I looked younger, cooler and more confident. I was determined to act the part. I called Jen and invited her out for drinks that night. Once we made plans, I settled in for a nap.

THE NEXT MORNING, I awoke feeling refreshed, despite my late night with Jen. I ate a granola bar and some coffee, then dressed in my new workout gear. Having cancelled the gym membership, I resigned myself to get in shape the old-fashioned way—jogging. It was a foolproof plan.

I used to run in high school. I mean, not on a team or anything, but we had to jog around the track in gym class and I survived. How hard could it be, really? One foot in front of the other foot, then repeat. Easy peasy.

I stretched inside my garage, then started with a brisk walk. After warming up, I transitioned to a slow jog. When that felt easy, I ran faster. It was a windy day, though, so I got breathless before too long. I decided to walk again. Interval training was better anyway. I jogged again after a few minutes and quickly fell into a rhythm.

Running was awesome. I felt energized, yet relaxed. Powerful, yet lithe. I should have started running instead of doing aerobics to start with. I gradually sped up, reaching a full out sprint after a few moments and maintaining that pace till I was gasping for air. Then, I stopped and looked around.

At some point during my running haze, I'd exited my

neighborhood. I didn't have a map handy, but it seemed I was miles and miles away from home. Now that I'd sprinted, I was exhausted. And I had to pee. Badly.

I stretched out my legs then started to walk back towards home, but that was getting me nowhere quickly, so I switched to a jog. My legs felt like mush, though, and there was the distinct possibility of peeing my pants if I maintained the bouncy pace, so I returned to the walk. A half hour later, I was home.

As soon as I'd peed, chugged some more coffee, and showered, I felt better. My back was a little stiff and the muscles in my legs ached, but I was fine with that. I was a runner. We runners had to deal with such discomforts.

I spent a few hours working, then called Nick to gloat.

"I ran like five miles today," I said as soon as he answered.

"You ran?"

"Yes."

"Was someone chasing you?"

I groaned. "For exercise. I quit the gym."

He laughed.

"You know, it's hard to be a serious athlete when people laugh at you."

Nick took a moment to compose himself. "You're right. I'm sorry. Running is a great idea. Maybe I could join you some day?"

"That would be lovely," I replied.

"Five miles, huh?"

"Approximately." I brushed my hair behind my ear, then remembered my other news. "And I have blonde highlights."

"I know."

"No, like really blonde. My stylist said I didn't have the complexion for platinum blonde, but she lightened it a lot."

"Do I get to see this new hair sometime?"

I started to say yes, when I remembered David's visit. "Oh, and David came by yesterday and he was fine with me taking the money to start my own bank account. He even said it was a good idea."

"Well, good," Nick said, starting to sound uncomfortable.

"He also said I should get an alarm system."

"Really?"

"Yeah. Will you help me pick one out? I don't know much about home security."

"I will."

"Good. So what's new with you?"

He told me about some stuff at work and then launched into a play-by-play story of the basketball game he'd played the prior night.

It was easy talking to him, almost like talking to Jen, except Nick was so obviously a guy. Pretty much every stereotype about men seemed true about him, from the macho attitude to the beer drinking to the love of sex.

When I hung up the phone, I was relaxed and happy. I grabbed a drink and plopped down with my laptop. I had already drafted a brief synopsis about my manuscript to email to my agent to see if she would represent my fiction career as well, and I had done the lion's share of the editing. All that was left was a final proofreading before sending it out and learning my fate.

I knew I had options if my agent rejected the idea. I could send query letters to other agents or I could even attempt to navigate the self-publishing world. But, especially in light of David's comments about my attempts to transition to fiction writing, I suspected that a rejection from my agent as well would signal the end of the road for me and this novel. So, it was with extreme hesitation that I clicked "send" on the email containing the synopsis.

Once it was done, I froze, staring at my computer screen as though waiting for it to explode. I realized my agent was unlikely to respond instantaneously regardless of her answer, but I still couldn't help watching my inbox for several minutes before finally minimizing my email and beginning the final proofreading. Just in case my agent did reply promptly and actually wanted to see the manuscript, I needed it polished in time.

I spent the next three hours reading and fine-tuning my work, taking breaks every few minutes to check my inbox, before calling it a night. I was exhausted, and I wanted to feel fresh and alert when I did the final read-through in the morning.

14

I awoke early, eager to check my inbox, but found no response from my agent. Discouraged, I plopped at my desk and powered through the final proofread before changing into my running gear. I was still achy from my last run, but I needed a distraction.

My second run started out well. Having learned from my mistake the first time, I started slow, knowing I could always choose to speed up later. Hah, like that would happen. It was a gorgeous day, sunny and warm with a cool breeze. I smiled, appreciating my luck at having a job that permitted me to just take off for a late afternoon jog while all the other schmucks were stuck in rush hour traffic. A bird flew overhead, and I lifted my gaze, watching the bird as it flew into the bright blue, cloudless sky.

I glanced back down to the pavement just in time to see my left foot catch on the edge of a raised sidewalk panel. I landed on the edge of my right foot, which promptly buckled and dumped me onto the ground.

"Aarggg!" My loud wail even stopped the canaries overhead mid-chirp.

I sat on the sidewalk, a slew of expletives streaming from my mouth as I focused on breathing. The pain in my ankle was more intense than anything I'd experienced before. It radiated up the side of my leg and back down through my foot. I reached to touch it, hoping to confirm it wasn't broken, but it was already swollen and looked a little bendy. I leaned back on the pavement, propping myself up on my elbows. The throbbing was dizzying and I was starting to see spots.

"Son of a bitch," I muttered. How was I ever going to get home? I'd only been jogging for fifteen minutes, but that put me right at the halfway point of my jog, the furthest spot from my house. I couldn't stomach the thought of standing, let alone walking home right now. And I didn't have a cell phone. Clearly, I was going to die on this stupid patch of sidewalk. Maybe my parents could at least sue someone over that damn lopsided concrete.

I heard a door slam in the distance and a man's voice call out.

"Ma'am, are you alright?"

I gritted my teeth at the "ma'am," but refrained from pointing out that, were I alright, I would not be sprawled out on a sidewalk cursing. I strained to see who was speaking. Of course, it was a uniformed police officer. Perfect.

"Is everything alright ma'am? Do you need me to call an ambulance?"

"No, God no," I said. "I mean, no to the ambulance." I looked closer at him. He couldn't have been much older than me and was exceptionally cute. What was with the local police department and their cute officers?

"I fell," I finally said.

"Can you get up?"

"Um, I don't know. My ankle," I said.

He crouched down and stared at my ankle. "That's really swollen," he said. "You sure about the ambulance?"

I nodded.

"Well, at least let me help you up then."

I winced, but reached my hand out to him. He pulled me up and I stood, balanced entirely on my left foot.

"Can you put weight on it?"

I barely tapped my right toes to the ground and shook my head, furiously. I weighed my options. I could either take a damn ambulance, beg the officer for a ride home, or ask to use his phone to call someone. I knew Jen was at work, though, and aside from David, I didn't know anyone else's phone number. I grimaced at my only remaining option.

"Do you know Officer Nick Gyllenhaal?"

"Uh, yeah," he said, his face displaying confusion.

"I think he's working today. Is there any way you could get a hold of him?"

The officer frowned for a moment, and then his face lit up. "Hey, are you the cookie lady?"

I winced at the description but nodded. "Most people call me Chelsea, though."

"I'm Officer Brown. Eric Brown. Come on," he said, helping me limp to his car. I plopped onto the curb next to his car to wait. With my luck, if I got in the car to wait, my neighbors would all drive by and think I was under arrest.

He emerged from his car a moment later. "Nick said he'll be here in five minutes."

I nodded. "Thanks. You don't have to wait. I'm sure you're busy."

This amused him for some reason. "No, I think I'll stick around. So, are you a runner?"

"Do I look like a runner?"

Officer Brown shrugged.

I guessed maybe that was a compliment. A lengthy silence ensued. "What exactly has Nick said about me?"

"Oh, nothing. I just remember the cookies. He said they were from some lady that lived around here."

I could tell from the look on his face that he was omitting something. "He didn't tell you how we met?"

He shook his head. Clearly, there was something he wanted to ask.

"We're not dating, or anything like that," I said defensively. Officer Brown nodded but didn't seem particularly convinced.

A moment later, we heard sirens in the distance. As the noise got louder, we could see flashing lights. "Oh God," I said, just before Nick pulled into the neighborhood. He turned the siren off, but the lights kept flashing. Just in case people hadn't already noticed Officer Brown's flashing lights.

Nick hopped out of the car and looked straight to me. "Babe," he laughed, an expression of pity on his face.

I shot a glance at Officer Brown, who now looked like he was sure he had enough evidence to arrest me for perjury on that not-dating comment.

Nick followed my stare and turned to Officer Brown.

"Hey, Nick," Officer Brown said, and they shook hands.

"Hi, Eric. What happened?"

"She fell. I didn't see it. I was just driving past on patrol and saw her lying on the sidewalk."

"Right here?"

"No, down that path about twenty yards." He gestured to the infamous patch of sidewalk, both of them still pretending I wasn't seated right next to them, well within earshot. "Seems like she might have broken her ankle, but she wouldn't let me call an ambulance."

Nick laughed again and caught my eye. "Did she ask you to call me?"

Officer Brown nodded.

"Thanks for helping her, Eric. I can take it from here."

Officer Brown waved to me. "You have a good afternoon, ma'am. Take care of that ankle."

"Thanks," I said. Then I turned to Nick. "Why do you people all call me ma'am? I'm not that old."

"I know, babe," he said, crouching down beside me.

"And why do you call me babe in front of people? They're going to think we're sleeping together."

He smiled smugly. "We are."

"No, that just happened once while I was conscious and I told you it couldn't happen again."

Nick nodded his head in a condescending manner.

"You didn't tell them we're sleeping together, did you?"

He laughed. "I had to say something to explain why you brought the cookies."

I was fairly certain he was joking. At least he better have been. I winced as he poked my ankle.

He sighed, then hoisted me up by my arm pits and carried me to the car. "Same ER as last time or do you want to shake things up?" he asked.

"Just drop me at my house," I said.

"You need an x-ray. It might be broken."

"Then it'll still be broken in the morning."

He buckled his belt and merged onto the street. "Maybe they'll give you good drugs this time," he said.

I sighed. "I need to get my purse first."

We drove past my house, where Nick ran in for my purse, and then he escorted me into the hospital where, thankfully, none of the staff looked familiar. Hopefully, it was a completely different ER crew than I'd seen the week before. He dumped me into a wheelchair, helped me to the triage desk, and said for me to call him when I was ready to be picked up.

I CALLED Jen once my foot was wrapped, but of course she was working late, so I reluctantly phoned Nick and asked him to come get me when his shift ended. I had roughly an hour to kill before he arrived, which gave me plenty of time to fill my pain medicine prescription and practice on my new crutches.

Nick was still in full uniform and still driving the police cruiser when he picked me up, but I didn't complain about the additional scene it made because it enabled him to park in the fire lane. The less I had to hobble around, the better. The stupid crutches were killing my armpits.

"What's the verdict?" he asked as soon as he'd helped me into the car, tossing my crutches in the back.

"Pizza," I replied. "With everything on it."

He laughed and started the car. "I meant with your ankle, not dinner."

"Oh." I guess I was hungrier than I thought. "Not broken. Just a bad sprain. The doctor said to stay off of it entirely for a week, then to just use it lightly for another week or two until it's completely healed. And he prescribed this." I held out my prescription bottle.

Nick eyed it warily at a stoplight. "That's some heavy duty stuff. Have you had it before?"

I shook my head. "But I'm in heavy duty pain. I want pizza, a shower, and drugs."

Nick smiled and handed me his phone. "It's speed-dial eight."

I phoned in the order, and since I was so grateful for the ride, I didn't even tease him about having a pizza delivery number programmed into his phone.

When we arrived at my house, Nick helped me out of the car and up to the door. "Thanks," I said. "You saved me. Again." I sighed. "You don't have to stay, though. I'm sure you had better plans tonight than babysitting me again."

He grinned. "Babysitting you turned out pretty well last time, and besides, you just ordered a large pizza, breadsticks, and wings. You can't possibly plan on eating all that yourself."

That was precisely my plan, actually, but Nick didn't need to know that, so I shrugged and swung the door open wide. He grabbed a duffel bag from the car and then followed me in. I hesitated at the bottom of the stairs, not certain how to climb them with crutches. Did the crutches go first, or my good foot?

"No way," Nick shouted, scooping me off my feet. He carried me and my crutches up the stairs and set me down delicately at the top. "If you need to go up or down the stairs when I'm not here, crawl!"

I rolled my eyes, not about to admit that his suggestion actually made sense.

"I need a shower," I said.

Nick eyed my neatly bandaged ankle warily. Then he shook his head and started the bath water. "I'll help you in, then you can just prop your foot on the side. Or I can get you a bag to wrap it in so the bandages don't get wet."

"The doctor didn't say it had to stay dry."

"It'll stink if you soak it."

I frowned. Bathing did seem more practical than showering, but I wasn't about to let Nick see me awkwardly bathing in the nude with a bum ankle. I considered my options, squirted a ton of bubble bath into the tub, then hobbled into the closet, shutting the door behind me. I emerged a moment later, wearing my black bikini.

Nick bit his lip to avoid laughing. "You do realize I've seen you naked before, don't you?"

I rolled my eyes. "Not flailing helplessly in the tub, you haven't."

He grinned, shut off the bath water, then delicately helped me into the tub. Every time I moved my leg, the throbbing in my ankle nearly caused me to scream, but I was determined to finish the bath.

Nick eyed me sympathetically, then started to unbutton his shirt.

"What are you doing?"

"Helping," he replied, taking off the belt that contained all his various tools and weapons. He set it on the counter next to his shirt and crouched beside the tub. He reached over the side and grabbed my calf, steadying my leg.

"I'll hold it still so you can wash your hair," he said, his voice soft.

"Thanks," I mumbled. It really did help, but what really struck me was how sensitive Nick was being. Not that he wasn't normally nice, but he hadn't even attempted to seduce me once since I'd changed into my suit. But no sooner did I think that than he spoke again.

"You know I could probably be even more helpful if I were in the tub with you," he said.

I splashed him just as the doorbell rang.

"That must be dinner," he said. "No matter what, do not move. Do you understand? You are not to attempt to stand up or leave that tub on your own."

"I'm not a child," I called after him as he dried his hands and left the bathroom.

He was gone a long time. I heard male voices for much longer than I would expect it to take to pay for a pizza, but I was determined not to break my promise about climbing out of the tub. I couldn't figure out the logistics of exiting on my own even if I wanted to.

After an eternity, Nick returned.

"No pizza?" I asked, panicked.

"I left it on the table downstairs."

"Thank God," I mumbled. "I'm starving and I'm desperate for my pills. This ankle is killing me."

Nick reached for a towel and then carefully helped me out of the tub.

"What took so long?"

"It, um, well, that initial doorbell ring wasn't the pizza guy. It was David."

"What? My David?"

"Yes, *your* David," he said, his voice full of disgust. "He said he saw the police cruiser and wanted to see what was wrong."

"That's bullshit," I said. "He just wanted to see if you were here."

Nick shrugged. "I couldn't exactly ignore the doorbell. He had already seen the car."

"What did you tell him?"

"The truth, that you had a little accident but were fine and I had just driven you home from the hospital."

"Did he seem worried about my ankle?"

Nick hesitated. "He seemed a little more concerned about my attire and the fact that I had bubbles on my shirt."

"What did he say?"

Nick helped me dry off, then handed me my crutches so I could get dressed. "Nothing of importance."

"Nick," I called from the closet. "Tell me!"

"He wanted to come in and see you and I said no. He called you some names, muttered some crap about how predictable it was, and then stormed off as the pizza arrived." He paused. "Look, Chelsea, he was a total dick, and I don't think you need to worry about it. You changed the locks so he can't get in anymore, and I can stay tonight anyway."

I was too hungry to fumble with a full outfit, so I slipped into some cute pajama shorts and one of those tank tops with the built-in bras. Then I hopped back to the bathroom so Nick could carry me downstairs.

We were both quiet while Nick plated up the pizza. He poured himself some wine then brought the food to the coffee table and helped me prop my foot up. Then he brought me an ice pack.

"I'm sorry about David, Chelsea. I should've switched cars. I just didn't want to leave you waiting any longer at the hospital."

I devoured half of a slice in a single bite. "It's not your fault. He's being a jerk, you're right. And maybe it's not a bad thing for him to be jealous."

I finished the slice and popped two of my pills into my mouth. I grabbed Nick's wine and washed the pills down with a large gulp.

"Chelsea you can't drink with those," he protested, snatching the wine away and handing me a glass of water.

I rolled my eyes but accepted the water, sneaking sips of the wine when he wasn't looking. I downed two chicken wings, a breadstick, and part of another slice of pizza before I was stuffed. I plopped my plate on the coffee table and scooted it away.

"You were hungry," he observed with a smile.

I shrugged, realizing the throbbing in my ankle was eons

better and that I felt ever so slightly buzzed. "It was all that running. I feel better now," I said.

Nick stared at me for a moment. "Do you want me to help you upstairs? You might be more comfortable in bed."

I nodded agreeably. Now that I was neither starving or in searing pain, I was feeling guilty about monopolizing another of Nick's nights because of a random injury. "You don't have to stay, though."

"Do you want me to stay?"

I bit my lip shyly but nodded again.

"Then I'll stay. Do you need more ice?"

"Not yet," I said.

Nick carried me up the stairs again, plopping me on the bed. He wedged a pillow under my foot then spied a deck of cards on the dresser.

"Want to play poker?" he asked.

I shook my head. I was in the mood for something now, but it was definitely not poker. Stupid David, spying on me. Who did he think he was, anyway? What I did—and with whom—was none of his business as long as he was with Traci. I reached my thumb around to wriggle the band of my engagement ring, an odd habit I'd developed for checking that I hadn't lost it.

Then an idea came to me.

"Can you get your shirt back on?"

Nick frowned.

"Please?"

He sighed and went into the bathroom. He was buttoning it up when he returned.

I smiled. Admittedly, I'd always had a thing for men in uniform, but still, there was something spectacular about this particular man in this particular uniform. The shirt was just tight enough to flaunt his muscular arms and chest and the pants were fitted just to the point where I was reminded of his amazing ass without it being too obvious.

I motioned for him to stop just before he got to the bed. He finished fastening the last button on his shirt and stared at me with a mixture of confusion and irritation.

"Thanks," I said. "Now take it off," I instructed, "Slowly."

Nick's eyes widened, and a broad grin broke out on his face. I suspected he was debating confirming that he'd heard me correctly, but he apparently decided just to go with it. He unfastened the buttons of his shirt, one by one, then stepped closer and slowly shrugged out of the shirt, his eyes trained on me the entire time.

I gazed down at his pants and he immediately began unbuckling them. He lowered them down and tossed them to the side of the room, now standing before me in a plain white undershirt and tight black boxer briefs that made it all too clear that he was in the mood for the exact same thing I was.

He reached for the bottom of his shirt and paused, grinning at me. I smiled back, loving the way his brown eyes sparkled when he was excited, and I nodded for him to proceed. He slipped the shirt over his head, revealing the washboard abs and chest I remembered so clearly.

I sighed wistfully, unable to focus on anything but Nick's statuesque physique, mere feet from my bed.

I raised an eyebrow, prompting for him to finish, but he shook his head and grinned.

"Nope, not until we even the playing field, missy." He crawled onto the bed, and placed one leg on either side of my thighs, careful not to bump my ankle.

I smiled and reached for him, running my hands along his stomach and up his chest, enjoying his perfection.

"May I?" Nick asked politely, his fingers tugging the bottom of my tank top.

I nodded and he pulled it up over my head.

He smiled and exhaled hard, his eyes focused on my breasts. I was oddly aware of my own absence of self-consciousness as Nick placed his hands on my body, gently cupping my bare breasts.

"Do you have any idea how unbelievably gorgeous you are, Chelsea? How breathtakingly sexy?" he asked, gazing back to my face.

I breathed a laugh.

Nick shook his head. "I don't think you do, and that's a crime."

Now I giggled loudly. "Oh is it, Officer? And tell me, what's the punishment?"

He grinned wider and slid my shorts off, seeming surprised that I had nothing on beneath them. "I think I can come up with something." He stretched out on top of me, staying slightly to the side of my good ankle, and kissed me lightly.

I reached to pull him closer, craving the sensation of his body pressed against mine, but he hesitated.

"Are you sure about this, Chelsea? Because I can go now, or we could..."

I covered his mouth with my hand to shush him. "If you go anywhere right now, I will hobble into the bathroom and shoot you with your own gun."

Nick raised an eyebrow curiously. "Are you sure you don't have another concussion?"

I groaned with frustration and reached for his boxer briefs. He laughed, but cooperated. Then he kissed me and didn't pull away, his lips reaching for mine over and over until we were both breathless and eager for more. His hands gently caressed my breasts before wandering lower, his fingers deftly exploring and probing until I was dizzy with excitement.

The rest was a blur of sighs, moans, and overwhelming sensation. Nick had a way of bringing me right to the peak of pleasure and keeping me there, as long as I could handle it, before letting me explode into waves of exquisite relief. I fell asleep satisfied, totally oblivious to my swollen ankle, and happier than I'd been in a long, long while.

MY BLADDER WAS full when I woke up, but before I'd even opened my eyes fully, the throbbing in my foot reminded me that I couldn't walk. I turned to see if I'd left my crutches within an arm's reach of the bed and instead, all I saw was Nick.

"Whoops," I said quietly, as flashes of the previous night came back to me. I lifted the covers and confirmed my suspicions—I was still naked. Given that Nick had now tricked me into sleeping with him three times, I was confident that waking him so he could help me to the bathroom would result in yet another inappropriate encounter.

I gingerly scooted down the covers and placed my good foot on the ground, lowering myself down to a crawling position. I peered over the bed to verify that Nick was still asleep and then began inching my way across the room to the bathroom on all fours. Just as I reached the tile bathroom floor and was debating trying to spare my knees by hobbling the remaining four feet to the toilet, I heard laughter. Crap.

"What are you doing?" Nick asked.

I flipped to a seated position, confident that a naked

crawling cripple was not on the top ten sexiest things to wake up to list. "I had to pee and I don't have my crutches," I said.

He smiled and left the room, returning a moment later with my crutches. He pulled me up and helped me onto my crutches. Then he stepped out of the bathroom and closed the door. I went about my business then brushed my teeth, washed my face, and applied makeup, but I couldn't get dressed because my bras and panties were all in the dresser in the bedroom. The thought of limping back out in front of Nick, naked and on crutches, wasn't too appealing, but my pain pills were also in the bedroom, so I knew staying in the bathroom forever wasn't an option.

Nick was already dressed when I emerged, his gun visibly poking out of the waistband of his jeans on top of his tee shirt. I saw a hint of a smile when he looked at me, but I was determined not to let on how much I was enjoying looking at him. I hobbled to my underwear drawer and grunted as I balanced on the crutches while pulling the drawer open.

"Let me help," he said. He began rifling through the contents of the drawer. "Ooh," he said, retrieving a particularly skanky thong, one that tied on both sides and was likely worn for about ten minutes, max, years ago on my honeymoon.

"No."

He laughed, then pulled out a plain black thong.

I shrugged, so he tossed it to me.

"Bra?"

"The drawer right below it. There should be a black one."

He helped me into the bra and fastened it for me.

"Thanks." I hobbled back to the closet to get some clothes and then returned for my pills.

"You should eat something before you take this," he said.

I snatched the bottle out of his hand.

"Seriously, you get wacky on medication. As much as I'd like to, I can't stay in bed with you all day, satisfying your every sexual desire, so promise you'll take it with food."

I nodded solemnly. While I was pretty sure my wackiness came from the alcohol I'd had on top of the pills, perhaps combined with the pain, I was planning on switching to plain old Advil after the next dose anyway. I didn't like being doped up, especially when it led me to do crazy things like sleep with Nick. Although, now that I'd already ruined my loyalty to David by sleeping with him once, it didn't seem like there was much additional harm in doing it again. Besides, every time I had sex with Nick, I felt a little less bitter about David's affair with Traci.

"Do you have to work today?" I asked him as I crutched my way to the top of the stairs.

Nick grimaced at the stairs before picking up me and my crutches and slowly trudging down. "Not exactly. I need to get my hours in at the gun range before the end of the month to stay on track for this promotion, and then I have a date." He plopped me back down at the foot of the stairs.

I nearly fell off my crutches at this. "You tricked me into having sex with you last night and now you're telling me you have a date?"

"First off, it's not that kind of date. My mom set me up with her friend's daughter or something like that. It will be awkward, unpleasant and will definitely not lead to sex. And second, you seduced me last night. After that whole 'I thought I was dreaming' debacle from last time, I wasn't about to make a move on you, but you practically forced me to." He paused. "That's why you need to eat something first. Because I don't have time to have sex with you two more times this morning after your pills make you all randy."

"Two times? We did it twice?"

He grinned and peered in my fridge, finally selecting muffins. He popped them in the microwave and then made coffee.

"Well, at least you're finally taking responsibility for the last time," I said.

Nick shrugged. "You're right. You had a head injury. I should've known you were only fantasizing about ravishing me." He placed one of the muffins on the counter in front of me and wolfed down the other in three big bites. "Do you have a travel mug I can borrow?"

I pointed to the cabinet by the sink. He grabbed a lidded, metal mug with the letter C stamped all over it and a regular striped coffee mug for me. Once the coffee had brewed enough for two cups, he poured it and then replaced the pot to finish brewing.

"I should run. Are you going to be okay? Is there anything else you need from upstairs before I go?"

I shook my head.

"You're sure? Because I don't think you should go up or down the stairs on your own."

I hesitated. There was one thing I'd forgotten upstairs that was fairly important, but I really didn't want to make him rummage around in my medicine cabinet. "I'll have my friend Jen come over soon. She can get it for me."

"What is it?"

"My birth control pill is in the medicine cabinet," I said, cringing.

He was gone in a flash, and I could've sworn less than

three seconds passed before he had returned, pill in hand, to watch me swallow the sucker.

"Thanks," I said warily, a little offended at his level of panic. Then I read into it further. "We really should have used...protection last night," I said, embarrassed by my inability to say the word "condom."

"We did," Nick replied, pointing to the pill I was placing on my tongue.

"That only protects against pregnancy."

Nick sighed. "I thought we had this talk already."

"You have a date tonight!" I reminded him. "Even if you don't have any STDs now, it isn't responsible for me to have unprotected sex with you when you're dating other people!"

He laughed at my franticness, which only flustered me more. "Babe, it's just a date, not sex. I promise." He looped his finger around the hem of my shirt and tugged me closer, ensuring that I reciprocated eye contact. "Just because I don't like commitments doesn't mean I sleep around."

"I'm pretty sure that's exactly what it means."

Nick's expression darkened. Clearly, I was annoying him. "Chelsea, you are the only one I am sleeping with. I will not touch another woman in a sexual way until whatever this is," he paused and gestured back and forth between us, "is over. Boy Scout promise."

I turned away and scoffed. "So you do have some sense of morals?"

Nick laughed. "It's nothing to do with morals. I'm a practical guy, and women are complicated. I can only handle one at a time."

I had to commend his honesty at least.

I caught him glancing at the clock and knew he really did need to go. "I really appreciate you taking care of me last night," I said.

He flashed me a mischievous grin before leaving. "Yep, I'm pretty good at taking care of things for you, huh."

I ate my muffin in peace and then called Jen. She had a hair appointment but was coming by the house later, so I wrote to pass the time until she arrived.

That was one of the perks of working from home. I could work whenever I felt like it, without worrying about toting supplies to and from another office. Of course, it was also the downside, as there were days when I'd do anything to have a "snowed in" style excuse. I'd never really had a nine-to-five job, though, and I wasn't sure I was cut out for it.

Some days, I really got into my work, tapping away on my laptop for hours without a break, but others, each sentence was painfully tedious, and I'd catch myself finding little chores around the house that just had to be done, preferring to iron curtains or vacuum under the bed rather than finish a chapter. Usually, the days where the writing came easily occurred when I was writing humorous articles that involved little research. Today was one of those days, a fact which I realized when the doorbell rang and I looked to the clock, seeing that I'd spent the last three hours working.

I rose from the computer and made my way to the door. I immediately noticed Jen's hair, chopped just below chin length and dyed auburn brown, but before I could compliment her new style, she gasped at my crutches.

"Oh my God, you poor thing. When you said sprain, I didn't think it would be this bad. Does it hurt? Why didn't you call me last night? I would've come over!"

I glanced down at my ankle. It was still wrapped in the oversized ice pack I'd strapped on after calling her, which had long since ceased being cold. "It's okay. Nick came over last night."

She raised an eyebrow but didn't say anything until

she'd helped me to the couch. I propped my foot on the coffee table and began unwrapping the ice pack. The ankle was purplish black and swollen to about three times the size of the other foot.

"There's another ice pack in the freezer," I said. She took off for the kitchen, returning with the ice pack. While I wrapped my foot, she turned on the kettle for tea, wiped down the kitchen counters, and then jogged upstairs to make the bed. This is why she would always be my best friend.

"Love the new stove," she called.

She brought the tea in and sat beside me on the couch. "So where's your knight in shining armor today?"

The pills must have been making my brain slower than usual because it took me several moments to realize she was asking about Nick. "Oh, he had to go shoot stuff and then he had a date."

She ignored the odd first part of the sentence and immediately followed up on the rest. "Your new boyfriend is on a date?"

"He's not my boyfriend."

"You're sleeping with him," she reminded me.

"I am not." I'd told her about the first time, but I'd been so embarrassed about the last one that I hadn't mentioned it yet.

"He slept over last night," she said.

"How do you know that?"

She shrugged, and I remembered that she had just made my bed.

"Fine, but he only stayed to take care of me. Nothing happened."

"Yes it did."

The trouble with best friends is that they know when

you're lying. "Fine, we had sex twice last night. And once last week after I got a concussion at the gym."

Jen smiled. "You sure are accident prone lately."

"You're not going to get all judgy now?"

She shook her head. "No way. He's super hot. I'd sleep with him if you weren't already."

"What happened to your construction worker?"

"Eh." She glanced down at my foot. "God your nails are horrible. Want a pedicure?"

I sighed. "Sure, why not?"

She filled me in on her love life, or lack thereof, and on work, while doing my toenails. Then we each painted our own fingernails while I rambled on about Nick.

"I think you like him," Jen teased as we blew on our wet nails.

I giggled at her schoolgirl tone. "I do feel better about everything with David now," I said. "You were totally right. I could have never forgiven him for what he's done to me with Traci, but now that I've been doing...things...with Nick, well, it's all even."

Jen wrinkled her nose. "Yeah, except he cheated on you and then moved out. What you're doing with Nick isn't cheating."

I wasn't so sure about that. In fact, I was positive that my mother, pastor, and spouse would all definitely consider it cheating. And something about the relationship with Nick felt naughty and forbidden. But even if it was cheating, David did it first, which seemed like a fair moral argument. "I'm still married," I finally said.

"I know, sweetie," Jen smiled warmly at me. "And I know all of this is really confusing and complicated and not how you pictured your life to be at this point. But you seem happy lately, and more relaxed."

I smiled back, delicately tapping on my pinky nail to test the firmness of the polish. I loved how succinctly Jen phrased it all. She really understood me and she never judged me. "Thanks," I said. "This was exactly what I needed today." I thought about my agent—and the lack of response to my email—but dismissed it. Today was Saturday, so she probably wasn't at her desk anyway.

"Something on your mind?" she asked.

Sometimes it was scary how best friends could do that. I shook my head quickly and focused on something else. "I want to take some cookies to the station for the officer who helped me off the sidewalk yesterday."

"I thought that was Nick."

"No, it was another guy, Officer Brown, who showed up first. He called Nick for me." I saw Jen's confused expression, so I explained further. "I've been taking cookies to anyone who helps me out. Usually it's Nick, but I'm worried the people at the station are starting to think Nick and I are involved."

"So you want to bring cookies to someone else to throw them off the trail?"

I nodded.

Jen looked perplexed. "But you and Nick are involved."

"Not officially," I clarified.

She laughed, but seemed to realized I couldn't be convinced not to do this. "Are yours dry yet?" She gestured to my nails.

I nodded, so she handed me my crutches and we made our way to the kitchen. I sat on a barstool while Jen preheated the oven, retrieved the cookie sheets, and defrosted the dough.

"Your stash is running low in here," she commented. "Must have been baking for lots of men lately."

I giggled, although it was the truth. I had been baking less lately and gifting more. Hence, the need for greater supply. "I'll have a baking day once my ankle is better."

I plopped the dough onto the sheets and instructed Jen on positioning them in the oven. "Will you come with me to drop them off?"

She glanced at my crutches. "Is there an alternative?"

I shrugged.

"I wouldn't mind meeting some hot policemen anyway," she said. "We can pick up dinner on the way home."

I smiled, then flipped through a magazine while Jen ran upstairs to get me some better clothes, makeup, and hair brush. She took the cookies out of the oven for me, and I hobbled into the downstairs bathroom to change and make myself semi-presentable. We packaged up the cookies once they cooled, and headed out to the station.

As soon as we entered the station, the desk clerk glanced up at me and shook her head. It was Marge. I had seen her several times before. "Officer Gyllenhaal isn't here," she said warily.

"Oh, I know, he's..." I started, thankfully cutting myself off before saying he was on a date.

Jen held the cookies up to remind me of our mission.

"These are for Officer Brown. I hurt my ankle yesterday," I gestured to the bandaged leg with my crutch. "Well, obviously. Haha. Anyway, he helped me out so I thought I'd bring him some cookies."

"Any of the macadamia nut ones you brought last time?"

I nodded shyly. "A few."

Jen handed the plate to Marge.

"Which Officer Brown? There are two," she asked.

"Oh. Eric?"

She nodded curtly. "He's on duty now, but he's out on patrol."

"That's fine. Can I just leave them with you for him? I'll write a note," I said. I motioned for Jen to hand me my purse and I tugged out a mini notepad.

"Officer Brown," I wrote. "Thanks for all your help yesterday. My ankle is not broken, but it's a severe sprain so I am still stuck in crutches for a bit. Hope you enjoy cookies."

I handed the note to Marge just as several young officers came through the door. I noticed Jen's eyes perk up instantly as she spotted the cute one.

"More cookies?" a voice behind me asked. I swiveled around, but it was an awkwardly slow movement with the crutches. It was one of the officers who had helped with my owl problem.

"Oh, hi, Officer Wellington," I said, grateful for the name placard on his uniform. "This is my friend Jen. We were just bringing some cookies as a thank you to Officer Brown. He helped when I hurt my ankle."

"Call me Marcus," he said, shaking Jen's hand. He turned back to me. "Is Nick on tonight?"

"No," I said. "I mean, I don't keep track of his schedule," I quickly added, trying not to sound like we were dating.

Jen laughed. "We should get going. It was lovely meeting you." She dragged me out of the station before I could make myself look any dumber.

Jen left shortly after dinner, on my insistence. I was dying to check my email, but of course it was still empty. I sighed, slowly made my way into the kitchen, and maneuvered my crutches around so I could pour myself a glass of wine. Getting back to the couch while holding the wine was challenging, but I was highly motivated, so I managed.

I flipped through the few stations I got on the TV, but

soon found myself thinking about Nick. He was probably on his date now, although I wasn't sure what exactly he had planned. Maybe dinner and a movie. Or was that too cliché for him?

I wondered if his mom set him up often. Then I wondered if she knew about me. Surely not, right? What would he tell her—hey mom, there's this hot soon-to-be divorcée that I sleep with on occasion? Every mom would love to hear that.

I turned back to my laptop and tapped my fingers nervously on the base of the keyboard. Then my phone buzzed with a text message. It was from Nick. He wanted to know what firm David worked at.

I answered, and his reply of "thank god" came within seconds.

That seemed odd. "How was your date?" I texted back.

"Currently ongoing," he replied.

"That's redundant," I messaged back, then added "Why are you texting me about David's job while you're on a date?"

There was a pause, and I set down my phone just before it buzzed again.

"My date is a paralegal!" came his response. "Different firm though."

"Ugh!" I typed.

"She's nice tho" he wrote.

"I have to work now," I tapped angrily into my phone.

"Really? On a Saturday? I could sneak into the bathroom and we could have phone sex..."

"GO BACK TO YOUR DATE, PERV!"

He replied with a smiley face, then left me alone.

I chugged my wine, took some more ibuprofen, and went to bed.

15

The next morning, the pain in my ankle had subsided enough that I made it through breakfast without taking any pills. I took that as a sign that I could phase out the crutches. It was Sunday, my normal cleaning day, so I made some meager attempts to tidy up without putting too much pressure on my ankle.

My parents had invited me to join them at church and then lunch, but with my injury, I had a solid excuse to skip church. The lunch was trickier to avoid, since my parents simply offered to come to me.

They arrived shortly after 11, with a full spread of fried chicken, biscuits, mashed potatoes and corn. Even though I really wasn't in much pain, I pretended I was, figuring that I should garner as much sympathy as possible to avoid my mother harping on me about my marital woes.

My father helped keep the conversation light, and we all ate quickly. I gave my mom a few minutes to handle the cleanup for me before faking a long, drawn-out yawn.

"Gosh, the medicine they've got me on for my injury sure has me sleepy," I said.

My father, probably eager to get home to watch the football game anyway, immediately took the hint. "We should get out of your hair so you can nap." He scurried my mom along and they were gone before two p.m.

Having survived that ordeal, I checked my email again, fully expecting nothing. Instead, there it was—the response from my agent.

I inhaled sharply, then held my breath while clicking on the message. It was suspiciously short, I noticed. My heart sunk. Short agent responses were much like college application responses—filled with bad news.

I said a silent prayer, then read: "Hi Chelsea- I'm honored you thought of me when seeking representation for your novel. I'm intrigued by your premise and would be delighted to read the full manuscript. Please email it to me at your convenience."

"Yes!" I screeched, leaping out of my chair. "Yes! Yes! Yes! Ouch!" I quickly sat back down, having perhaps misjudged my ankle's ability to support me jumping up and down with excitement.

I re-read the email a few more times, then tried to decide if there was any benefit from playing hard-to-get and waiting a few days to respond. I concluded that there may be, but that I was too impatient to try that, so I quickly set up a reply, attached my full manuscript, and hit send. Then I stood and, carefully balancing so more weight was on my good leg, did a victory dance.

I knew this meant nothing, really. She was my agent, so even if she thought my book sounded dumb she would at least have to offer to read it just to appease me. She probably wouldn't even read it. But still, I was excited. I needed to celebrate.

I immediately called Nick. He answered on the second

ring, but there was so much shouting and noise in the background that I couldn't hear him.

"Hang on!" he shouted. A moment later, it was quiet.

"Hey, Chelsea, what's up?"

"Where are you?"

"Sports bar. Watching the game," he replied.

"Oh." Suddenly I felt bad for interrupting him for my stupid news. "You can call me back later."

"I stepped outside so I can hear now. What's up?"

"Well, I just got some good news and I was in the mood to celebrate."

"What kind of good news?"

"My agent wants to read my full manuscript," I said, hoping he remembered enough to know what I was talking about. David's eyes always seemed to glaze over when I talked about writing.

"Are you serious? Chelsea, that's awesome!"

I beamed at his sincere enthusiasm.

"Did you send it to her?"

"Yeah, about five minutes ago."

"That is really great," he said. "So what kind of celebration did you have in mind?"

That was a good question. I couldn't drive for a few more days still, and I didn't feel like dressing up with a giant bandage wrapped around my ankle.

"I don't know. It can wait. I just wanted to share the news with someone. I didn't mean to interrupt the game."

"How's your ankle? Want to join us here? I'm just with some of the guys from the station. You've probably met them all already."

I grimaced at the thought. "Gee, as tempting as that is, I probably shouldn't. I still can't drive."

"But you wanted to celebrate," he reminded me.

"It can wait. It's not that big of a deal anyway. It's not like she said she'd represent me, just that she wanted to see it."

Nick sighed. "Chelsea, it is a huge deal, and we need to celebrate. Stop being such a girl and just tell me what you want. Are you thinking fancy dinner? I can go home and change and pick you up."

I giggled at his calling me a girl, then realized I wasn't sure what exactly I wanted. "I guess I don't feel like anything fancy with my ankle still wrapped up," I finally said. "I was just feeling good and wanted someone to share my excitement with."

Now it was Nick's turn to laugh. "Why Chelsea Craig, was this a booty call?"

"No!" I replied. But then I considered it and realized that actually was why I had called. "I mean, you can come over if you want, but don't leave before the game is over."

"It's not even half-time yet," he said.

I frowned. "So I'll see you in a few hours."

"Really?" Skepticism filled his voice.

"Yep. Bye." I hung up before I could ramble more.

True, I had wanted someone to celebrate with immediately, but it's not like I wouldn't still be excited in a few hours. Until then, I'd just relax and pamper myself.

I needed to change the bandage on my ankle anyway, so I started the bath water and perched on the edge to unwrap it. My ankle was still purple in spots and swollen, but looked —and felt—markedly better. I poured some bubbles into the tub, grabbed my shampoo and conditioner from the shower, and slowly inched into the steamy bath.

As soon as I'd settled in comfortably, my phone buzzed. I wiped my hand on a dry washcloth and carefully glanced at the screen. It was a text from Nick. I smiled and read it.

"What are you wearing?" it said.

I laughed. "Bubbles?" I wrote back.

"???" came his speedy reply.

"Taking a bath," I typed.

"U r killing me," he said.

I wasn't sure how to respond to that, but fortunately, I didn't have to.

"Having trouble concentrating on football," he continued.

"But you love football," I replied. "Football is your favorite."

His response took a little longer, but made me laugh out loud when I read it.

"Nick's favorite things, in order of preference: 1) Sex. 2) Oral sex. 3) Any other form of foreplay or fooling around. 4) Watching football. 5) Playing basketball. 6) Drinking beer with guys. 6) Watching or playing any other sports."

"Thanks for the informative text," I replied. "But I should get back to my bath now."

He didn't respond, so I relaxed back into the water. A few minutes later, my phone rang. I dried my hand again and answered.

"Where exactly are all these bubbles?" Nick asked, his voice deep.

"Where aren't they?" I teased.

"What are you washing now? Tell me about it," he urged.

I blushed, knowing exactly what he wanted but definitely not feeling confident enough to deliver. "Hey, how come it's so quiet now?"

"I left the bar," he said. "I'll be at your place in ten minutes. You still have the key by the door?"

"Yes."

"You really need to find a better system," he lectured.

"But for now, stay put. I want to see those bubbles when I get there."

I laughed and hung up, nervously awaiting his arrival.

When I heard the key in the door, I carefully arranged the bubbles around my body. It seemingly took Nick less than ten seconds to make his way upstairs. He grinned widely when he saw me, and I felt my heartbeat quicken at the sight of him. He was wearing dark jeans, a football jersey, and clearly hadn't shaven this morning. Everything about him was sexy.

"You unwrapped it," he said, eying my ankle.

I nodded, squirming eagerly in the tub.

He groaned. "You're killing me Chelsea."

"What?" I asked innocently.

He lifted his shirt off over his head. "You have to know how sexy you are," he said.

I gazed admiringly at his smooth abdomen and well-defined chest and arms. I could say the same thing back to him, except something told me Nick did know how sexy he was. He slipped out of his jeans and socks, then sat beside the tub in only his boxer briefs.

"How's it feel?"

His eyes had returned to my ankle, so I knew exactly what he meant. "Better. I think I'm done with the crutches."

"But no more running for a while?"

"No more running ever," I said, absentmindedly wiping the bubbles off my breast.

"Oh dear God, Chelsea," Nick groaned. In a flash, he was naked and in the tub on top of me. His mouth pressed into mine, and my whole body tingled. He shifted awkwardly, then traced his tongue around each of my nipples in turn. He grazed his teeth along the edge before drawing the entire nipple into his mouth playfully.

I groaned, the pressure at the apex of my thighs growing almost unbearable. I reached a hand out and grazed Nick's firm erection, eliciting a loud moan from him as well. I tried to think through the mechanics of us making love in the bath, but with my limited ankle mobility, I didn't see any logical solution. Then, I remembered item number 2 on Nick's list of favorites. We hadn't actually done that yet.

I shifted gradually upwards, guiding his hips until he was kneeling over me in the tub, his massive manhood right where I needed it. I tentatively licked him, tracing my tongue along his sizable length, then, reassured by his panting and groaning, took him further into my mouth. He came within minutes, thrashing so much with the final pulsating pleasures that he caused waves of water to splash over the side of the tub.

"You're sure that's second on your list?" I teased.

Nick groaned again and stood, lifting me out of the tub, and setting me on the countertop. He wrapped a towel loosely around me, then wiped himself off, still breathing heavily. Before I could even dry off, he knelt in front of me, forced my thighs apart with his hands, and circled his tongue along each of my inner thighs before diving into his goal.

"Oh," I murmured, caught off guard by the suddenness of the action. Surprisingly, my body was ready, meeting the intensity of his tongue's strokes quickly with increasing pressure taking me higher and higher until I finally fell, unraveling into a series of pleasurable shock waves.

"Oh my God," I breathed, letting my head fall backwards against the mirror.

Nick stood and leaned over me, kissing the top of my head while I caught my breath.

"That was definitely better than football," I murmured.

"You don't even like football," he whispered. He pressed closer to me until I realized he was already fully aroused again.

Our eyes met briefly, then Nick shifted my hips and entered me. I cried out as he filled me so completely and so suddenly. He paused, letting our bodies melt together before withdrawing slowly and then slamming back into me.

I braced myself on my hand, and tried to resist as I felt myself slowly giving into that now familiar aching desire. My breath quickened along with Nick's and we both came soon, my nails clenching into his shoulder at the peak of the intensity.

Neither of us moved or spoke for a moment. When Nick finally withdrew, he raised his hand to his shoulder and rubbed it tentatively. "Ouch," he murmured, drawing my attention to the reddened claw marks I'd left.

"Sorry," I mumbled.

He laughed, wiping himself off with a tissue before wrapping the towel around his waist. "That'll be hard to explain at the gym."

"You could just wear a shirt," I said.

Nick grinned and kissed me.

"Do you want to watch the rest of the football game?"

"What's football?"

I giggled.

"I like your hair," he said.

I smiled, having completely forgotten about my new color. "Thanks."

"I liked it before too, though," he added. He started to dress himself. "You're pretty spectacular the way you are, you know? You don't need to keep changing things."

I slipped off the counter and searched for some clothes

to put on in lieu of answering. I noticed Nick checking the score on his phone, and saw that it was still early in the third quarter.

"You should get back to the bar. Your friends are going to miss you."

He considered this for a minute. "Not unless you come with me. We're celebrating, remember?"

I did feel like getting out, now that I had worked through the sexual tension eating away at me, but I still wasn't sure. "Nick, is that a good idea, for us to show up together at a bar after you disappeared? You said all your coworkers are there."

Nick shrugged. "Are you afraid they'll think we're dating or are you afraid we'll see someone you know and they'll think we're dating?"

"Both," I admitted, starting to re-wrap my ankle with a new bandage. Nick snatched the bandage from me and wrapped it himself.

"Why do you care what they think? You and I know what we're doing, and isn't that all that matters?"

I fastened my jeans while formulating a response. "Do we know what we're doing?" I finally asked.

"I thought so. Friends with benefits?"

I shrugged.

Nick pulled me close. "Look, as long as you don't force me into the bathroom for a quickie, no one will know what is going on with us. And if it's any consolation, there's mostly cops at that bar anyway. I didn't see David or anyone else who looks like a lawyer. When we get there, you can scan the room for anyone you don't want to see you. If someone is there, I won't touch you the whole game. I work every day next week and then have extra training most evenings, so I'm not going to have much availability after today."

"What if I want you to touch me?" I asked finally.

Nick growled with a smile. "That's my girl," he said. "I'll be downstairs when you're finished getting ready."

I did my hair and makeup in under five minutes and we were out the door.

I was nervous on the way to the bar, but Nick was right. There was no one I knew there, and besides, so what if there was? David was living with Traci. That meant I was allowed to date without judgment, right?

The guys didn't pay much attention to us when we arrived, the game having just entered the fourth quarter. Nick ordered us drinks and then pulled a chair up to the table with the guys. True to his word, he didn't touch me or do anything else to suggest we were more than friends. That got boring fast, so I casually placed my hand on his thigh, inching it upwards and squeezing slightly until he turned and acknowledged me.

"You're literally ruining football for me," he whispered, his breath hot in my ear. "You ready for that quickie?"

I swatted him playfully, then caught Marcus eying us suspiciously.

When the game ended, a few of the guys left, but we stayed, along with Marcus and a few other officers I hadn't met before. Nick introduced me to everyone, then made some casual jokes in response to their pointed questions about his sudden disappearance and subsequent reappearance with me. Marcus seemed curious about my friend Jen, but Nick seemed determined to shoot that down.

"So how long have you guys been dating?" Marcus asked finally.

"We're not," Nick and I both said simultaneously. Then we turned to each other and grinned.

"Oh," Marcus replied, his eyes focused on Nick's arm that was casually draped over my shoulders. Nick picked up on the cue and moved his arm.

"Speaking of dating, how was your date last night?" I asked Nick.

He shrugged. "Better than most my mom arranges."

Marcus raised an eyebrow but didn't say anything.

Nick glanced at me, then spoke. "Chelsea here is married. To a lawyer."

Suddenly, I was mortified. I realized Nick thought I was concerned people would think we were dating, but frankly that was a better possibility than people thinking I was in an open marriage or cheating on a loyal husband.

"We are separated," I said through gritted teeth, glaring at Nick. "He moved in with his paralegal."

Marcus was obviously uncomfortable. "I should be getting home," he said. "You on tomorrow?"

Nick nodded and said goodbye before turning to me. "Should I not have said that?"

I shook the rest of my drink into my mouth. "I don't even know anymore. This is just complicated. I thought you said it was simpler to not have relationships."

"No. Nothing with women is simple. That's why I can only handle one woman at a time. It's commitment, not complications, that I avoid at all costs."

"Right," I mumbled, holding up my glass. "Refill?"

He grinned and walked up to the bar to get us another round of drinks. "I ordered us some nachos and wings while I was up there," he said when he returned with the beverages. He started to scoot mine across the table to me and then paused. "You're not still on the narcotics, are you?"

"No, Officer," I replied tartly, snatching my drink. "Speaking of that, how's work going?" I knew Nick was on the vice squad, so drugs were one of his areas of expertise.

He shrugged. "The price of heroin is ridiculously low these days, which is likely to start impacting crime rates at all levels."

"I thought meth was the big problem lately."

"It is. And controlled drugs like your little ankle prescription were out of control for a while, too, but now it's cheaper and easier for people to get heroin than morphine."

"Catch any hookers lately?"

Nick grinned, likely remembering my concerns the night we met. "Not too much prostitution in the suburbs here. That we know about, anyway."

"What's the other thing you deal with?"

"Traffic stops?" he joked. We both knew he hated that aspect of his job. The tedium of traffic patrol was not so thrilling. "Gambling."

"Oh, right. That's illegal?"

"Sometimes. That's not usually an issue around here either, though. We had a dog fighting ring about a year ago, but it's been slow since then."

We talked about his upcoming training some more and I got his thoughts on my alarm system while we waited for the food to come.

"Hey, will you teach me to shoot sometime?" I asked, pulling a tortilla chip off of the plate and twisting it to separate the extra cheese.

Nick hesitated. "Sure," he finally replied, his tone conveying the opposite message from his words.

"Hey, I'm offended. Why the uncertainty?"

"I don't want you to shoot me."

"Are you really busy all week?"

He shrugged. "I'll have to work during the day and I want to do as many training sessions as I can at night. I need to get the hours in if I want to be considered for this promotion."

I nodded.

"I mean, I'd have to sleep at some point, though. And it probably wouldn't hurt if I spent maybe a half hour of my sleep time in bed not sleeping."

Now I smiled. "I'll be around. Just call."

16

I worked more hours than normal over the next three days. I hadn't seen or heard from Nick, and I hadn't heard from my agent. The suspense was killing me. Making matters worse was the fact that I still couldn't drive, thanks to my bad ankle, and Jen was fully entrenched in tax season. By Thursday, I was so desperate for a distraction that I agreed to dinner with my parents.

The meal went smoothly, but then as we were cleaning up, my mom started to pester me about David.

"Have you spoken with David lately?" she asked.

"Briefly."

"How's he doing?"

"Who cares?"

My mother let out an exaggerated sigh of exasperation. "He's your husband."

"Right. I guess I forgot, seeing as how he is not here."

"So you're just giving up?"

"No, Mom, I'm not giving up. I took cooking classes, dyed my hair, tried to grow out my nails, joined a gym. I've done everything he always wanted me to do and there's nothing left that I can do. It is out of my control. The mandatory waiting period is almost over and if David wants a divorce at the end of that time, there's nothing I can do to stop him."

"Leave her alone, Marcia," my dad barked.

She sighed, but returned to her cleaning silently.

Right as my mom was drying the last dish, my phone rang. She reached it before I did and, in typical nosy-mom fashion, checked who was calling instead of just handing it to me.

"Who's Nick?" she asked.

I snatched the phone from her and quickly rejected the call. "You met him actually. He's that cop I interviewed for that book," I answered, remembering that the closer you stick to the truth, the harder it is to get caught in a lie.

"What's he calling about?"

"I don't know. I'll call him back later and see."

She rolled her eyes and folded the towel by the sink.

"Be right back," I said, limping into the bathroom. I shut the door, switched on the fan, and texted Nick: "With my parents now. They should be leaving shortly. What's up?"

His response came quickly. "Got some new equipment this evening. Thought you'd like to help me practice with it."

I flushed the toilet without ever having opened the lid and flipped on the faucet so my mom wouldn't get suspicious. "I'm intrigued," I typed. "Explain?"

"You'll have to be patient. I like surprises."

"I hate surprises."

"This surprise works best when your clothes are off."

"Fine. I'm sold."

"Text me when your parents leave."

"I'll kick them out as soon as I can. Come in an hour?"

"Deal."

I wedged my phone into my back pocket and tried unsuccessfully to stop grinning before returning to my parents. Fortunately, they left on their own accord about ten minutes later.

I made my way upstairs and changed into lacy panties and a matching push-up bra, brushed my teeth, and fixed my hair. When I heard a car in the driveway, I glanced out the front window and grinned. It was Nick. I scurried down the stairs as quickly as I could with my bum ankle and opened the garage door for him. I wasn't sure if he planned to stay the night, but if his car was inside, I didn't have to worry about David driving by and seeing it.

He took the hint and pulled into the garage, and I closed the door once he cut the engine. As he angled out of his car, I was surprised that he was still in uniform.

"I thought you were at training?"

"Equipment training," he said, "So we needed to be in uniform. Besides, I thought you liked the uniform."

It would be hard not to like him in that uniform. It was crisp and clean and showed just enough of his muscles to make me want to see more. I grinned and rose to my toes to kiss him. "I do. But uniforms make me do crazy things."

"I'm banking on that."

Nick followed me into the house calmly, but started kissing me as soon as we shut the door. His mouth was warm and I eagerly greeted his tongue with mine.

"I've missed this," he whispered, moving his lips down to my neck, then collarbone. His hands squeezed my hips, then slipped beneath my shirt. Goosebumps spread across my body as his fingers grazed my sensitive, bare flesh.

"I thought we were going to go shoot stuff first," I murmured, acutely aware that I was already breathless from the kissing.

Nick pulled back slightly, chuckling. "Babe, I just spent the last two hours shooting. That's the last thing on my mind."

"You said you wanted to try out some new equipment."

Nick raised his eyebrows seductively and led me upstairs. "Technically, I'm pretty experienced with this particular piece of equipment, but this specific set is brand new, issued to me today," he began. He set his gun on my dresser then reached onto his belt and unhooked a shiny silver pair of handcuffs. He tossed them onto the bed, then retrieved another, slightly larger, pair and placed it beside the first. "These have never been used on anybody for anything."

"So you're wanting to break them in?"

"I thought you might have fun with them."

I retrieved the smaller pair and turned it around in my hand. The metal was cold and shinier than a new appliance. "You have the key?"

Nick nodded.

"Why two pairs?"

"Professionally, it's for different sized perps."

"And recreationally?" I asked, having already figured why he'd need two pairs on the job. It was the appearance of two pairs in the present moment that stumped me.

He narrowed his eyes and gave me that seductive look of his that nearly brought me to orgasm without any physical contact. "Do you trust me?"

I nodded without hesitation.

"Then you'll find out," he said. He pulled me close and kissed me hard. I started to kiss him back, eager for more, when he broke away, slipping my shirt up over my head.

His eyes grew wide at the sight of my bra. He exhaled hard.

"The panties match," I said with a smile.

Nick unfastened my jeans and tugged them down, steadying me while I stepped out of them. He grinned happily and kissed me through the thin material of my panties, then worked his way back up my body to my bra. He kissed the tops of my breasts that were trussed above the lacy edge of the bra, then guided me back to the bed.

"But you're still fully clothed," I protested. As much as the uniform turned me on, I knew I liked what was underneath even more.

He winked, unfastened my bra, and shoved me onto my back. Tossing my bra onto the ground, he grabbed the smaller pair of handcuffs. With a flick of his wrist, the cuff opened. He fastened it around my left wrist, kissing my palm as it clicked shut. Nick then straddled me and raised both of my arms above my head. He looped the chain of the handcuffs around the bar at the head of the bed and fastened the other cuff securely against my right wrist, kissing that hand too.

He let go of my arms, and I immediately pulled them for some reason. The cold metal pressed into my skin and my arms didn't budge.

"Careful, there, girl. Those will leave a mark if you struggle."

I bit my lip, still ridiculously aroused, but starting to feel nervous about the restraints. I found the idea of handcuffs sexy, though the reality of being completely at the whim of a guy, especially one who happened to have a gun, was intimidating.

Nick must have sensed my apprehension, because he leaned closer and kissed me gently. "You okay?" he asked softly.

I nodded, and his lips returned to mine, briefly, before

working their way to my breasts. His hand slid across my body, pressing downward from my stomach. I clenched my thighs together around his hand, quivering from the friction of his simple movements. He tucked his finger under the silky material and slowly lowered my panties over my feet.

Nick pulled away suddenly. I had a limited view, with my arms stretched above my head, so I wasn't sure what he was doing until I felt the cold metal band around my ankle. I heard the click as he secured the cuff around my left ankle, securing the other cuff to the post at the foot of the bed.

"If only I had three pairs," he mumbled, eying my free leg. Then he laughed.

He crouched near my free ankle, kissing it tenderly. I remembered then that this was my injured ankle, and realized that probably had more to do with his decision to leave it untethered than a lack of equipment. Nick inched his way back up my body, kissing every inch of my leg until he reached the top. He hesitated, then traced his tongue ever so slightly across my core.

I sighed audibly from the pleasure, raising my hips ever so slightly in hopes of increasing the pressure from his mouth. He breathed a laugh against my sensitive skin, then pulled away.

"Patience isn't your strong suit, is it?" he teased, slowly removing his flashlight, mace and other items on his belt. Then he turned to face me, slowly unbuttoning his shirt. Once it was off, he folded it and set it on the dresser with all of his other stuff. I watched as he lowered his pants to the ground, still facing the dresser, and then folded them. He repeated the slow removal and folding process with his undershirt. It was clear from his pace that Nick was trying to drive me crazy. It was working.

He swiveled back to face me. "Where is my camera when I need it?" he mused.

"I'd kill you," I said, surprised at how raw and breathless I sounded.

Nick grinned mischievously and returned to the bed. He straddled me, ran his hands up the length of my arms, then back to my breasts. He shifted lower, crouching between my legs again, and lifted my free leg so his mouth could better reach his goal.

This time, he wasn't messing around. I groaned unabashedly at the exquisite warmth rapidly spreading throughout my body. I longed to run my fingers through his hair while his tongue darted back and forth, but every time I forgot and tried to move my arms, they were yanked back into place by the unyielding metal cuffs. I saw my chest rise and fall with my increased breathing as his fingers traced across my nipples, gently at first, then firmer and pinching.

When I couldn't bear the pressure any longer, I cried out, my body exploding into a million pieces around his expert touch. Nick collapsed onto me without hesitation, his frantic kisses reminding me how aroused he was by my pleasure. I raised my hips again, feeling his erection through his boxer briefs, but he pulled away.

"That made me thirsty," he said. "Would you like a drink?"

I didn't answer, couldn't even formulate words while my body still felt like I was on fire.

Suddenly, he disappeared.

"Nick!" I screeched, but he was gone. I listened for sounds downstairs, but heard nothing telling. Finally, I heard footsteps entering the room.

"Miss me?" he asked.

I turned my head to watch him open a bottle of white

wine. He poured some into a glass and took a large, leisurely sip. "Want some?"

I nodded eagerly, surprised he was drinking white since he always preferred red.

He held the glass near my lips and poured the smallest of sips into my mouth. I swallowed, then felt cool liquid in my belly button.

"Whoops, spilled some," Nick joked. He leaned closer and lapped the wine off of my stomach, then repeated the process.

"That's cold," I whined. "And you're making me all sticky."

"Yeah, but at least I'm not staining your sheets burgundy," he replied, explaining his choice of wine.

I saw him holding the bottle of wine over my breasts and I tensed, anticipating the harsh cold liquid that soon fell onto my sensitive nipples. I groaned as he licked it off, surprised by the unexpected satisfaction from the mixture of sensations. He repeated the process, then offered me another sip from the glass.

"I have to admit, I like having you restrained," he whispered. "I wish there were some way I could prolong this, but I can't imagine holding off too long once we get started."

I bit my lip so hard I nearly drew blood. The anticipation was killing me, and talking about it wasn't helping.

He kissed me again, sipped more wine, then set the glass on the dresser and removed his only remaining article of clothing. I smiled, already appreciating what he was about to do with his valuable member.

"Next time we're blindfolding you," he said with a mischievous grin. He sat beside me and I would've given anything to be able to touch him—to trace my fingers along the firm ridges of his stomach, to touch the soft hair on his head, and to squeeze the firmness of his manhood. But all I could do was watch and wait.

"Waiting is such sweet torture, huh," he mused. He stretched out beside me and lifted my right leg, effectively pinning it between our bodies. He aligned himself with the top of my thighs and shifted closer, causing my body to tingle with the knowledge that he was less than an inch away from entering me.

"You'll tell me if I'm hurting you?"

I groaned with frustration. "You are killing me now. Fuck me already," I said, stunned to hear the coarse words coming from my mouth.

Nick licked his lips. "Yes ma'am," he replied, quickly complying.

I moaned eagerly as soon as he entered me, feeling my breath turn to panting within a few short thrusts. I tried to rope my left leg around him, forgetting the cuffs, and groaned again with frustration. With the position Nick had forced my free leg into, I couldn't even leverage my hips against anything to raise my pelvis to meet his without forcing the cuff to press into my ankle. I was completely at his mercy, and he knew it.

As soon as I felt myself start to topple over the peak of pleasure, Nick stilled. I told myself his breathing was every bit as frantic as mine, so he couldn't possibly play this game much longer, but then he still did, time and time again.

Finally, I couldn't take it any longer. "Please," I begged, and he complied, thrusting into me harder and faster until we both came with a jolt that shook the bed.

"Fuck," Nick murmured, letting my leg drop down beside the other and collapsing on top of me. He didn't move until I felt my pulse level out.

When he finally raised his head up to face me, he was grinning victoriously.

"What?" I asked, irritated by the smirk as much as the fact that I still couldn't move.

"I made you talk dirty *and* beg for it," he gloated.

I squeezed my eyes shut, embarrassed.

"You aren't on medication are you? Or suffering from a concussion?" He paused, then laughed. "See, and normally you'd probably smack me for teasing you, but you can't now, can you?"

I groaned.

Nick kissed my forehead then climbed off of me. "Well, I consider those pieces of equipment thoroughly tested and fully functioning."

"And you have the key?"

"Yes," he said.

He retrieved a small key from a pouch on his belt and unlocked my wrists. As soon as they were free, I lowered my arms. They felt heavy and weak from the decreased blood flow in having been above my head. I circled my wrists to loosen them up as Nick unfastened my ankle.

"Oh shit," he exclaimed.

"What?" I sat up.

Nick set my foot on the bed and directed his attention to my wrists. I followed his panicked expression to see dark red bruising around my wrists. The bruise was wider along the outside, where I'd kept pulling against the metal every time I wanted to move freely.

"Chelsea, you should've told me I was hurting you. I didn't mean..." he rubbed my wrists. "This doesn't happen when I arrest people."

I giggled. "Hopefully most of this scenario doesn't

happen when you arrest people," I said, gesturing at both of us.

He smiled slightly. "I'm really sorry. I didn't realize you'd be pulling against them so much. That might be why they pad the recreational cuffs."

I sat slowly, eager to be closer to him. "It's okay. It doesn't hurt, and that was fun."

He scooted off the bed and disappeared into the bathroom for a few minutes. I poured a little more wine into his glass and drank it, then started to redress just as he emerged.

"Can I stay here tonight?" he asked.

I nodded, oddly relieved he was staying. Something about the intensity of that whole experience made me crave more attention from him.

"Thanks. I'm exhausted. This week has been brutal, and I work at the club Saturday night."

I wrinkled my nose but refrained from complaining since he was already clearly bummed about it. "Mind if I shower? Somehow I got all sticky and I smell like Riesling."

Nick grinned.

I took a quick shower then changed into a sexy slip before brushing my teeth and returning to the bedroom. Nick was in his boxer briefs, in bed, with the lights off. I thought he might already be asleep, so I silently crawled into bed beside him.

"Sweet dreams, Chelsea," he whispered, scooting closer to drape his hand across my hip.

I snuggled back against him, feeling warm, satisfied, and safe. I drifted to sleep quickly and slept deeply.

NICK WOKE early in the morning, somehow managing to shower, shave, and dress without waking me. When he was all ready to go, he leaned over me and softly kissed my forehead.

I fluttered my eyes open slowly then jumped, startled to see him already dressed.

"Don't get up," he said. "What's your garage code? I'll close it behind me."

"You're headed back to work?"

He nodded.

I pouted, then told him the code.

"Sorry again about the bruising," he said.

I smiled as the memories of the prior night rushed back to me. "It's okay," I said. "Something tells me I'll have a good time remembering how I got these marks whenever I see them."

He laughed. "I'll call you sometime next week."

I WORKED ALL DAY FRIDAY, finishing two freelance articles before lunch. Then, finally feeling recovered enough from my fall to be able to drive, I did a much overdo grocery store run on Saturday. I stocked up on the essentials, plus enough supplies to fully restock my cookie dough stash.

I spent the rest of the afternoon baking, then met up with Jen for dinner and a movie. We picked a Mexican place in the same outdoor shopping mall as the theater so we could fill up on margaritas then sober up at the chick flick.

Jen was in good spirits, as was I. She had updated her online dating profile the prior night and had finished some huge return at work that had been monopolizing her time over the past week.

"So now you'll actually have some free time again?" I asked her.

"Not if my new profile is successful," she joked.

I reached for another tortilla chip and Jen leaned closer.

"What's that?" she asked, grabbing my wrist. I blushed as she released it and looked for the matching bruise on the other.

It was too hot for long sleeves, but I thought I'd successfully covered the marks with chunky bracelets and a watch.

"Handcuffs," I mumbled.

"What?"

"Handcuffs," I said louder.

Her eyes grew wide. "And it left marks?"

I shrugged.

"This was consensual, right?"

I rolled my eyes. "Of course." I shivered as memories of the experience floated back to me. "It was the most amazing sex ever," I said, grinning. Then I realized what I'd just said and added, "I mean other than David, of course"

Now Jen rolled her eyes. She ran her finger over the mark and shook her head. "You do know they make toy handcuffs for this sort of thing," she said.

"All we had were the real ones." I cleared my throat to get her attention, slipping my leg out from under the table and raising my jeans just enough to reveal the matching mark on my ankle.

"Oh my God," she murmured. "I don't even know you anymore. This is insane. I am actually intrigued by your sex life now and I never thought that would happen. I think I'm even a little jealous."

I giggled, trying not to be offended by the implications of her words, then quickly changed the subject.

17

Several days went by with no word from Nick. I was keeping busy with edits on the Olympian's book in between my freelance assignments, so it wasn't like I was pining away at the phone. And he had warned me he would be busy for a few days. But still, since the whole point of a friend with benefits was to have someone to help me not feel so lonely, I decided I'd given him enough time away from me.

I texted him, but it took him over an hour to reply. When he did, it was terse, reading "Shitty day. Can't talk now. Watch the news."

I went online and looked up the local news. The story popped up instantly, with the headline reading "Suburbs rocked by tragic death." I winced, realizing this type of occurrence was precisely why I didn't normally read the news, but I forced myself to keep reading. Apparently, a toddler had ingested a lethal dose of meth and died early that morning. The dad had been arrested and had prior convictions, and according to "sources," police had been called to the house numerous times for domestic violence complaints.

I shuddered. No wonder Nick's day stunk. If the cops could've prevented this, he surely felt guilty, even if he wasn't involved. I tried to think of what would help me feel better if I were in his shoes, but I decided a hug and a massive batch of cookies probably wouldn't solve much for him.

I texted him again later that evening, offering to help cheer him up. He responded quicker this time, simply saying he was still at work.

I sighed, and switched gears. Checking my email, I flagged a few sales that I might want to shop, and then froze as I saw an email from my agent. I clicked it, biting my lip in anticipation.

"Chelsea- I wanted you to know I LOVE your manuscript so far. Hoping to finish this weekend and have lots of potential publishers in mind for you. Let's talk Monday."

I flew out of my chair and shrieked and screamed like a crazy woman for a good fifteen minutes.

When I finally calmed down, I called Jen, not wanting to bug Nick again.

We met up for a celebratory shopping spree, and it was early evening when I finally headed home.

I was about to turn into my neighborhood when I noticed the flashing lights behind me.

"Shit," I mumbled. I glanced down at the speedometer to confirm that I was cruising at almost ten miles above the speed limit. My mind of course thought of Nick, but I didn't have time to devise a plan to use my connection to him to get me out of the ticket. I slammed on my breaks, flipped my signal on, and maneuvered the car to the side of the road, slinking down into my seat as I rolled down my window so none of my neighbors who happened to be passing saw me.

It had been nearly a decade since my last speeding ticket, and then I was really speeding. Maybe this time I'd just get a warning. I looked up in the rearview mirror as the officer stepped out of his cruiser. Within a second, my mood went from anxious to irate.

"Are you kidding me?" I snapped as soon as Nick reached my window, in full uniform. "I nearly had a heart attack."

His dark sunglasses blocked my view of his eyes, but I could tell from the half-dimple on his cheek that he was trying not to smile. "Do you know why I pulled you over?"

"Because you're a stalker on a power trip?" Really, he could have just called me.

Nick leaned in, resting his forearms on my window ledge. "Your registration is expired," he said. "And you better cool that attitude because you were speeding, too, and you failed to pull over right away."

I frowned. "How long were you behind me?"

"Long enough to confirm my suspicions that you need a driving class. Do you ever look in your rearview mirror?"

I sighed.

He shrugged and glanced around him at the passing cars. "I went by your house to see if you'd heard back from your agent, but you weren't home. Then I saw you driving by and was just going to follow you home, but you clearly didn't notice me behind you."

"So my registration isn't expired?"

"No, it is. You need to go to the Bureau of Motor Vehicles first thing tomorrow and pay to renew your plates. There will be a small fine for renewing late, but they'll give you a little sticker to put on your plates so you don't get pulled over again."

I shook my head. "It's David's car."

"You want me to ticket him?" he teased. "He might have gotten the renewal notice and just not told you. Or you might have gotten it and just disregarded it."

I nodded reluctantly. "Fine. I'll pay it. But you really shouldn't go pulling people over when you're not serious about ticketing them. I nearly had a heart attack."

"I like watching you squirm." Nick grinned. He stood upright. "Go check your mail. I bet you have the notice about your plates mixed in with all that random crap in your laundry room."

"It's not crap. I have a system," I insisted.

He rolled his eyes and started to saunter away.

"How's everything at work now?"

He walked back over and wrinkled his nose. "Pretty rotten. Have you been following the news?"

I nodded.

He leaned in the window, placing his elbows on the ledge. "I went to that house once. Several of the guys had. Honestly, I never even realized they had a kid. I knew something was going on but the woman would never press charges or even speak up."

"It's not your fault."

Nick shrugged. "Doesn't really matter whose fault it is when a kid's dead."

There was nothing I could say to refute that.

"Anyway, there is just a lot more pressure on the department now to make sure we're doing everything by the books and with the mayoral race in the fall, everyone is eager to make sure we keep the city crime free."

"Sorry," I mumbled.

"Hey, what did your agent say?"

I swallowed and raised my eyebrows excitedly. "She loved it!"

Nick looked genuinely happy. "Can I read it now?"

"We'll see."

He laughed. "Can you manage the rest of the drive home without breaking any laws?"

"Goodbye, Nick," I replied, starting my engine.

NICK SENT me a text later to apologize for being incommunicado for so long.

I forgave him, since it seemed like that was what friends with benefits do. I asked him if he was still working nonstop and he said yes. Then my phone rang.

"My thumbs are tired," Nick said when I answered.

"Hmm, guess that's what happens when you avoid your sex slave for ten days and have to handle things the old-fashioned way."

"Is that how long it's been? Geez, no wonder I'm stressed."

I laughed.

"So you're not pissed?"

"About you pulling me over?"

"No, about me not calling for so long."

"You were busy," I said.

He was quiet for a moment before speaking again. "This is another reason why I don't do relationships. If we were actually dating, I'd feel guilty about being away from you and you'd be pissed off."

I figured he was right, so I didn't answer.

"Most days I love my job. It's never boring, as long as I'm not on traffic patrol, and even when I have bad days, I can still tell myself I made a difference. But then when something happens, even if it's not something I could've prevented, I still feel like shit. And everyone blames the police even though no one seems too appreciative about all the crimes and crap we prevent that they don't even know about." He sighed. "Everyone here is shitty and on edge, the Chief is putting tons of pressure on us, and the media is driving us crazy. I just want to punch something and get really drunk."

"Wow," I said. "That was a very honest, yet macho response to stress."

He laughed.

"I don't have a punching bag, but maybe we could meet up later and I could help you work out some of the stress another way?"

He groaned. "I wish, but we're all putting in overtime this week."

"And you couldn't spare ten minutes?"

"It's just going to make me feel like an even bigger jerk if I drop by for a quickie and then leave again."

"Hmm. Well, it's your call. I'm home now, just sitting around in my lingerie. Remember that black bra you like? I got a matching one in white. Didn't you say white lace turns you on?"

Nick growled. "I'll be there in ten minutes. Meet me in the garage."

He hung up before I could question this. Pleased with my success at persuading him to come over, I couldn't stop grinning as I changed into the white lingerie I'd referenced. I brushed my hair, dabbed on some lip gloss, and massaged vanilla lotion into my thighs, then heard the car pull in.

I arrived in the garage just as Nick pressed the button to shut the overhead door. I started to greet him, but he grabbed me by the waist and plopped me onto the hood of his police cruiser before I could protest.

"I need to be back in ten minutes and it's a five minute drive," he said, kissing my neck between words. "You look hot." He lifted my breasts out of my bra and massaged one with his hands while using his tongue to taunt the other.

I felt the familiar tingling already, which was good since Nick was not wasting any time. He unzipped his pants and tugged my panties off. His mouth moved down my body, kissing and licking me for only a moment, but somehow bringing me close to the peak of pleasure. Then he stood up, hoisted my legs higher, and pushed into me.

We both moaned initially, and our hips quickly took over, meeting each other again and again at a relentless pace. The delicious burning intensified and I couldn't hold off any longer. I cried out, desperately squeezing his body further into mine, and he instantly found his own release as well.

I closed my eyes, dizzy with satisfaction, and Nick pulled away slowly. I heard a breathy laugh and opened my eyes.

"Three minutes to spare," Nick whispered. "Not bad." He reached into the car and grabbed a handful of tissues, offering some to me and keeping the rest. "And I do like white lingerie," he added.

I slowly sat up, suddenly aware that I'd just made love on a police car. Jen would just die when she heard this.

"Here's the part where you tell me you feel used and that I'm a sexist jerk," Nick said, zipping up his pants and smoothing the front of his uniform.

I smiled and rose to my toes to kiss him instead. His lips were warm and soft in a way that made me want to squeeze in another round before he had to leave, but I resisted. He bent to pick up my panties, but when I reached for them, he simply shook his head.

"Souvenir," he whispered. "In case tomorrow is stressful too."

I rolled my eyes but smiled, oddly certain I could trust him not to embarrass me with his souvenir.

"Thank you," he said, kissing me again. "I do feel better now."

"Me too," I said.

He grinned and started to climb in his car.

"Hey, tomorrow night, if you're free, Jen and I are getting together with some friends at a bar to celebrate my book."

Nick nodded. "That sounds good. Can I meet you there?"

"Yeah. See you later," I said, ducking back into the house as soon as I'd opened the garage door so the neighbors wouldn't see me in my bra.

THE NEXT NIGHT, Jen and I had been at the bar for almost an hour when Nick arrived. He greeted her politely, and we moved to a nearby table. Jen asked him some basic questions about his work, he asked her some questions about hers, and slowly they both relaxed and the conversation flowed a little easier. By the time the second round of drinks arrived, Nick's hand was on my thigh, under the table.

The simple, though not exactly innocent, touch sent chills up my spine, and I suddenly lost all train of thought. Jen raised an eyebrow, then started to laugh. Thankfully, our friend Erin arrived then, along with one of Jen's coworkers named Mike. Jen introduced them both to Nick, then dragged me to the bathroom.

"Okay, what is going on?" she asked the moment we were alone.

"What do you mean?"

"You said you and Nick are just friends who occasionally fuck."

"Jen!" I blushed and glanced under the stalls, certain someone had heard. "That's not exactly true."

She stuck her hand on her hip. "No, shit. Friends with benefits do not act that way."

"What way?"

She rolled her eyes. "He stares at you whenever you talk. You laugh excessively at everything he says. And don't think I don't notice that inner thigh rub he was giving you under the table."

"What's your point?"

"Nick likes you, Chelsea. And you like him. And you guys have this amazing chemistry that is abundantly clear to everyone around you."

I turned away from her and pretended to check my hair in the mirror.

"Chelsea, why can't you just let David go? Sign the papers and move on. He did you a favor by leaving. You deserve someone like Nick, and he is ready and willing to step up to the plate!"

I shook my head. "No, he's not, Jen. Nick has made that perfectly clear. He is not interested in a relationship. The only reason he even goes out with me is because he thinks I'm unavailable."

Jen stared at me for a long moment. "You're wrong," she said. "The only thing standing between you and a really good relationship with Nick is your nonsensical obsession with winning back David. I hope you figure that out before it's too late."

She stormed out of the bathroom and I waited a minute before following.

"Everything okay?" Nick asked when I returned.

I nodded hesitantly. Jen was already over with Erin and Mike, doing shots like she was back in college.

He wrapped an arm around me and kissed the side of my head. "You're supposed to be celebrating tonight, not pouting," he said.

His lips lingered near my ear, and I shivered.

"I am. Jen just, well, nevermind," I said. "I need a drink."

Nick ordered for me and we rejoined the rest of the group.

As Erin launched into a story about her last blind date, Nick leaned in closer to whisper.

"I've been meaning to tell you that I really liked the whole thing, but I was especially impressed by your creativity in the bedroom scenes. I did have some questions though. Maybe we could reenact a few of those scenes just to confirm I'm reading it correctly."

I couldn't figure out what he was talking about, and frankly the proximity of his tongue to my ear was distracting. "What?" I whispered back.

"Your book," he breathed. "It was amazing."

I turned to him, my cheeks pulled so widely by my smile that it practically hurt. "You read it? Already? I just emailed it to you yesterday."

Nick shrugged. "I couldn't put it down."

We had stopped lowering our voices, so the rest of the group was watching us now.

"I never pegged you for the romance novel type," I teased.

"I just hadn't found the right author yet, I guess," he replied.

"Hey, how come he got to read it before me?" Jen whined.

"He asked," I said. "But I can give you a copy now if you want."

"I do!" she replied, enthusiastically.

The conversation gradually shifted away from my book, when Nick leaned in again.

"I'd like to be first in line to volunteer as a tester for your next book. Surely you can't write those scenes without trying them first."

I felt myself blush, and turned back towards Jen.

The next hour was a blast. I almost forgot what Jen had said, but I remained acutely aware of every glance and touch from Nick.

Before long though, Jen started talking to another guy at the bar and Erin and Mike went to play darts. "I'll play the winner," Nick called as they headed across the bar. Then he gestured to Jen and chuckled.

"She's good at picking up men," he observed.

I smiled. "It's a special talent of hers."

"Have you ever picked up a guy at a bar?"

"Sure. The night I met you,' I replied.

"Really? I'm impressed," he said. "What line did you use?"

I wrinkled my nose. "Okay, maybe Jen introduced us."

Nick laughed. "I bet even in college you didn't have to pick up men. I bet they all just flocked to you."

I sipped my drink, trying to remember the last time I'd even been hit on by a stranger.

"You should practice. Come on," he urged. "Use a pickup line on me."

I thought for a moment, then gave Nick a quick once over, smiling when my eyes landed on his groin. "Okay, stranger, here goes." I turned to face him and flipped my hair seductively behind my shoulder. "Is that a gun in your pocket or are you just happy to see me?"

Nick laughed. "Sweetheart, if you're hitting on a guy with a gun in a bar, you've got bigger issues than your pickup line."

I pouted. "But you wear your gun in bars."

"Only because I'm a police officer and never when I'm drinking," he replied.

I considered this for a moment. "Wait, so you're completely unarmed now?"

He nodded and leaned forward. "I guess I'm just very happy to see you," he whispered.

"I'm a loser," Erin said suddenly, startling me. "You get to play Mike," she said to Nick. He looked at me, licked his lips, then stood.

I watched him saunter away, wondering exactly which exercise he did at the gym to achieve that appearance from behind.

"Sorry," Erin mumbled, jutting me out of my daydream. "I hadn't meant to interrupt you guys. It looked like you were hitting it off."

"You didn't interrupt," I lied. "He's just a friend."

She seemed skeptical, but changed the subject anyway. When the guys finished their game, though, she wandered back over to Mike.

Jen collapsed into the seat next to me the moment Erin stood to leave. "I was talking to your man," she slurred with a wink.

"Oh yeah? Which man is that?"

She glanced over at Nick, who was chatting with another guy near the bar. He gazed over, raised an eyebrow, and grinned as I looked at him.

"You're drunk," I told her.

"Nick and I agree on something."

"Really? And what is that?" I took another sip of my drink, realizing how much I missed the days where Jen was drunker than me.

"We both think David is an idiot and that you are an even bigger idiot for trying to win him back."

"Nick called me an idiot?"

Jen attempted a shrug but nearly fell off the barstool. "Not in so many words. He said you could do better, but that you didn't realize that yet." She reached for my drink and I slid it out of reach. She pouted.

"He really likes you," she said.

"No, what he likes is no-strings-attached sex."

She shook her head, but Nick approached us before she could explain further. "Anyone need a ride home?" he offered.

"I'm sorry you got stuck being the designated driver," I said after we dropped Jen off. "You probably could've used a drink after the week you've had."

"It was your night to celebrate. And I did have a drink, two actually, when I first got to the bar. And then I switched to soda so I'd be energetic enough for whatever you had planned."

"Oh, so you think you're coming in with me?"

"Unless you want to try another part of the car," he replied.

I tried picturing that.

"I'm glad you've stopped making me work for it. It was really a struggle back when you pretended you weren't going to sleep with me every time you saw me."

"Hey, I was never pretending. I'm just not very good at resisting temptation."

"And I'm just really persuasive," he agreed, reminding me of some of our first conversations.

"I am tired, though," I said.

"Then I'll tuck you in right away," he offered, leading me into the house. I ducked into the bathroom for a moment, and when I came out, I found that Nick had stripped naked, unmade the bed, and dimmed the lights.

"Turns out I forgot my pajamas," he said. He stepped up behind me and brushed my hair to the side, kissing the back of my neck. His erection pressed into my lower back as he traced his tongue behind my ear, then reached around to fondle my breasts through the lacy cups of the bra.

A slight moan escaped my lips as Nick unfastened the bra, letting it drop to the floor. He then slid my panties down to my ankles and I stepped out of them, gingerly.

"You are so hot," he whispered.

He nudged me forward, lifted my leg and placed my foot on the edge of the bed. He licked his finger then traced it down my body. I shuddered as his moistened skin brushed across my nipple, and I drew in a sharp breath as his fingers continued to move lower, circling the entrance of my sex. His mouth lingered on the back of my neck for a moment and his fingers disappeared, only to be replaced by his firm erection.

He moved slowly, entering me gradually so I could truly

absorb every exquisite sensation of him filling and stretching me. After a moment, he gripped my waist and hoisted me onto the bed. I remained on my hands and knees as he scooted behind me, soon resuming his slow, delicious torture. My breath quickened, and I relished the unfamiliarity of this position, how it freed up his hands to massage my breasts or even to rub the apex of my thighs while he gently thrusted.

Nick wrapped an arm around my waist, lowering me down to my chest and placing my arms behind me. The sheets rubbed against my nipples as we rocked back and forth and I groaned again with delight. The sensations in my body were intense, and without Nick's lips on mine or his body wrapped around me, I could do nothing but absorb each pleasurable movement.

I knew I was close, that I couldn't tolerate the increasing tension much longer without a release. Nick kissed my neck, whispered "let go," and I did, moaning loudly as I came. He straightened my legs out longer without leaving my body, so that I was stretched out on my stomach and he squeezed my buttocks as he increased the pace. The friction was even more intense now, and Nick's pleasure was palpable as he came loudly, collapsing on top of me right after.

The second I caught my breath, I burst into tears. At first, I was able to hide it, simply keeping my face buried in the bed. But I couldn't exactly breathe in that position, and Nick figured it out anyway. I felt him shift beside me in the bed, then slowly slide his hand up and down across my back.

"Um, Chels, do you want to talk?" he asked, kissing my shoulder blade lightly.

I sniffled loudly, trying not to wipe my nose on the pillowcase.

"Was I that bad?" Nick continued. "I mean, I suspected it

wasn't my best work but it was still pretty good for me. Maybe I should watch some instructional videos, brush up on my technique…"

I giggled, despite my best efforts not to.

"Will you turn over so we can talk, Chelsea?"

"No," I cried into the mattress. "You hate crying women and I'm a total wreck."

"I see that," he said softly. "I'm trying to figure out what's wrong before you suffocate."

I sighed then reluctantly turned onto my side, facing away from him. I half expected Nick to leave, but instead he scooted closer and draped his arm around my waist.

"You don't have to stay," I told him.

"I'm not leaving while you're upset."

"It's not your fault. I'm just a mess," I explained.

"That's a relief. So the sex wasn't that horrible?"

I groaned. "Of course not. That's the problem. It's never horrible. Sex is always good with you. Really good."

There was a silence.

"So you're crying because the sex was too good?"

"No. I'm confused."

"Me too."

Nick kissed the back of my neck. I knew he was only trying to comfort me, but it made things worse. I wriggled away and sat up.

"Is this about whatever Jen said to you earlier tonight?" he asked. "Because I talked to her later and she seemed excited about your book."

"She is," I said. "And I don't know if that's what it's about. She just pointed out that you and I seem to have good chemistry. She said we're always flirting and we seem really happy when we're together."

"Oh," he said. "And like great sex, that's a bad thing?"

I wiped my eyes on the back of my hand and turned to face him. "No, and Jen is completely right. I do have fun with you and we do get along well and the sex is amazing. If I were even remotely rational, that would be enough for me. Any other woman in these circumstances would be head over heels in love with you." I paused, sniffling. "But as it stands, I still want David." I sighed. "And it doesn't matter anyway because you're not into commitments, which is fine."

Nick was quiet again for a moment. "Let's take my feelings out of the equation for the moment. How you feel about David has nothing to do with what I want." His hand froze on my upper back. "So you're saying that you're still not over him?"

"Correct. And because of that Jen thinks I'm crazy, and let's face it, she's obviously right. It's embarrassing to tell anybody because what sane person would want someone who cheated on them?"

Nick sighed and rubbed my shoulders for a length before answering. "That doesn't make you crazy, Chelsea. He was your husband. You guys have a lot of history together and you're surrounded by reminders of him and you probably had some happy times together. Sure he's an asshole of epic proportions now, but he couldn't possibly have always been a complete jerk, right?"

"Do you have a point?"

"Yeah. There is nothing to be ashamed of in wanting to be with someone even after they've done something horrible."

I shook my head. "You're just saying that because I'm crying. You've told me countless times that I'm crazy to still want him."

"You are," he agreed. "But it's understandable. I had no

logical reason to want Katelyn back after the way she left and humiliated me, but I still did. It's just part of being a human."

"I am happy when I'm with you. Why can't I just stay angry at him? Why can't I curse him out, key his car, and dump his shit on the curb?"

Nick dropped his hands to my thighs. "Maybe what you're feeling isn't about getting him back, maybe it's just about winning."

"What do you mean?"

"Maybe you don't really want him back and all you really want is for him to pick you over Traci."

"I wish," I mumbled.

Nick swallowed loudly. I turned to face him, pulling the covers over my stomach.

"I'm sorry I cried again."

He shrugged nonchalantly, then glanced down at the bed. "Do you still love him?"

"I think I do."

"Does this mean we're not having sex anymore?" he asked.

"I like having sex with you. How ironic is that?"

Nick didn't answer.

"I don't want you to feel like you're just a placeholder, keeping me occupied until David is back in my bed. I really do like spending time with you outside the bedroom, too." I sniffled. "Besides, isn't this your ideal relationship now? Sex without the risk of a future with the woman?"

There was a long silence and then Nick shifted in the bed. "I have to work in the morning, but I can stay the night if you need me to."

"You can go home," I said, recognizing from his tone that while he might be willing, he didn't actually want to stay.

He hesitated, then kissed my forehead and crawled out of bed. I watched him dress without talking, then forced a smile as he kissed me again and assured me he'd lock up on his way out. As soon as I heard his engine start in the driveway, I stopped holding back the tears.

18

The next morning, I texted Nick to apologize for crying. He didn't reply until afternoon, and even then, it was a terse "don't worry about it." I didn't want to be that girl, the one who sensed she'd screwed things up with a guy and then instead of letting it go just kept pushing him and ignoring his hints until he finally thought she was a stalker and took out a restraining order. So, I didn't text or call at all for two days.

I wasn't sure what to say to him anyway. Neither of us could deny that our relationship was weird. On the surface it seemed perfect, but in reality, it was completely unsustainable and we both knew it. I was trapped in the classic love triangle—where I still loved David yet still desired Nick. Only in my triangle, neither of the other participants wanted a happily-ever-after with me.

I tried to sort out my feelings, to play out a few hypothetical scenarios in my mind. Option A involved David coming home and begging for forgiveness. My immediate response would be to accept him back, obviously making him work to truly earn my forgiveness, forget about Nick, and live happily ever after. So far, though, there were no signs indicating David was about to go this route. Option B seemed more likely, and it involved David and I finalizing the divorce, now that the waiting period was up, and me eventually moving on out of necessity. Having no one else to distract me, I'd become horribly obsessed with Nick, but as a divorcée, I'd be totally available and up for a relationship so he would avoid me like the plague and I'd end up alone.

I couldn't devise any other options in my mind. At least not without wine, but before I could pour any, my phone rang. I was so grumpy I answered without checking the caller ID. An unfamiliar female voice greeted me warmly. I didn't answer immediately, so she repeated herself.

"Chelsea? It's Katherine Grater."

It was my agent. I perked up immediately. "Oh hi, sorry I couldn't hear you at first there."

"No problem. How have you been?"

"Good, thanks," I lied. "You?"

"Great," she said. "Busy actually. We sent your manuscript out to a few different publishers the week before last."

Her assistant always copied me on the emails, so I already vaguely knew this information. "I saw that. Thanks."

"Are you sitting down?"

"Yep," I said, still clueless.

"I just got off the phone with Marla and she said they love your work!"

I was too hung up on trying to recall which publishing house had an editor named Marla to process what Katherine had said.

"Chelsea? Did you hear me?"

"Yes. Wait—did you say she loves it?"

"Uh huh," Katherine paused, but I could hear the happiness in her voice now. "Chelsea, this is really terrific news. We never hear back from editors this quickly. She said her beta readers finished your manuscript on Monday and stuck it on the top of her desk and she hadn't yet finished but she's really interested."

"Oh my God!"

"We don't have an official offer yet," she cautioned. "And you can always try to get them to wait a bit to see if another publisher shows any interest, too. But in the meantime, Marla said she'd love to meet with you to discuss the book once she's finished."

"Meet with me? What does that mean?"

"Well, they'd fly you out to New York and probably take you out to lunch to discuss your vision for the book, and go over some ideas. I'll be honest, usually when they want these meetings, they have some proposed changes, but they also probably wouldn't bother if they weren't interested in buying the publishing rights."

"They want me to go to New York?"

"Yes."

"Oh my God!" I was panting and pacing the room now. "They liked my book?"

"Yes, Chelsea. Loved it. Congratulations."

"Thanks," I said, still dazed.

"I'll let you go process this now, maybe celebrate some, and then we'll touch base tomorrow. I'll send you some details from Marla and see if we can get an itinerary and then you can decide if you want to go."

"Okay."

She hung up, but I was still frozen, clutching my phone

like a baby. Once I snapped out of my trance, I started cheering. I called Jen, then my parents, and then paused, oddly uncertain about calling Nick. I finally settled for a text. I wrote "I got good news. Call me asap."

When Jen picked me up for drinks two hours later, I hadn't heard back from him.

THE NEXT MORNING, I was hungover from drinks, excited about my potential book deal, and bummed about Nick. He should've called me. It seemed he was trying to break up with me, or whatever it would be since we weren't really a couple. But what kind of a person just stops calling and texting someone? Couldn't he at least have the decency to dump me in person?

I deserved answers. I dressed and made myself look cute but casual, picked up sandwiches, and brought them to the station. Unless Nick's schedule had changed, he was working today. I had my laptop in the car, so if he was out on patrol when I arrived, I could head across to the library to work while I waited for him to return to the station.

Fortunately, I was in luck. When I asked for him, the clerk said he'd just returned a moment before. I smiled triumphantly, then waited patiently by the door.

"Chelsea, you didn't have to do this," he said when he saw the bag of food.

"You've been too busy to call or text, so I figured you were too busy to go out for lunch too," I chided him.

He sheepishly accepted the sandwiches.

"You've been avoiding me," I said.

"I have not."

I frowned, determined not to cry or pick a fight. "Nick, you've always been honest with me. I know you've been avoiding me. Please just tell me why or at least just tell me I'm right so I can stop bothering you."

He sighed and glanced at the front desk. "Karyn, I'll be back in a half hour," he said, turning back to me. "Come on." He swung the door open and waited for me to exit before following me outside.

Nick led me to a bench about fifty yards from the police station. It was a beautiful spring day, with birds chirping and a warm sun compensating for the slight chilly breeze. We sat and I waited for him to talk.

"I guess I have been avoiding you but I already feel like a dick about it, so I don't need a lecture." He opened the bag and pulled out a sandwich, offering me a bite. I shook my head.

"After everything you told me last time, about your feelings for David and everything, I guess I just don't know how to be around you."

I nodded. Obviously, given the timing of his sudden disappearance in my life, I had figured there was a connection there. "You told me everything I was feeling was completely normal."

Nick shrugged. "And it is. That's why I feel like such a jerk. It took me months to get over my fiancée, so I'd never expect you to be over your husband so quickly." He took a few more bites.

"Nick, from the start, you told me the reason you were fine with hanging out with me so much was *because* I was still in love with David and now you're saying we can't hang out at all for that exact reason. That doesn't make sense!"

"Okay, if you want honesty, my issue is with David.

Everything I've seen and learned about him makes him seem like a worthless piece of shit. He's verbally abusive and manipulative and doesn't appreciate what you have to offer. I don't like how he treats you and I don't think you should get back together with him." Nick paused to catch his breath.

"I have no problem with you still having feelings for him, but I can't be part of Team Win-David-Back anymore." Nick said.

"Oh."

He reached over and rubbed my back. "You deserve better than David, Chelsea. Everybody sees that except you, and the worst part is that you're going to get exactly what you want. Any day now, he's going to come crawling back when he realizes he lost the best thing in his life, and I'm not sure I can handle seeing you take him back after everything he's done."

I slumped my head into my hands. I had no options, basically no friends now, and couldn't see any route that wasn't lose-lose at this point. "Are you saying we can't be friends if I go back to David?"

Nick laughed. "Chelsea, it takes all the self-control I have not to punch him in the jaw every time I see him. I seriously don't think I can hold it together if he moves back in, especially when he starts making you miserable again, which he will." He paused. "And I'd be lying if I said I didn't like the sex part of our friendship."

I shook my head. "That isn't fair."

He shrugged. "You asked me to be honest."

I grimaced as the old "be careful what you wish for" adage floated through my head.

"You can't actually think we would still be doing this if

you went back to your husband. How exactly would that work? You think David would ever be okay with us hanging out if you got back together? Would you just lie and tell him we were never intimate? Because if it were me, I wouldn't want my wife being friends with a man she'd recently had sex with."

I knew he was right, but I wasn't back with David now. And I possibly wouldn't ever be. I'd done everything I could think of to win him back and yet I was no closer to my goal than the day he left.

"Here's the thing, Nick. All of my married friends are also David's friends, so I don't feel very connected to them right now. It's just too awkward. And aside from Jen, I don't have many single friends, and Jen is completely incommunicado until after tax season. So you are literally my only friend right now, and I really need you."

He sighed, dropping his hand down to my waist, still eating with the other hand. "I've really missed hanging out with you," he finally said.

"Me too. And if anybody can help me get over David, it has to be you."

He grinned. "I'm that much better in bed than all your other men, huh?"

I rolled my eyes, nudging him playfully. "I just want things to go back to normal between us. I miss the friends with benefits thing."

"Me too," he agreed. "But I'm serious—I'm not helping you win back that asshole. I don't even want to hear about your ridiculous plans."

"Deal," I agreed quickly.

Some voices came over his walkie talkie then, and he reached to lower the volume.

"It's still the perfect arrangement," I continued. "I mean,

as long as I'm still hung up on you-know-who, you still get to have sex without those pesky commitments you're so afraid of. That's exactly what you said you wanted."

Nick stared down at the ground, then wiped his mouth on a napkin and checked his watch. "That is what I said," he agreed. He shook his head and stood. "I should get back. Thanks for lunch."

I nodded, but detected a slight change in his demeanor that concerned me. "Want to come over for a drink later?"

"I really do have plans already tonight," he said. "Promise. But maybe tomorrow? I could bring pizza. There's a game at 7."

"I could cook," I said.

He shook his head furiously. "I don't need to see the fire department tomorrow."

"Fine."

Nick grinned, and walked me back to my car.

"Hey, you never even asked about my good news," I said.

He narrowed his eyes. "I assumed it involved David."

I scoffed. "Hardly. No, my agent called yesterday and there's a publisher in New York who wants to meet with me to discuss my manuscript. I might have a publishing deal!"

Nick frowned with disbelief. "Are you joking?"

I shook my head.

"But that's so quick. They just sent it out!"

"I know. And now I have to figure out what to do with marketing plans and book covers and exclusive rights contracts and blah blah blah. I'm so excited!"

"I knew you could do it," he said. "I'm proud of you for having the guts to send it out. That couldn't have been easy."

I remembered how nervous I was about sending my hard work to my agent for rejection and criticism, but it all seemed so distant now. I smiled proudly.

"Forget the game then. Let's go out someplace fancy to celebrate tomorrow night. Dinner, drinks, dancing, whatever. I'll make reservations and I can pick you up at a quarter till seven. Deal?"

"Deal."

19

———

The next evening was perfect. I felt beautiful in the short black dress I'd chosen, Nick looked mouth-watering in his shirt and tie, and conversation flowed smoothly over drinks and dinner. Every aspect of our meal felt like a traditional date, except that neither of us was awkward or nervous around the other.

But tonight, I wasn't letting my confusion about our relationship get the best of me. I was living in the moment, enjoying my martinis and steak, gazing dreamily into Nick's eyes while he spoke, and squeezing his butt on the dance floor when no one was looking. It felt good to relax and just enjoy the night.

Nick must have felt the same way because as soon as we left the restaurant, he suggested stopping someplace for coffee.

"Nobody drinks coffee at night except in the movies. How would you ever fall asleep?"

He laughed. "Maybe I don't plan on falling asleep."

The implication of his words gave me goosebumps. "Fine. But I'm ordering decaf."

I shivered, and Nick wrapped his arm around my shoulder, pulling me closer. As we turned the corner, the wind blasted into us and I tucked my face into his shoulder. A moment later, he stopped abruptly and I looked up to see a man with a black, hooded sweatshirt standing right in front of us, a gun pointed directly at me.

"Gimme your purse," he said.

I froze. Nick dropped his arm from my back and then nudged me. "Give him your purse."

I loosened my grip on the purse and Nick tossed it to the guy. My eyes grew wide. Wasn't the benefit of sleeping with a cop that you don't get mugged? Well, that and fewer parking tickets.

"You got what you wanted, leave us alone," Nick said, stepping slightly in front of me.

The man considered this, then waved the gun. "Gimme your wallet."

Nick sighed, glanced at me, then reached around to his back pocket. In an instant, his gun was out. "Police! Drop your weapon!" he shouted.

The man cursed and took off running.

"Damn it," Nick mumbled. "Get inside that store, Chelsea. I'll be right back." And he took off after the guy.

I weighed the pros of heading into the store like Nick suggested—warmth and safety being the first that came to mind, but I decided instead to keep my eyes on Nick—and my purse. I started off after them, my heart pounding. Just as I was beginning to think through the scenario and realize, with panic, that Nick could get shot, I saw them collapse up ahead. I inched forward slowly and then heaved a sigh of relief.

Nick was straddling the guy's back, cuffing him. He had

both guns wedged visibly in the back of his pants as he stood up, tugging the guy to a standing position and then forcing him down against a nearby wall. "Don't even think about moving," he said. He retrieved his cell phone and made a call to his station and then stepped back.

"Jesus, Chelsea," he jumped when he saw me. "I thought I told you to wait inside. This isn't safe."

"You seem to have the situation under control," I said.

He picked my purse off the pavement, dusted it off, and handed it to me.

"Yeah, she hot," the handcuffed guy said. "You hitting that?"

Nick kicked the guy's foot. "Shut up."

"Do you always carry handcuffs when you're off duty?" I asked, surprised. I knew by now that he always carried a gun, sometimes two, but I thought I would've noticed handcuffs.

Nick shook his head and smiled. "No, actually, I had this pair in my coat pocket thinking it might be fun for later," he said softly so the mugger couldn't hear.

"Yeah, dude, what's up with these cuffs? They so tight my hands can't breathe."

"They're smaller than the standard," Nick admitted.

Within a few minutes, a police car arrived, followed shortly by a second. Nick spoke with the officers for a few minutes and then they loaded the guy into the car. My teeth were chattering uncontrollably by this point. Nick turned and saw me, gave me a quick hug, then told me to get in the police car to warm up.

"I don't want to ride with him!" I said, gesturing to the guy, now cursing wildly from the backseat.

"The other car," he said, helping me in. An eternity later,

he came to get me. He ducked his head into the first car before closing the door.

"I'll see you in the morning," he said to the mugger.

"You better be hitting that tonight," the guy replied.

Nick slammed the door and we began the walk back to his car. "I guess coffee is out of the question now," he said.

"Coffee?" I laughed. "I can't stop thinking about how crazy you are, chasing some guy down for my purse."

He reached for my hand. The gesture was nice, but oddly out of character for him. Nick must have thought so too, because he quickly dropped my hand and draped his arm across my shoulder again. "I wasn't just about your purse, you know. He was a kid, and he was high."

"Um, and armed."

Nick shrugged. "I want to know where a kid gets guns and drugs. That's why I chased him. I'll talk with him in the morning."

"Will he go to jail?"

"Depends. If it's his first offense, we might be able to get him into a special school or some transitional rehabilitation center." He paused. "And you'll have to decide if you're pressing charges."

I shuddered. "He came out of nowhere. I can't imagine what would've happened if I'd been alone, or even with..." I didn't want to mention my ex's name, so I stopped.

"He would've taken your purse and left," Nick assured me, the look in his eyes less certain than the tone in his voice.

"You're sexy when you work," I said.

We stopped walking and Nick guided me a few steps backwards until we were off the sidewalk. I stared into his rich brown eyes as he reached his hands up, placing them on my cheeks. And then he kissed me, pushing my back against the wall of the building, his hands firmly holding my face against his until he was certain I wasn't going to stop the kiss, and then wandering down my body, landing at my hands, which he pinned to my sides. His body pressed into mine and all I could think about was the warmth of his tongue against mine, the tantalizing smell of his cologne, and the familiar ache in my groin.

The kiss ended gradually, Nick slowly retracting his tongue and inching his lips away, leaving his face so close to mine that his quickened breath still poured out onto my cheek. He stared back at me and our eyes locked. Finally, he licked his lips and dropped my hands.

"We should get back to the car before we get mugged again," he said.

I stumbled, my legs weak from his kiss. "Another kiss like that and I'll just give them my purse."

Nick paused and grinned, and we walked to the car quietly. As he drove, the excitement of the evening started to wear off and I was feeling a bit more like myself.

"Hey, why have I never been to your apartment?" I asked. "You've stayed at my place tons and I've never even seen yours."

He breathed a laugh. "It's not that impressive. The reason we always end up at your place is because you insist that I'm just dropping you off and that I won't be staying. If you acknowledged the possibility of sex up front, then we could go to whichever place is closer."

I considered this and then reached my hand to his lap and resting it firmly over his goods. "Which is closer?"

"Mine," he said, inhaling sharply.

We were kissing again before he'd finished unlocking

his apartment door. It was dark and smelled clean, but other than that, I didn't form any impressions because Nick was already nudging my coat off my shoulders. I helped him, and he quickly yanked my dress up over my head. Within seconds, I was down to my bra, and Nick hoisted me onto the counter. I unfastened his belt while he worked on the bra, Nick reaching around to grab his gun right before I let it drop to the ground with his pants. He placed it on the counter a few feet away, tugged down his boxer briefs, and pulled me to him.

I wrapped my legs around his waist, arched my head back as he kissed and sucked the tender skin around my neck, moving his way down to my breasts. A minute of fore-play was enough. I wanted him then.

I dug my fingers into his back, gave him a pleading stare, and we made love, quickly and breathlessly. My whole body shook as I came, and Nick lifted me off the counter onto his body until we both stilled, satisfied.

He gently placed me back on the counter and kissed my neck one last time. He breathed a soft laugh. "Damn, girl."

I smiled. "I guess the hero thing works for me."

We were quiet for another minute before Nick cleared his throat and spoke again. "Well, this is my apartment. Do you want the tour?"

I scooted off the counter and dressed. Nick pulled on his boxer briefs and left the rest of his clothes on the floor, switching on a light. The apartment was much cleaner than I'd expected from a bachelor pad, and larger.

"You've met the kitchen," he said, leading me out to a larger room with a leather couch, oversized chair and ottoman, and gigantic flat screen TV. "Here's the living room, here's a bathroom, laundry, and extra room," he said, as we walked past a half bathroom that was clearly never used, a closet-laundry room, and a small extra bedroom equipped with a futon, desk, and workout equipment. "Here's the main bathroom, and here's my bedroom," he said.

I peered into his bathroom. It was decent sized, with a tub-shower combo and walk in closet. A few pertinent toiletries were on the counter, but other than that it was neat. His bedroom was also orderly, with a queen-sized bed, a bookshelf, and a dresser. Another smaller flat screen TV was on the dresser. I was pleasantly surprised at the size and cleanliness of his apartment. Either he wasn't home much or he had a cleaning lady. Another perk of the suburbs, apparently, was that even the apartments were nice.

"Make yourself at home," he said. "I'll just be a minute." He stepped into the bathroom.

I glanced at the two photos on his dresser, one clearly of family and the other of him skiing with some guys, and then caught myself remembering the evening, how he'd bravely chased down a hooded gunman without a second thought.

By the time he emerged from the bathroom a moment later, I had stripped naked and was sprawled out on his bed. He seemed surprised, but shrugged and smiled. "I can work with that," he said, lowering himself over me. We made love a second time, and then lay in bed long after, my leg draped over his body, his arm roped around mine.

"So do you like my apartment?"

"Mmm hmm," I said, feeling drugged from the sex.

"I'm glad we skipped the coffee," Nick said.

I moaned softly in agreement and kissed his chest gently. He brushed my hair out of my face and our eyes met. "I love," I began, "that you're so into your job." As I spoke, I swear I saw his eyes widen hopefully before he blinked, a vivid but brief flash of disappointment crossing his face. He opened his mouth as though he were going to respond, but instead he kissed the top of my head.

We went to sleep shortly after that, but I woke up several times in the night, adrenaline from the mugging still coursing through my veins. By three, I was jittery and bored. I glanced over at Nick, who seemed to be sleeping soundly. Typical man.

He was on his back, and even in the dark, I could see his perfectly sculpted chest muscles. I lifted the sheets and glanced downward, watching his toned stomach rise up and down with each calm breath. I couldn't see much past that, but now I had an idea of what might help me fall back to sleep. I reached my hand downward and gently stroked his penis.

He groaned almost immediately, and then his eyes opened groggily. He reached for my hand and clasped it, halting my movement. "I'm sleeping," he said.

"Well, at least one part of you is awake now," I said, giving him a firmer squeeze.

He moaned again, then moved my hand. "You can't possibly want more."

"I can't sleep," I explained, and then I ducked under the covers, my mouth picking up where my hand left off. I couldn't have been down there for more than a minute or two when Nick's hands reached under my armpits and pulled me upwards until I was straddling him, my face even with his.

"Fine," he said. "You win."

I sighed with relief as he pushed into me, his warm length filling me, bringing me instantly to the peak of desire. Nick's hands gently caressed my breasts and my hands roamed his chest, my nails digging into his firm skin with every ecstatic tingle jolting through my body. We locked eyes, and then waves of pleasure shook through me, rocking my hips faster and faster until we both lay still.

I slumped onto his body, exhausted. He didn't say anything, and somehow, we both went back to sleep. When I awoke, it was morning, and Nick was trying to slither out from underneath me.

I sighed happily as flashes of the previous night came back to me. He playfully smacked my butt and then scooted me off him.

"Where are you going?"

"Shower," he said. "I'm all sticky."

I gave myself a once over. "Me too." I sat up. No sense in wasting water by showering separately.

He stared at me like a deer in headlights as I followed him into the bathroom a minute later when I heard the water running. He shook his head. "I'm going to need IV fluids if you attack me again. Chelsea, I'm spent."

I giggled. "That sounds like a challenge."

He was already shampooing his hair when I climbed in. He shook his head again, but smiled and handed me the shampoo. I lathered my hair, then turned to face the water as I rinsed out the suds. Right as I was about to step out from under the water, Nick pressed his body against my back. I smiled. He was all slippery from the soap, warm from the water, and hard in all the right places.

"Fine," he whispered into my ear. "But this is the last time for at least twelve hours, deal?"

"Deal," I mumbled, as he we made love one more time.

The water was starting to get cold by the time we climbed out of the shower. Nick tossed me a towel, then helped dry me off. He handed me an unopened toothbrush from the cabinet under the sink and then began to shave.

"I get my own toothbrush?"

"Babe, after last night, I'd give you your own yacht if I could afford it."

WITHIN AN HOUR, we'd finished breakfast and dressed, him in a sexy professional but non-uniformed cop outfit, me in the same clothes I'd worn the night before, minus the underpants which I'd decided were better off in my purse than being worn again. Nick drove me to my neighborhood, and I squeezed his thigh as we approached my driveway.

"That was fun," I said. "We should do it again."

"Minus the mugging, right?"

I smiled and started to lean in to kiss him goodbye, but then I noticed the car parked in front of my house. It was David's red Acura. "Fuck."

Nick slowed, as though trying to debate if it was too late to simply drive on by, but then pulled into my driveway.

"Were you expecting him?" he asked.

I shook my head.

"I can come in with you," he offered.

"No, you go on to work. It's okay."

"Are you sure?" Nick asked, that police-officer level of concern clear on his face.

I nodded. "Positive. You go gloat to that kid about your sexual exploits."

He laughed. "Call me when he leaves."

I climbed out of the car and stared at David for a moment. He was sitting in the driver's seat, looking straight ahead. He wasn't watching me, and he didn't appear to be on the phone or anything like that. I followed his stare, my stomach clenching when I realized he was glaring at Nick. I took a deep breath and let myself into the house, expecting David to follow soon after. He did.

I glanced quickly around the room, confirming there wasn't anything that revealed I hadn't been home all night. David closed the door behind him. He looked furious, but as always, handsome.

I poured myself a glass of water and waited for him to speak.

"Where the hell were you?"

I narrowed my eyes. "Good morning, David. How are you?"

"Why doesn't my key work?"

"I had the locks changed ages ago."

"Then give me a new key."

"No."

"Chelsea, it's my house, too."

"You moved out, remember? If you ever need anything, you can call and find a time that I'm here. I don't want you barging in during the middle of the night again."

"I only came over then because I wanted to see if you were having an affair."

I rolled my eyes, but he continued. "And now I know the truth."

"What truth?" I asked. "That I went out to breakfast with a friend?"

"It was that cop, right? The one who's always at your house. Did you spend the night with him?"

"How's Traci?" I asked.

He shook his head dismissively. "I've been honest with you, Chelsea. We're still married, and I deserve to know the truth."

I sat at the breakfast bar. "Fine. I was mugged last night, and I was pretty shaken up after, so Nick waited to get my statement this morning. Now he's on his way to the station to interrogate the guy."

David's expression altered immediately. He stepped closer. "You were mugged? Are you okay?"

I nodded. "He took my purse at gunpoint, but the cops caught him." I held my purse up. "And I got my purse back."

"Jesus, Chelsea. Why didn't you call me?"

I snorted. Did he really think calling him and having Traci answer his phone would make me feel better?

"Chelsea, even though we're separated, you know I still care about you. You should've called me."

"Yeah, well, I didn't." I shrugged and stood. "Why did you come by anyway? Shouldn't you be at work now?"

David frowned, his expression so sheepish that I almost felt bad for snapping at him. "I just thought we should talk. The 60-day waiting period is over, so…"

He didn't need to finish the sentence. I knew what he wanted. He wanted to know if I was going to contest the divorce when he filed. I'd been waiting for this moment, for this precise conversation, but I just couldn't do it now. I just didn't have it in me to fight for him this morning.

"You really didn't spend the night with him?" David asked, his face softened.

I looked him straight in the eye. "Yeah, David. Actually, I did. I got mugged and then went straight to the cop's house and we fucked over and over the whole night long." I panicked as soon as the words left my mouth, but within an instant, it was clear that David thought it was sarcasm.

"Whatever, Chelsea. Look, we need to talk sometime, but maybe when you're not so worked up over this mugging."

I took a deep breath and nodded. He was right. "I could meet you for lunch sometime this week."

"Why don't I come by the house instead? We could get dinner. How's Wednesday?"

I shrugged in my most noncommittal agreement, and he left.

I TRIED to work once I was alone, but was too exhausted, so I finally gave in and took a long nap. When I awoke, I decided to offset my feelings of laziness by attempting some housework. I was barely into my first load of laundry when my phone rang.

I glanced at the caller ID and smiled. "Hi Nick," I answered sweetly. "Have you cured the bad guy of his purse snatching ways?"

He chuckled. "I don't know about that, but he gave us the name of his dealer and the guy who sold him the gun, so it's a start at least. It's not gang related, so I might get to head up this investigation, too, which would mean a promotion."

"Oh my God!" I shrieked. "You're going to make detective!"

"Nothing's definite," he said. "Just a hunch. So, everything went okay this morning?"

"Yeah, I told him about the mugging and he even looked a little concerned." I didn't mention that he was also insanely jealous when he saw Nick. "Anyway, the mandatory 60-day waiting period is over, so he just wanted to finalize the divorce details."

There was a long silence before Nick spoke. "Does that mean you're going through with it?"

"I guess." Suddenly, this discussion felt strange and uncomfortable. I decided to change the subject. "I couldn't really focus anyway. I was a little distracted."

"Oh yeah? By what?" There was a smile in Nick's voice.

"I couldn't remember if I shampooed my hair this morning," I lied.

"Mmm, you did. And you rinsed really really well."

I sighed happily.

"If you're not too busy, this might be an appropriate time for you to bring some cookies by the station. I did save you from a mugger, after all."

"I'm pretty sure I already adequately thanked you for that heroic endeavor."

"Yeah," he agreed. "But I'm starving. I ate lunch early and my stomach is still growling. It's like all my energy and nutrient resources were depleted in the last twelve hours."

I giggled and checked the time. "Drink more liquids. It'll take me an hour."

We hung up and I began selecting the ingredients from my pantry, still smiling. I mixed the batter and scooped the first half onto the sheets in neat rounded balls. I was trying a new kind, chocolate cherry almond, so I dipped the spoon back into the bowl of dough for a taste before sliding the cookie sheets into the warm oven. Perfect.

I set the timer and sprinted upstairs to change clothes. I hadn't dried my hair at Nick's, so it fell in casual, loose waves. I rubbed a little shine-enhancing serum on the ends and decided it looked good enough. I dabbed on a little more makeup and dashed back down the stairs with a minute left on the timer. While the cookies cooled, I dialed Jen.

"I got mugged last night," I said when she answered. "And then I had sex with Nick four times and spent the night at his place and David was here to talk about the divorce when Nick brought me home."

Jen didn't answer.

"Jen? Jen?"

"Yeah, I'm here. That's just a lot to process. I don't know where to start."

"I'm bringing cookies to the station in a little bit."

"Of course you are," she laughed. "Did you say four times?"

"Yep. In roughly eight hours."

"Jesus, he really is good."

"Yep."

"And then David…?"

"Came to tell me that we can file for divorce now. Pretended he just wanted to know if I was going to contest it, but he seemed super jealous when he saw Nick."

"So your plan might be working?"

"Hard to say." I paused, tempted to admit I wasn't that focused on my plan anymore, but I held back. It didn't matter, she knew me too well anyway.

"Has this thing with Nick changed your mind?"

"It's just sex with Nick."

"Mmm hmm," she agreed, in the same tone she used when I told her I could keep gummy bears in the pantry and only eat a few each day.

I sighed. "I've got to go."

"To see Nick," she supplied. "Hey, Chels, did you say you were mugged?"

"Yep. I'm fine though. Nick chased down the guy, tackled him, got my purse back and then held him until backup arrived."

She laughed. "Of course he did. Be careful Chelsea."

I hung up, not sure what she meant, and began arranging the cookies onto a plate.

~

THE STATION PARKING lot was on the empty side, typical for a Sunday. I marched in, comfortable with the routine now, and held up the cookies so Marge could see them. She slid the plexiglass window open. "Who are these for?"

"Nick," I said with a smile.

She nodded and disappeared for a minute. The door behind her opened and in walked Officer Brown with another officer. He smiled at me.

"More cookies?" he asked.

I nodded. "These are for Nick, though. I was mugged last night."

"I heard. They've still got the guy locked up here if you want to go rough him up a little." He leaned forward and grinned.

I smiled. I was really starting to like cute, flirty cops.

"Hey, that's mine," Nick shouted, popping through the security door with a smile.

Officer Brown glanced at him. "The cookies or the lady?"

I turned to Nick, expectantly awaiting his response.

He blushed and his eyes narrowed. "The cookies," he finally said.

Officer Brown laughed and started to the door just as Nick tilted his head down and kissed me. It wasn't a lingering kiss, but it was familiar and telling nonetheless.

"Mmm, you taste like cookies," he said.

"And you just kissed me in front of your coworkers." I said nervously, nodding my head towards Officer Brown who had paused by the door, seemingly surprised. "I already told him we weren't dating."

Nick laughed. "That's right. We're not dating, Eric. She's just using me for sex."

Officer Brown laughed now and went back into the station. I felt my cheeks turning bright red.

"I can't believe you just said that."

He grinned proudly. "He thinks I was kidding."

"You were kidding."

Now Nick laughed outright. "No I wasn't, but I'm not complaining either." And before I could protest, he kissed me again.

20

The next few days were a blur. Katherine called to tell me they wanted me in New York as soon as possible. Having no other pressing plans, I agreed to leave the next day and immediately set about packing. I would only be in town for two nights, so I wasn't going to have time for much sight-seeing, but I still packed several casual outfits just in case I had free time in between my meetings. Once I had most of my wardrobe strewn about on my bed, I realized I lacked an attractive business suit.

Jen was trapped at work for the most part but agreed to meet me at the mall once I'd narrowed it down to my final two selections. One was a tailored grey pantsuit, and the other a more traditional black suit with a skirt. Jen immediately voted for the grey.

"Even though it's pants, it looks more feminine," she asserted. "Plus your ass looks amazing in that material."

I blushed and disregarded the disapproving look from the mom waiting to use the large mirror when I finished.

Suit in hand, I returned home to finish my packing and called Nick to see if he could sneak away from working the night shift to say a proper goodbye before I left. Sadly, he was busy, so I took it as a sign that I was meant to arrive in New York well rested and went to bed early.

The next morning, as my cab arrived at the airport, I realized I was supposed to have dinner with David that night. I paid the cabbie, checked in for my flight, then called David once I was comfortably seated with my coffee at the gate.

I chewed on the edge of my lip as the phone rang, dreading the tone his voice was sure to have since he would assume I was simply trying to stall the divorce by postponing our dinner.

"Hello, Chelsea," he said warmly, completely throwing me off from my prepared speech.

"Hi," I stammered. "How are you?"

"I'm well, thank you. How are you?"

"Uh good. So listen, I actually had something come up and wanted to know if you'd be free next week for dinner instead. Maybe Tuesday night?"

There was a silence and I assumed he was either checking his calendar or thinking evil thoughts about me. "Sure, that would work for me. Shall I pick you up, say 7 o'clock?"

I wasn't sure I could handle riding in a car with him. If things went horribly wrong in our discussion, I'd be stranded at a restaurant. "I'll meet you there. You can pick the restaurant, just text me the name."

"Oh. Okay, so..."

Just then I heard the pre-boarding announcement for my flight. "Sorry, got to go. See you Tuesday," I interrupted.

My phone buzzed right as I disconnected the call.

It was a text from Nick. "Knock em dead," he wrote, followed quickly by, "Bonus points for sending me nudie pics from the hotel. Triple points for nudie pics by the Statue of Liberty."

I giggled and typed, "unless you have some connections to the NYPD, I don't think I'll try that one."

We wrote back a few more times as I boarded the plane and then I switched my phone off for the flight, pulling out a magazine and daydreaming the duration of the short trip.

A car met me at the airport and deposited me at my hotel, where I had a few hours to freshen up before I met my agent for pre-dinner drinks. Although she'd represented my work for years, I'd never actually met Katherine. I had seen her picture on the agency website and we'd spoken many times, so I felt like I knew her, but at the same time, this was different.

I slipped into the same black dress I'd worn for my pre-mugging dinner with Nick, pairing it with a trendy denim jacket and lots of jewelry to keep it casual, then took the elevator downstairs to the lobby where I spotted Katherine immediately.

"Chelsea, how are you?" she gushed, rushing forward to hug me as though we were old friends. "You look gorgeous. It's so good to finally meet you!"

"Thanks, you too," I mumbled, starting to question if I was in over my head.

She flashed another excessively eager smile and led me towards the hotel bar. "I thought it would be good for us to chat some before we meet with your editing team, just to make sure we're on the same page. So let's have a drink here and then we'll head out to meet up with the rest for a drink and dinner. Sound good?" She nodded enthusiastically at her own question.

"Perfect!" I replied, mimicking her peppy attitude and following her to a barstool.

We ordered and made small talk for a bit before she launched into her canned lecture.

"Tonight is about getting to know each other, Chelsea, so don't worry too much about the business side of things. At this point, they want to know that you're going to be easy to work with and that you'll be an asset to your sales when it comes to marketing and publicity. You want them to like you," she said, pausing emphatically.

"Okay..." I replied uncertainly.

"Don't worry!" she gushed. "Just be yourself. You've got this," she patted my hand. "Tomorrow we will meet up for lunch and discuss what to expect. They might get into some edits, which is fine, and you should be amenable to all of their suggestions but agree to nothing. They might bring up the contract, too, but don't you worry about that—I'll hammer out all of those details. Most of the work can be done remotely, so they'll likely send some cover designs to get your input on and can deal with all the final revisions via email, but don't be surprised if they want to discuss your preferences and vision now."

Katherine paused to take a breath before continuing, "Friday morning they want to do a photo shoot. It might end up on the jacket of the book but more likely will just be for some preliminary publicity."

"I didn't bring anything to wear to a photo shoot," I interrupted, panicked.

"Just be yourself," she reiterated. "If you hate the pictures, we can get them redone at a local photographer's when you return home. Readers want to see you looking like you anyway."

I nodded nervously and chugged the rest of my martini.

The rest of the evening was overwhelming and wonderful. Katherine treated me like a friend she'd known for years the entire time, and by the end of the night, her can-do attitude was really rubbing off on me. I wasn't sure if it was the magical black dress, the sparkle of the big city, or my cheerleader-sidekick, but I felt more confident than I had in years.

As soon as I returned to my hotel room, I called Jen to give her the full play-by-play and then called Nick with the abbreviated version as I wolfed down half the contents of my mini-fridge without even worrying if the publishing house would cover that, too, when they paid my hotel bill.

When I fell asleep, I felt relaxed and powerful, and I awoke in much the same mood. I grabbed a bagel and coffee in the hotel lobby on my way out the door early the next morning, ready to do some sightseeing and shopping before my late lunch. Certain I'd never master the subway system in time, I stuck with stores I could reach on foot, confident I could justify at least one nice outfit for my photo shoot based on my publishing advance.

I returned to the hotel to freshen up before lunch and then met up with Katherine and a slightly different group of people from the publishing house for a delicious seafood lunch by the harbor. I spent the evening sightseeing and sampled local cuisine from several food trucks near Times Square before tucking in early, not brave enough to immerse myself in the big city nightlife or to risk looking hungover in my photos.

The next morning, I packed my bags and spent extra time getting ready for my photo shoot and then checked out of the hotel. I went straight from the photo shoot to the airport, barely having time to update Jen on the rest of my trip before the flight took off.

As soon as the cab dropped me off at my house, I called

Nick, who immediately agreed to come by with pizza when he got off work.

That left me just enough time to run to the grocery and then unpack. I changed back into my new suit, omitting the blouse under the suit jacket and pairing it with a pair of reading glasses that just screamed sexy schoolteacher.

Nick walked in the door shortly after seven, still in his casual work attire and carrying a box of pizza with two large paper sacks on top. "I wasn't sure if you wanted breadsticks or wings, so I brought both," he said, plopping it all down on the counter. "I didn't stop by the liquor store, though, so do you have any..." His voice trailed off as he glanced up and saw me leaned over the counter in my sexiest pose.

"I have lots of beer, if that's what you want," I said, trying not to smile at the bewildered look on his face.

"What's beer?" he mumbled, lunging across the kitchen and sweeping me into his arms.

He kissed me firmly, immediately making me feel, as always, like it had been too long since I'd last been kissed that way. He quickly unbuttoned the suit jacket, revealing the rest of the black satin bra, and he roamed his cool hands freely across my warm skin. He had just begun to nibble the side of my neck and unbutton my pants when I pulled back.

"The pizza might get cold," I cautioned. "Aren't you hungry?"

"Not for food," he murmured, gazing up at my face. "Are those your glasses?"

I laughed and shook my head. "I can't see a thing with them. They just seemed to complete the look, though."

I slid the glasses off and freed my hair from the elastic band, tousling it behind me as they do on shampoo commercials.

Nick grinned. "If this is what you wore to your meeting, I

bet they gave you a very warm welcome." He pulled my suit pants down and dropped to his knees in front of me, kissing my thighs and working his way upward.

"Not quite this friendly of a welcome," I replied. My pulse quickened as his mouth reached the apex of my thighs and I gripped the counter for support as Nick's tongue reminded me exactly what I'd been missing the past few days.

He gently nudged me further apart with his hands, tracing a finger through the dampness before plunging it into me. I bit my lip to avoid groaning with pleasure but soon felt too dizzy to control myself. Nick held firmly to my thigh with his free hand and then the moment I began to explode into exquisite waves of pleasure around him, he gripped my waist with both hands so I didn't collapse.

I let him support me for another minute while I caught my breath and then began undressing him. He let me do some of the work but then carried me to the couch and finished undressing himself. We made love fervently, as though it had been weeks rather than days since our needs had last been met.

After, Nick flipped me over on top of him and delicately brushed my hair off my forehead while I lay on his chest. "So the meeting went well, I presume?"

I glanced up at him and smiled. "Yeah, it really did. I thought I'd be stressed about all the changes they'll want to make to my book, but really it was just fun. They all flattered me the entire time, and it felt like we were all collaborating on something really good."

"Well, you were. And I don't think it was flattery, Chelsea. Your book is really great. They're lucky to get to work with you."

I flashed him a dramatic eye roll. "I already slept with you, so you don't have to say things like that."

"Maybe I want another round," he teased.

The mere thought of that sent shivers up my spine. But then my stomach growled. "I'm starving," I admitted.

"Me too."

I climbed off him and retrieved my bra and panties. He pulled on his boxer briefs and pants, but I hesitated before handing him his shirt and instead pulled it over my own head. It wasn't the softest material in the world, but it was large enough to mostly cover my butt and then I wouldn't have to worry about dry cleaning my suit.

Nick nodded approvingly.

"Would I make a good cop?"

Nick chuckled. "You would make a terrible cop. But you're sexy as hell in that. Just don't get pizza sauce all over it." He kissed me slowly, slipping his fingers up the back of the shirt to let me know he wasn't too concerned about his uniform.

He didn't stay the night, but that was fine with me. I needed to rest up from my trip anyway. Plus, the publisher had wanted to move along with a local launch party, to get a little pre-publication publicity going for my book, so Katherine was flying in Wednesday morning to finalize the preparations. I'd worried it was all moving too fast, but she assured me this was just a small gathering for a few local writers and then my close friends and family. Apparently, there would be a real launch party once the editing was finished and the book was ready for release. Still, that left me no time to buy a new dress.

I stared into my closet, flummoxed, until I spotted the sparkly red dress I'd bought for David's work party. I traced my finger along the slick fabric, debating whether it would spoil my special night to wear a dress intended for a much different event, but finally concluded if anything, it would just redeem the dress. It would tell the world I didn't need my spouse's fancy parties to justify a new dress—I have my own awesome career. Well, or it would if anyone but Jen knew what I'd purchased the dress for originally.

21

I awoke on Tuesday morning still basking in the glow of great sex and a promising book deal. I spent a few hours calling to invite people to my party and hashing out catering details with Katherine's assistant and totally forgot about my dinner with David until a text arrived from him at five o'clock with the name of a local restaurant. I debated postponing it again, but knew he'd accuse me of stalling if I did that, so instead I just called Jen for a last minute pep talk and some wardrobe advice.

"Chelsea, just remember what we discussed and you'll do great. Just go into the dinner assuming you're going through with the divorce and don't let your emotions get the best of you. Nothing is final until you sign the paperwork, but now is not the time to show weakness."

I agreed and hung up, sighing. She'd helped me pull together the perfect outfit, specifying even what jewelry I should wear, but her advice as to David seemed vague. We had talked about the financial side of things before, so I knew what to expect on that front, but I had no idea what to think about the rest.

I'd been so caught up with my book lately that I hadn't had a chance to focus on the progress—or lack thereof—on my plan. Tonight was when I could see if I had any remaining chance at all of winning David back. That was huge. I should be excited, nervous, and hopeful. But instead I was just, well, blah.

I arrived at the restaurant promptly at seven, knowing how much it peeved David when people were late. He greeted me warmly with a kiss on the cheek, complimented my appearance, and guided me to the table with a hand on my back. I interpreted all of those as good signs, but then again, if there was one thing my experience with David had taught me, it was that I sucked at reading his signs.

We made small talk while perusing the menu, and I forced myself to order a respectable wine instead of the bubbly sweet wine I craved. I felt myself becoming more nervous by the minute. As David spoke about some case he was currently wrapping up, I gazed into his bright blue eyes, trying to siphon some of the comfort I used to feel from him, but there was nothing.

Our food arrived, and it was obvious we both were focused on the business we still had to discuss—the divorce. I took a deep breath while cutting my chicken.

"You wanted to get together so we could discuss the details of the divorce, right?" I said.

David seemed taken aback, and his eyes widened. He chewed a bite, then cautiously answered. "Well, I wanted to know if we would be able to work this out on our own or if we would need a third party to be involved."

"I already consulted with an attorney, but as long as you're prepared to be reasonable, I don't see any reason we can't resolve things amicably."

"You aren't planning on contesting the divorce?"

I took a few small bites, chewed, and swallowed. I felt like I was really holding my own with him, and I wanted to relish every moment of it. "I'm not opposed to getting a divorce, if that's what you mean. I'm keeping the house and the car, of course, but I'm sure we can work something out with that."

David choked on his asparagus. I scooted his water glass towards him as he raised his napkin to his mouth. When he finished coughing, his face was beet red. "When we spoke two months ago, you said you would never agree to a divorce."

I shrugged. "You're living with your paralegal. It's really just a formality at this point, isn't it?"

He winced. We ate in silence for a moment.

"You are still living with Traci, right?"

David cleared his throat awkwardly. "I think I'll be looking for my own place soon."

It took every ounce of self-restraint I could muster not to jump on the table and cheer. "Aww, trouble in paradise?"

David sighed. "You can't afford those mortgage payments on your own," he said. "Especially not when you factor in property insurance, taxes, health insurance, and the car insurance."

This I was prepared for. Jen might occasionally be a flakey friend, but she was a kickass accountant, and she had reviewed all of my finances for me. Between the regular column I'd nailed in lieu of freelancing and the advance I was anticipating on my novel, I could easily cover all my expenses for at least the next two years. And by that time, I would hopefully have another novel ready to sell or at least some royalties from the first one.

"Actually, I can." I replied confidently.

He seemed surprised.

"I'm no longer freelancing. You see, I finally sent my novel in to my agent, and it was going to take so much of my time to work through the editing process with them that I didn't want to waste time on freelancing anymore. When I told the magazine editor that, they were so eager to keep me on that they offered me a regular column."

"Oh, wow. Congratulations. That's what you wanted, isn't it?"

I nodded. "Of course, it's not as exciting as I always figured it would be because I'm so tied up in the publishing process now with my book."

"Which book?"

I smirked. "Oh, you know, the novel I wrote. In my own name. The trashy unpublishable romance, I think you called it."

He blushed. "You found a publisher?"

"More like they found me. We're still negotiating the details, but I think I'll be fine with the house payments." I chewed a few more bites and then realized this was going well. Much better than I'd ever dreamed. I needed to end it before I screwed something up. "You know, I probably should head out soon. I'm still exhausted from my trip to New York."

David was flabbergasted. I'd never before seen the man speechless, and it was priceless.

I stood slowly, smiling as I watched his eyes scan down to my butt. Jen was right—these jeans were definitely worth every penny. "It was nice seeing you. I assume you'd like to draw up the divorce papers yourself, so just send them over whenever it's done. I'll have my lawyer look it over, but like I said, as long as you've got the house and car down correctly, I don't anticipate any problems. Have a good night!"

And with that, I left.

As soon as I'd tipped the valet and pulled out onto the street, I dialed Jen. "It was perfect!" I gushed as soon as she answered. I narrated the key details of the evening, feeling more pumped up and victorious with every rehashed moment.

"You should've seen his face when I walked out," I finished. "Those jeans were perfect. He's definitely coming back to me now."

Jen was uncharacteristically quiet.

"Jen?"

"Yeah, sorry. I'm here. Just thinking."

"Ha! You didn't think I could do it, did you?"

"Chels, you could have any man you wanted, so I never doubted you'd win back David. I just..."

"What?"

"Well, are you sure you still want him?"

I groaned.

"I know you think I was never supportive of your nutty plan to win him back, and that's true, but only because I love you and I think you could do better than him."

"Jen..."

"Hear me out, okay? It's just that you've been really happy this past month. Happier than I remember seeing you when you were with David. I wonder if maybe you don't want to go back to him now. Just because he might agree to take you back now doesn't mean you have to let him move back in. I just want you to think about it before you jump back into something with him."

"Are you kidding? Jen, I called you to celebrate. I'm about to get what I wanted, what I've been working for the past few months, and you can't even be supportive for a minute?"

"I'm sorry Chelsea, but I think you…"

"No," I interrupted, fuming that she'd ruined my good mood. "This has nothing to do with me. This is about you. You're jealous."

She sighed audibly. "You know what Chelsea? You're right. I am jealous. But not because of David. And if you'd stop being so stubborn, you'd see what I mean." And then the line clicked off.

I stared at my phone, appalled. Jen had never hung up on me before. I was tempted to dial her back just so *I* could hang up on *her*, but then I spotted a car in my driveway. It was David's car.

He was standing awkwardly beside the car, his hands in his pockets. David would never lean against a car and practically thought even touching a car was an offense against its pristine paint job.

I pulled past him into the garage and grabbed my purse as he held the door open for me. "How did you beat me here?"

He shrugged. "You don't exactly take the most direct route places. You really should get GPS."

"I like my routes," I insisted.

"Listen, I didn't come here to argue. I just, well, I hadn't just wanted to talk about the divorce at dinner, but then I lost my nerve."

"What did you want to talk about?" I asked, purposefully

dropping my purse so I could bend down in my jeans to retrieve it.

"I, um, I..." he stuttered.

I grinned. "Well?"

"Can I come in?"

"Sure." I unlocked the door and he followed me in.

"Oh wow, you got a new chandelier," he said, pointing to the replacement I made after the owl break-in. "And a new stove."

I shrugged, glad to use my mishaps to my advantage. "I felt like a change. And I've been cooking more. So what did you want to discuss?"

He took a deep breath and I knew he was about to say it. I smiled in anticipation.

"I want to make sure we're not rushing into anything. Divorce is so final, you know? And I admit we've had some rough patches, but we had a lot of good times together, too. Now that we've both seen what else is out there, it seems like we might both be realizing that separating wasn't necessarily our best decision."

I raised my eyebrows at his misuse of the term "our," but decided, in the interest of reconciliation, that I wouldn't mention it. I cleared my throat. "So what are you saying?"

David shuffled his feet nervously. "I think we should try again, Chelsea."

My heart thudded uncontrollably at the sound of those words...the words I'd been waiting to hear for well over 60 days now. I wanted to shriek with glee, to jump around shouting "take that, Traci," but before I could say anything, he kissed me.

I kissed him back, eagerly waiting for the sparks to fly, but I was just too overwhelmed to focus.

"I missed you," he said, between kisses.

"I missed you too," I whispered back.

We kissed again, but my phone buzzed loudly and I pulled away to check the text. It was from my agent. "I should probably call her in a minute," I said.

"Now?"

I shrugged. "It might be urgent. This is a critical time for the book."

"Yeah, you'll have to tell me more about that. It sounds really, uh, time-consuming."

"It's pretty exciting, actually. It's always been a dream of mine, so.... Oh! I almost forgot. There's a reception tomorrow. Just a little party my agent is throwing to celebrate the book and kick off the marketing campaign. You could come if you want."

He nodded hesitantly. "Of course. Yes. That sounds great. But we have a lot of other things to discuss, too. Like living situations, for example."

My phone buzzed again. "Right." I tried to read the message without seeming too obvious. "We should sit down and hash that all out sometime. Maybe we could grab a coffee after the party tomorrow?"

David looked taken aback, but quickly agreed. "I'll let you get to your call now. Text me the details for the party tomorrow."

I nodded and he kissed me chastely before leaving.

THE NEXT NIGHT, I felt like a princess. When I walked into the room, my friends and family clapped. My agent gave a short, embarrassing speech, and then I was free to mingle. There were waiters carrying around trays of hors d'oeuvres that looked fantastic, but every time I tried to snag one, someone pulled me aside for a chat. Luckily, I was able to get my hands on plenty of white wine. I was just about to reach for another glass off a passing tray when an arm reached around my back and guided me away.

I turned to see Nick, smiling. "I got you a drink," he said. "And a small present. Come here." He motioned towards the balcony with his head. I happily let him lead me out.

I sipped the drink he handed me and scowled. "This is water!"

Nick smiled. "I thought you could use a break from the wine. But look what else I got you." He pulled a napkin out of his jacket and unfolded it, revealing one of every one of the appetizers that had passed by me.

"Oh yum! You are awesome," I squealed, snatching the napkin and biting into the first appetizer.

"You look stunning tonight," he said, his breath so close to my neck that it sent shivers down my spine.

"Thanks. This is all a little overwhelming. I'm not quite used to the attention."

"You can't tell. You're a natural in the spotlight."

"Thanks." I rubbed my arms for warmth.

"Here," Nick draped his suit jacket over my shoulders.

I eyed his back, under the pretense of checking for visible weapons, but secretly just glancing at his ass.

"On the ankle," he said with a chuckle. "You think I'd ever dare go unarmed near you? Crazy shit follows you around, lady."

I smiled and leaned closer. "I could show you crazy," I began seductively, but then I stopped myself, remembering. "Shit, I forgot to tell you."

"Tell me what?"

I hesitated. I hated to ruin the moment but knew it would be worse if I didn't warn Nick and he ran into David at the party. "Well, I met with David last night to talk about our divorce. He said he broke up with Traci and he wants me back."

"Oh." Nick looked surprised, initially, but then he turned away, gazing off into the distance over the balcony. "That's good news, right? I mean, congratulations."

"Yeah."

"So how did you guys leave it? Is he moving back in?"

"Oh I don't know about that. But I did invite him here."

Nick was silent.

"Nick? Sorry. Was that weird, for me to invite him? It just didn't seem right not to tell him about it."

He turned back to me but didn't make eye contact. Instead he pulled me in for a quick hug. "No, of course not. It's your party. Your husband should be here. Everyone who makes you happy should be here tonight." His voice sounded off, then he paused. "You should get back in there, though."

I nodded. "Right. Thanks for the food. Oh, and here's your coat." I started back in, then turned. "You won't leave without saying goodbye, will you? I mean, I'd really like you to stay longer."

"Sure," he agreed, a less than genuine smile on his face.

I was headed into the lady's room to check my makeup and I ran into Jen.

"Oh, hi!" I greeted her. "I wasn't sure if you would still come after…"

"After I hung up on you? Sorry. I still think you're insane for choosing David over Officer Sexy but tonight's your night. I wouldn't miss it for the world."

I pulled her in for a long hug. "Thanks, Jen."

She led me into the bathroom. "You okay? What's wrong?"

"Oh nothing. I just told Nick about David and he didn't take it well." I paused. "I mean, he did. He said all the right things and seemed totally cool with it, but I could tell he was upset."

Jen frowned. "You weren't expecting him to be upset over you dumping him?"

"I hardly dumped him. We were never together."

"Right. You've just been spending almost every day with him, having mind-blowing sex with him, and not dating other people, but now that you've told him that's all over, you're surprised that he's bummed?"

"I didn't tell him it was over, just that I invited David tonight."

"You don't have to be a detective to know that means you're getting back together with him."

I rubbed my forehead, trying to smooth the wrinkles that were quickly appearing. "I'm just overwhelmed."

"I imagine. Just take it slow, Chelsea. You don't have to pick up with David where you left off. Start slow. Make him take you on some dates first."

"You think I should date my husband?"

She nodded. "Have you talked to him tonight?"

"Not yet. I didn't see him earlier."

"Well, he's here now."

I hugged her again, checked my makeup, then walked out to find my husband.

I glanced around but didn't see him initially. Then I spotted him with Nick. The two were engaged in what seemed to be their best attempt at concealing a heated discussion. Oh boy. I scurried over as fast as I could in heels.

"Chelsea," David greeted me warmly, kissing my cheek. "You look beautiful. And this is all amazing," he said, gesturing around the room.

Nick cleared his throat. "It was nice chatting with you David, and Chelsea, congrats again on well, everything. But I need to head out. I have some business I need to attend to."

I reached for him and gave him a quick parting hug, feeling panicky that it would be our last.

"Well, he's feisty," David said as soon as Nick was gone.

I smiled, agreeing with that description to some extent. "What were you two discussing?"

"Nothing of importance, dear. Now I need a drink."

David followed me around the rest of the evening, like the dutiful husband he'd never exactly been. At the end of the party, he offered to drive me home.

I stepped into his car and noticed his bag packed in the back seat. "Are you going somewhere?"

"Well, I don't have any clothes at the house anymore."

My eyes widened at the realization that he planned to stay. "Oh no, you can't move home yet. We need to take it slow. Date or something."

"Date?"

"Yes. Rekindle the romance."

At the next stoplight, he placed his hand on my thigh and turned to me. "Chelsea, I already said I'm sorry. I know I screwed up and I know I hurt you. You've clearly been lost these past couple months without me and I want to make that up to you." He paused and turned back to the road as the light turned green. "But I just don't see how me sleeping in a hotel fixes anything. We've already been apart long enough. As soon as I'm settled back in, I promise I'll start making it up to you. I remember a certain necklace you had your eye on..."

He had a point. I tried to remember why else Jen thought we should take it slow. After all, I did like new jewelry.

"We made a great team, you and I. I think we should try to pick up where we left off and forget about these past few months. Let bygones be bygones."

I started to say I hated clichés, but then I thought of Nick, and how sad he looked leaving the party. I shook my head, determined to stay focused. "David, we obviously had some problems or you wouldn't have cheated on me."

"I said I was sorry," he snapped. "Look, we've both cheated, so let's just move on."

"I never cheated!" I shouted. "I was faithful to you the entire time you lived in our home."

David's expression changed. "So I was right then, you were sleeping with that guy?"

I rolled my eyes. "He has a name. And I didn't even meet him until after you and I had separated."

He parked the car in the driveway and leaned towards me. "I'm sorry, Chelsea. The thought of you with another man just kills me. I love you, and I never stopped loving you. I know I messed up. Can we just move on?"

His cerulean eyes pleaded with me and I found myself nodding, and then we kissed.

He walked me to the door and hesitated. "You should at least come in for some coffee," I said.

David followed me in and I started to make coffee.

"You are so beautiful, Chelsea. And so amazing, I mean everything you've done with the house and your book..." His voice trailed off as he looked around him. "I think I just got scared, you know, because everything was too perfect. I never want to lose you again."

I started to tell him that he didn't exactly lose me so much as leave me, but David pressed his lips to mine before I could speak a word. Everything about him was so familiar —his musky smell, the smoothness of his chin against mine, even the predictable way he moved his tongue in my mouth. It was like nothing had changed between us.

David loosened his tie and started unbuttoning his shirt. I reached over to help, then yanked it open instead, sending the buttons flying.

"Jesus, Chelsea. What the fuck?"

I froze. "Sorry, I was..."

"This shirt cost ninety dollars."

I bit my lip.

"Crap. I'm sorry, look, Chelsea, you just caught me off guard."

I turned away. "I'll make the coffee."

As soon as I hit "brew" on the pot, I felt David's hand on my back. He slowly unzipped my dress and kissed my neck. He lowered my dress down, reaching his hands across to my breasts, and I started to close my eyes, but instead focused on the oven. And that made me think of Nick.

"I'm sorry, I can't do this," I mumbled, pulling my dress up and shimmying out from between David and the counter.

He frowned, but nodded agreeably. "Okay, we can take it slow."

I was about to protest, to tell him that wasn't exactly what I meant, but I hesitated. "When did you end things with Traci?"

"I moved out last week," he said, sitting at the table.

"So you knew then that you wanted to get back together? I mean, that's why you broke up with her?"

He squirmed in his seat. "Technically she broke up with me, but it was only a matter of time before..."

"Wait, so you came back to me because she kicked you out?"

"It isn't like that, Chelsea. I know I made some bad

choices. But I am sure of what I want now, and it's right here in this kitchen. I want you. I want our old life back."

"But it wouldn't be our old life, David. I've changed."

"I know you've got your book deal right now, but I mean, for the most part, I want things to be the way they used to be."

"I get what you're saying, but that's not what I want. I'm not sure I was happy before."

"Of course you were, Chelsea. You were devastated when I left."

"I know. But then I realized I was fine on my own. And I started to explore things that I'd been interested in but couldn't pursue with you, like my writing."

"You wrote that book during our marriage."

"Yeah, but I never would've sent it to publishers if you hadn't left me."

"You don't know that."

I frowned. "You're right, but it doesn't matter. Since you've left, I've learned that I don't need you."

"You do need me, Chelsea. And besides, that's not the point. I know you still want me." He stood up and grazed my cheek with his hand.

I stared at him silently for a few minutes. Looking into his eyes, I could still see the man I married so many years before. I saw the scar by his chin from our first—and last—kayaking trip, I remembered the time I cut his hair for him, the way we made love on the bathroom floor after, surrounded by the disembodied strands of his fine blond hair. Watching his breath quicken, nervously, I felt the familiar longing for a child—the desperate need to have something pure and good come from the union—but it was distant now, almost as though I were watching someone else experience the urge.

I concentrated on David's lips, on his eyes, on the familiar wrinkle above his brow, and I desperately tried to reconcile my memories with my current feelings. But I couldn't. There was an odd, disembodied sense about it all, like I couldn't connect the couple we used to be to the people we were now. It just didn't feel right.

"I can't do this," I said finally.

"Can't do what?"

I took a deep breath, afraid to hear the words come out of my mouth. "I can't get back together with you, David."

"What, because of your book? Or because of Nick?"

I nearly smiled at the sound of his name and realized instantly how wrong I'd been all along. I thought David guaranteed happiness, security, and a family, but he left me. There was no security there. Thank God we didn't have a family when he left. And as for happiness, well, I hadn't even known how unhappy I was until I met Nick and actually felt happy.

"I looked into him, you know," David said, his voice patronizing and bitter. "Nick is a womanizing loser. He makes no money and he'll never settle down. You're just mad at me now and that's fair. So let's just start over and take things slow."

I shook my head again. "You might be right about Nick not settling down, but honestly, I had more fun in a month with him than in a year with you, so even if I just spend another week or two with him, it'll be worth it."

I inhaled sharply, filled with relief as David's reaction completely validated my decision. "And I'm fine on my own. I don't need a man anyway."

"You don't mean that, Chelsea. You're pissed at me and I get that. But we had a great relationship. You don't want to just throw that away."

"Maybe we did, maybe we didn't, but either way, that's all in the past. I'm not in love with you anymore, David. I think you should leave."

"Chelsea, you're making a big mistake. Call me in a few days when you cool down and come to your senses."

I shut and locked the door behind him and went upstairs to take a long, cold shower.

22

———

I slept terribly that night, groggy from too much wine, but jittery from the excitement of the party, and thoroughly depressed and confused about my conversation with David. I didn't call Jen that day to update her on my talk with David, nor did I reply to any of David's many text messages apologizing, complimenting me, and even offering some vacation proposals.

I wasn't second guessing my decision at all. Now that I'd spoken the truth to David, I knew it was the right thing. That part of my life—the part which revolved around him—had ended long before he moved out. I just hadn't been ready to accept that yet. And now that I was, I still needed to mourn it. I wasn't so much sad at the end of the marriage we actually had, but rather processing the loss of the marriage and life I had wanted.

Yes, I had dreamt of being a writer and that was coming true, but as pathetic as it sounds, I'd also dreamt of being a wife. And a mom. And I knew it wasn't at all modern or feminist to admit that, but it was the truth. So while I could now see that I'd never be happy married to David, I couldn't help but feel even further from those dreams now that I was officially single.

I'd been tempted to call Nick when I woke up, initially thinking he could help me celebrate my divorce in a very personal and fun way. But then, as unhappy as Nick looked seeing me with David last night, he still wasn't interested in a real relationship with me. Most likely he wouldn't even continue our friends with benefits arrangement now that I was truly available. I couldn't even blame him for his commitment phobia, since he had warned me more than adequately over the past four months.

I'd be happy continuing things as they were with Nick, but I didn't know how to convince him of that. Sure, in an ideal world, I'd want more, but was I willing to pass up time with Nick in hopes of "more" elsewhere? No way. If there was one thing I had learned from the past few months, it was that what actually made me happy was different from what I thought would make me happy. Well, that and not to leave the room while frying chicken.

I just needed to make it clear to Nick that I was fine with keeping it casual. That way, nothing would have to change. I gave myself the rest of the day to sort my emotions and ruminate and then texted him. "Good news... Want to meet up for drinks tomorrow?"

I stared at my phone for a full five minutes before concluding he was too busy to immediately respond. Instead of waiting longer, I grabbed a bottle of wine from the fridge and a novel from my nightstand and took a bath. When I emerged an hour later, Nick still hadn't responded. Fortunately, the combination of the heat and the wine had wiped me out, so I went to bed.

When I awoke in the morning, there was a missed call from Jen from the previous night, two messages from my mother, and a text from Nick sent in the last hour. I clicked on the text first.

"Sorry. Working," was all it said.

I rubbed my eyes groggily and scrolled up to see if I had missed anything else from him. Finding nothing, I texted back. "No problem. Today is busy for me, too. Maybe another day or we can chat later." I reread it a few times before clicking send to confirm that it was casual.

Then I listened to the voice mails from my mother, which is never a good thing to do before coffee. Next, I dialed Jen while trudging downstairs to make said coffee so it had time to fully infiltrate my system before I called my mother.

"Hey, how are you?" Jen asked.

"Fine. You?"

"Sick of taxes," she replied. "I was worried about you. I haven't heard from you since the party."

"Oh, yeah, I hibernated yesterday."

"Hibernated?"

"Yes. You know, like a bear."

"Oh. Okay. So... how did everything go with David?"

I yanked the coffee carafe out and poured myself a quick cup while it continued percolating. "It's over. We are officially getting a divorce."

Jen didn't speak right away, which is highly unusual for her. I poured a generous helping of hazelnut creamer into the coffee while awaiting her response.

"Chelsea, I'm so sorry. Do you need anything? I'm still swamped at work but I can come over later tonight. I know it doesn't seem like it now, but this is a blessing in disguise. He's doing you a favor by ending it now."

"Oh, he didn't," I interrupted. "My plan worked perfectly.

He said he and Traci split up, and he admitted he screwed up and he apologized and begged me to come back."

"Wait—for real?"

"Yep."

"Wow. Okay then. So what happened?"

"We made out a little and I said we could try to start over."

"But I thought you said you were getting divorced?"

"Oh, we are."

"So the make-out session was that bad?"

I could tell Jen was joking, but I answered anyway. "No. I mean, it was fine, but I felt like I was kissing him because I was supposed to kiss him, not because I wanted to kiss him. It wasn't like I couldn't not kiss him, you know?"

"Uh, no. Actually you lost me."

"Oh come on," I said. "You know how sometimes you're with a guy and you just have to kiss him. Like nothing you do can distract you from the fact that you just have to touch him? Well, it wasn't like that at all. Which I guess is maybe normal for marriage, you know, that you get used to things being a certain way, but I decided I didn't want to settle for that."

"Good for you. So how did Nick react?"

I frowned, both at the question and my realization that I'd chugged my whole cup of coffee. I stood to pour another before snuggling back up on the window seat in my living room. "He doesn't know yet. I texted him yesterday, but he didn't even respond until this morning."

"So what are you doing talking to me? Call him! Go see him! Do something!"

"Geez, calm down. What's the rush?"

"Chelsea you finally realized what has been painfully

obvious to the rest of us for months—that you want to be with Nick. You can't wait any longer."

I sighed. "It isn't that simple. Even if I did want to be with Nick," I began.

"Which you do," she interrupted.

"He has told me countless times that he is not interested in a committed relationship. He does not want a wife or even a girlfriend."

"You don't know that."

"I do, too. We have discussed it many times."

Jen exhaled, clearly annoyed with me. "Fine. But what do you want? Stop focusing on everyone else's feelings and go for what you want, Chelsea."

"I am," I insisted. "Look, I'm not denying that I would be up for trying a relationship with Nick. But I've given it a lot of thought and I decided that if my only choices are continuing this whole friends with benefits arrangement we have going on and not being with him at all, I'll take the friendship. I don't need to be in an official, traditional relationship with him to be happy, and if I push for that, I risk losing him altogether. I don't want to scare him off."

Jen was quiet for so long that I thought the line might have gone dead. But then she finally spoke. "Chelsea, you told me when David first left you that your biggest regret was not fighting for the things you wanted. So you started to fight and, well, maybe you hit a few snafus along the way and maybe you didn't end up where you expected, but you can't deny that you're happier now."

"What's your point?"

"Keep fighting, Chelsea. You deserve it all."

I let her motivational words wash over me like a dorky cat poster and then heard shouting in the background on her end.

"Oh shit, I have to go. Some software emergency."

"Okay, thanks. Bye," I said, hanging up, still bewildered.

I texted Nick again later, asking him to call when he had a chance, and I called my mother to tell her I was officially getting divorced. Then I decided I should probably tell David the same. I didn't want to talk with him about it, though, so I sent a text. It seemed cheesy, really, but it wasn't like I was breaking up with him via text. We had broken up long ago. This was just sealing the deal.

I wrote, "Thank you for dinner the other day. I have many fond memories from our marriage and would someday like to be friends with you, but we have gone through too much to rekindle our love at this time. Please finalize the divorce papers and send them to me for review. I wish you well."

I read over it a few times, decided it was good, then sent it. Moments later I got a response—a simple one word "whatever."

"Well, that's mature," I said aloud.

I forced myself to work on my column the rest of the afternoon so I wouldn't be tempted to text Nick again but by dinner time, I was going crazy. Why hadn't he written back? I quickly dialed his number but it went to voice mail, so I hung up. I hopped in my car and went to the mall to do some errands and pick up some food court delicacies and then called Nick again. Still no answer.

I called Jen and we agreed to meet up for a movie under the conditions that we not discuss men (my terms) or taxes (her terms). After the movie, I still had no missed calls. I went to bed agitated and a little queasy from too many Twizzlers.

The next morning, I called Nick again. His voice mail picked up after several rings. Again. Clearly not leaving a message wasn't an effective way of communicating with him. I sighed loudly after the beep, then spoke. "Hi Nick. It's me, again. I wanted to tell you that David told me he wants me back. My whole plan worked. He wanted to sleep over after the party, but I...oh geez. I can't do this on your voice mail. Can you just call me back? Please?"

I showered and got dressed, then decided to go pick up a bagel for lunch. I sat at the café trying to brainstorm new book ideas by people-watching. There was a cute elderly couple next to me holding hands while eating breakfast burritos and a harried looking mom with two small children. The rest of the café patrons were reading the paper. I smiled, thinking back to my attempt to read the paper, and that, of course, made me think of Nick. I glanced down at my phone and confirmed he still hadn't called.

"This is bullshit," I said, realizing too late, by the startled looks from the elderly couple, that I had actually spoken aloud. I called the police station and asked to speak with Officer Gyllenhaal.

"Oh, do you mean Detective Gyllenhaal?" the receptionist replied.

I nearly shrieked with excitement. He got the promotion. I mean, I'd known he would, but still...Wow! But why hadn't he called to tell me?"

"Hello?"

"Oh, yes. Sorry. Detective Gyllenhaal."

"He's not on duty today. I could direct your call to someone else if you provide me with more information about your situation."

"Oh, no thanks," I said politely, wondering why she hadn't just led with that. I hung up, and returned to the counter to order coffees to go.

Fully armed with caffeine, I drove straight to Nick's apartment and rang the bell before I could change my mind.

Nick took his time answering the door. When he did, I could hear the TV blaring in the background, with some football game on. He had a bottle of Fat Tire in his hand and residue from chips on one leg of his dark jeans. Despite that, he looked hot. He was wearing a black undershirt that hardly concealed the muscles in his chest and arms, and his hair was tousled in a sexy way that reminded me of the moments right after we made love, before he'd fully composed himself.

"I called you twice," I said. "You didn't return my call."

He glanced at his phone, resting on the countertop behind him. "Sorry, I've been busy."

"Yeah, I heard you got the promotion, Detective. Congratulations!"

Nick blushed. "Thanks."

I handed him one of the coffees I was holding. "Do you have a minute now?"

Nick seemed to debate this, which only made me more nervous. Finally, he nodded and swung the door open. I followed him in to his living room. He plopped down on the couch and lowered the volume on the TV.

"They sent me a tentative schedule for my book tour," I said as I sat beside him, hoping to break the ice.

He flashed me a genuine smile. "That's great, Chelsea."

There was an awkward silence.

"Have you been enjoying your new job, Detective?"

He nodded, a forced smile on his face. "It's not too different, yet. The money's better, though."

I sighed. "Are you going to tell me the real reason you haven't called?"

Nick frowned, clicked the TV off, and turned to face me.

"I'm happy for you that you got what you wanted, Chelsea. I just, I don't think we should hang out any more. It's weird, you know?"

"We can't hang out anymore because of my book deal?"

"No," he paused. "Because of David. Given our history, it just doesn't seem right to keep seeing each other now that you're back with your husband."

I took a long sip from my coffee. "When my agent requested my full manuscript, do you know who the first person I thought of was?"

He shrugged.

"You. I got the best news of my life and I wanted to share it with you first. Not David, not Jen, not my mother. You."

I waited for him to reply, but he didn't.

"Look, I know you don't do relationships or whatever, and that's fine. But you could've still called me back."

"Sorry," he mumbled.

"Yeah, you should be. Because if you'd returned my call, you'd already know that I didn't get back together with David."

It clearly took a moment for him to process this. When he did, he glanced up, shocked. "I saw you with him at your party. You told me he left his girlfriend and asked to move back in." He snorted. "He told me your plans for after the party."

"What plans?"

Nick made a face.

"Oh ewww. I didn't sleep with David. The rest is true—he did want me back, but I said no. I told him I wasn't in love with him anymore and that we weren't going to get back together."

Nick didn't answer, so I continued, my nerves growing more uneasy by the second. "We had divorce papers drawn up. I'm just waiting on David to sign and then it'll be official."

Nick's expression remained unchanged. "I don't understand. When I first met you, you were a mess over him leaving. And the past two months you've driven yourself crazy trying to win him back. Why would you turn him down when you got exactly what you wanted?"

I nearly laughed at his suggestion that I'd gotten what I wanted, knowing it couldn't be further from the truth. But I needed to stay focused.

"People change. I guess it's not what I want now." I paused. "I was devastated at first, granted. But the last sixty days, I've been happier than I ever was with David. I always thought I needed David, but I don't. And he's *definitely* not what I want."

"What do you want?" Nick's voice cracked as he spoke.

"You really don't know?" I reached for his hand and squeezed it. "I've had so much fun with you the past couple of months. You make me feel smart and funny, beautiful and sexy. You liked me even when I was a total disaster and never once asked me to change."

"You are smart and funny, beautiful and sexy."

I licked my lips nervously before continuing. "I know you're going to hate me for saying this, but I'm in love with you."

His eyes widened and his skin paled noticeably.

I took a deep breath, and continued, trying not to be discouraged by the heavy silence filling the air since my confession. "I want you in my life, even if it's just as a friend that I occasionally sleep with. I don't need to be a nagging girlfriend. I won't be. I promise. I know you don't do commitments, and I can work with that. I'll take whatever I can get as long as it's with you..."

"I can do commitments," he interrupted. "People change."

My heart rate skyrocketed. I tried to remain calm and not to jump to conclusions. "So…"

His lips curled into a small smile. "Sorry, I interrupted you. Finish what you were saying first."

"I think I covered it all." I said. "I want you. You're the one I love."

Nick smiled wider now. He leaned closer and I could feel his breath on my lips. "It's about time, Chelsea. I've been in love with you for two months now."

I reflexively smiled. "But you said…"

He interrupted me with a kiss—the kind of long, drawn out kiss with lots of tongue that always made me lose my train of thought. When the kiss ended, I was breathless.

Nick gripped my chin in his hands, his eyes boring into mine as he spoke. "I said I love you Chelsea. I can't take my eyes off you when I'm with you, and I can't stop thinking about you when we're apart. I want to spend the rest of my life with you."

My eyes widened. "But you don't…" I stopped myself before I could bring up all those things in the back of my mind, the things that I'd convinced myself didn't really matter as long as I had Nick in my life, things like marriage and kids.

"I do want that, Chelsea, all of it," he said, as though he could read my mind. "The only reason I thought I didn't want any of that before was that I hadn't met you." He brushed his hand against my cheek. "But I would marry you in a heartbeat. I'll have 2.5 kids with you, a white picket fence, and even give up my guns if it means I get to wake up next to you every morning."

I smiled and jumped onto his lap for another kiss. As

Nick's lips met mine, I realized how perfect this felt, how our mouths and bodies fit together like pieces of a puzzle, how it was all meant to be.

"You can keep the guns," I whispered, kissing him harder as he wrapped his arms around me.

The End

ACKNOWLEDGMENTS

The process of transforming a book from an intriguing idea to a polished ready-to-publish manuscript is time-consuming and daunting, and I never could have done it alone. I'm filled with gratitude for everyone who helped me and cheered me on along the way.

First, a huge heartfelt thanks to my husband and the hero of my own personal love story. I truly couldn't have achieved this dream without your support and patience. I also appreciate your willingness to supply me with a constant stream of caffeine while I work.

Thank you to my beta-readers, critique partners, and local RWA group. Your honest feedback is priceless.

Thank you to my editor, Kimberly. I'm so thankful for your attention to detail, ruthless cuts, and dedication to the Oxford comma. Your edits always strengthen my books.

Thank you to my cover artist, JD Book Designs. Your creation truly brought my vision to life.

Finally, thank you to all of the readers, bloggers, and other writers who support the literary industry and make it so fulfilling to create works of fiction.

ABOUT THE AUTHOR

Liza Malloy writes contemporary romance, new adult romance, women's fiction, and fantasy romance. She's a sucker for bad boys, dimples, and muscles, and she can't resist a man in uniform. Liza loves creating worlds where the heroine discovers her own strength and finds her Happily Ever After. When Liza isn't reading or writing torrid love stories, she's a practicing attorney. Her other passions include gummy bears, jelly beans, and the occasional marathon. She lives in the Midwest with her four daughters and her own Prince Charming. *Sixty Days for Love* is her first published novel. She has three more books slated for release in 2019.

Visit her website at: www.LizaMalloy.com

ALSO BY LIZA MALLOY

For Love and Italian

An education in amore? Yes please, Professore!

This new adult contemporary romance title is slated for release on May 13, 2019.

Forbidden Ink

Loving the bad boy never felt so good!

Look for this new adult contemporary romance in July 2019.

The Awakening

When worlds collide, can love truly conquer all?

The first title in this exciting new adult fantasy romance trilogy will be available in September 2019.